DANCING
WITH
THE
ICE LADY

DANCING
WITH
THE
ICE LADY

by
Ken Salter

An R. C. Bean Murder Mystery

REGENT PRESS
Berkeley, California

[paperback]
ISBN 13: 978-1-58790-386-1
ISBN 10: 1-58790-386-5

[e-book]
ISBN 13: 978-1-58790-387-8
ISBN 10: 1-58790-387-3

Library of Congress Catalog Number: 2017935718

Manufactured in the U.S.A.
REGENT PRESS
Berkeley, California
www.regentpress.net

Chapter 1

I WORK AS A PRIVATE INVESTIGATOR FOR NATE GREEN, A Berkeley divorce attorney and local legend. I do skip-tracing on deadbeat hubbies who fly the coop to establish new, secret lives elsewhere. I also root out hidden assets socked away by hubbies who let their faithful wives support them while they obtain their M.B.A.s or Ph.D.s at U.C., Berkeley, then woo a younger, childless mate on campus; all this in order to dump their unsuspecting wives as they set off merrily on their new careers with a new and often younger woman on their arm.

I was stumped while mulling over a complicated case involving one of Nate's "Berkeley Girls," as he refers to his women clients, when the intercom on my phone buzzed abruptly. "Mr. Green wants to see you in his office, pronto," rasped Saundra. Her strident tone caught me off guard. She's usually friendly and laid back with me. She's a very attractive black woman with an hourglass figure, winning smile and a down-home way about her that's non-threatening to Nate's predominately white, university-affiliated clients. She's a pro at establishing rapport with women who are angry and disillusioned to have been summarily used and abandoned by a cheating spouse.

Saundra will usually clue me in to what's up with the boss. Not today. Something unusual was happening and I'd have to play it by ear. I tried to ease out of my office to avoid Marcie, Nate's personal secretary and confidante, whose office faces mine on the hallway leading to Nate's office upstairs. Our offices are in an old Victorian house near the campus which he'd converted into law offices years ago. Marcie's door was wide open and she threw me a nasty look as I tried to sneak past.

I was apprehensive and curious but knew better than to poke my nose into it with either woman. Marcie's body language and Saundra's tone of voice signaled they were on the warpath together about something that involved me. Best stay out of their way. They'd been with Nate for years and I'm low man on the totem pole. They ran the show and let me know it.

I bounded up the stairs two at a time and knocked on Nate's closed door. Nate grunted, "Come in."

I eased the door open and stopped cold in my tracks, stunned to see an alluringly dressed, provocatively beautiful black woman seated crossways in front of Nate's desk. The woman looked me up and down and threw me a wry smile. Nate seemed to take pleasure in my moment of confusion before motioning me to a seat opposite the woman and continuing his stock recitation outlining the terms of his standard fee agreement.

It was not uncommon for Nate to summon me at this stage of his initial meeting with a client, especially if my services as an investigator will be required. It was unusual for him not to introduce me to a new client; today, he interrupted his fee pitch only briefly to wave in my direction and say, "My investigative assistant, Mr. Bean."

The woman graciously turned to me and said, "Nice to meet you, Mr. Bean. I'm Gloria Simmons." She locked her expressive, lustrous dark-brown eyes on mine long enough to send a mind-numbing shiver up my spine. Ping! In submarine warfare games, I was dead. She flashed me a bemused smile before turning her attention back to Nate who'd lost his concentration at the interruption.

Nate resumed his fee spiel designed to soften a client for the hardest part of the initial interview—paying a hefty retainer and signing a fee agreement. Normally, he was smooth at this part of the game. Not today. His hand trembled and his voice croaked like a frog. He was at the point where he makes his pitch for his standard, twenty-five hundred dollar retainer when Mrs. Simmons broke in on his rambling speech. "Do you think five thousand would be enough to get you started on the investigation of my husband's assets and the troubling doings at his mortuary that I spoke of earlier?"

The interruption left Nate open-mouthed with surprise. We both watched with bated breath as she leaned down from her chair to pick up a large Gucci shoulder bag resting on the carpet. She pulled out a thick manila envelope and tendered it to Nate. I felt my mouth go dry and suddenly realized I was staring brazenly at Mrs. Simmons. I was transfixed by the sight of her delectable, enticing curves straining against the flimsy fastenings of her breezy summer frock. Her flawless skin was silky smooth, the texture of soft, creamy caramel. She reminded me of photos I've seen of the tall, African model, Imam, the girlfriend of the singer, David Bowie.

Nate had to stretch awkwardly across his desk to grasp the manila envelope. As Mrs. Simmons resumed her seat, she tugged down the hem of her skimpy dress which had ridden up to the middle of her thighs. My heart skipped a beat as she sat down and crossed her legs. I noticed Nate's eyes were also transfixed by the rise and fall of her hemline instead of opening the envelope.

"Why don't you have Mr. Bean count the money while you fill him in on what needs doing. Just put the receipt for the funds in my file for now," she said, while flashing an exquisite smile my way. I was ready to melt. Fortunately for me, she shifted her attention back to Nate who struggled to get out of his chair to hand me the envelope.

Nate has never been overly graceful; now he looked all thumbs and elbows as he twisted awkwardly to hand me the envelope. I barely managed to intercept the packet before he stumbled prone across his desk and made a total fool of himself. I could now see why Saundra and Marcie were so out of sorts. Nate was smitten with his new client. He was acting like Dustin Hoffman in the presence of Mrs. Robinson.

Gloria Simmons watched this scene play out with a bemused smile. She didn't waste any time picking up the slack. "Don't you think you should fill Mr. Bean in on the nature of my problems? I'd like to hear how you plan to get the information we need to proceed."

While her words were addressed to Nate, it was clear she was used to telling men what to do and how to do it. Nate struggled to regain his composure by hacking into his handkerchief in an effort to clear his throat. "Mrs. Simmons may want to file a petition for divorce or legal separation depending on what information our office can develop with respect to her husband's business affairs."

Nate's lawyer-like tone surprised me. Normally, he spoke in a low-keyed, fatherly manner to his frightened, betrayed and vulnerable "Berkeley Girls." Then again, Mrs. Simmons was clearly not one of his girls. I was curious why she would choose to hire a frumpy lawyer like Nate instead of a high profile, slick divorce attorney who curried favor with the moneyed and sophisticated crowd in San Francisco and Marin County across the bay.

While Nate struggled to appear lawyer-like to summarize her case and Mrs. Simmons' attention was focused on him, I appraised our new client on the sly. My eyes registered one captivating feature after another. Her long legs were absolutely stunning; she'd showcased them in the latest sheer French hosiery with little diamond designs. Her stockings hugged her muscled calves and tapered down to perfectly formed ankles which were accentuated by low-heeled pumps with straps at the back.

Mrs. Simmons was not dressed provocatively. Everything she wore was in excellent taste and designed to stimulate the imagination as she moved. Her winsome features were suggested and accented rather than displayed. She was classy, unlike many of Nate's women clients who came to the office in drab and dowdy outfits or ones designed to reveal more than a healthy glimpse of cleavage and flesh.

Mrs. Simmons was in a class all by herself. She had no need to use artifice to attract interest. She would have had the same mesmerizing effect on Nate and me if she'd been dressed in a sweater and slacks or even a business suit. She exuded a simmering, primitive sexual heat that couldn't be contained by garments. It was pulling me like a magnet. While I counted the pile of hundred dollar bills, I couldn't keep my eyes off her. My every glance revealed something new to fire my imagination.

She was well aware of her effect on us; she didn't flaunt her wares like so many women often feel compelled to do. She had to know that her short, breezy, summer frock with straps that criss-crossed her back and a hem that stopped six inches short of her kneecaps was more enticing than a dress that showed more skin. Dressed as she was, heads were going to turn at forty yards. Dressed in anything more risqué, Gloria Simmons would cause a riot.

I tried to concentrate on Nate's monologue but only bits and pieces were getting through. I struggled to stop imagining what Mrs. Simmons would look like once those flimsy little back straps were unhooked and allowed to slide slowly down her body.

What I did learn was that Mrs. Simmons had married into one of Oakland's two large families that controlled the black mortuary business. I don't know much about the cas-ket-to-graveside trade other than it's very lucrative. Everyone is going to die eventually, but in Oakland, one of the murder capitals of the West, lots of folks were dying like flies. When you have the regular folks dying on time and then add the kids and young men who were killing each other in gang warfare and turf disputes, business had to be jumping in our local mortuaries.

Nate finally got around to me in his monologue. "I'll have my assistant run a check on ownership of your husband's many business interests. Title to the real estate and mortuary busi-ness will be on file with Alameda County tax authorities. Other assets may be harder to trace. We'll try to put a monetary esti-mate of what the funeral home business is worth, but without access to your husband's business records at this stage, we can only speculate. Should we proceed with an action for divorce or legal separation, we will be able to compel him to reveal his assets. You've indicated your husband is very secretive about his business dealings. Do you think you might access your husband's tax returns?"

"My husband owns the business with his brother and they don't use an accountant. They do all their tax filings themselves with the help of bookkeepers they employ in the funeral home." Mrs. Simmons now raised her eyebrows and gave me a penetrating look as if to say, "How do you plan to pierce the veil of secrecy surrounding my husband's business affairs?" Ball in my court.

I was surprised initially at the way she'd coolly sized me up when I walked into the room. She didn't seem to notice or care that I, like she, was a person of color. Usually African-Americans acknowledge each other in subtle, perceptible ways, even in the presence of the Man.

"You must gather your information very discretely, Mr. Bean. My husband must never suspect that he's being investigated. He and his brother are very tight-lipped about their business. If Jimmy had the slightest suspicion that I might be preparing to divorce him, he'd throw me out of the house and cut me off without a dime."

I smiled my smile and nodded my understanding. I had a hard time imagining Mrs. Simmons destitute for long. But with five thousand dollars in big bills sitting on my lap, it was no time to play coy.

"Did you ever file a joint tax return with your husband?" I asked.

"No, Jimmy always files a separate tax return. He doesn't bring any of his work home either. Keys to the business are locked in his briefcase at all times."

I had to suppress my amusement. If Mrs. Simmons couldn't get her hands on her husband's set of keys with all her charms, there was no way in hell I was going to get hold of them or access to his business records either. "Is your separate tax return also prepared by your husband's business?"

"No, I do it myself. It's really not complicated. I still have some residual income from my modeling and I do a Schedule "C" for my design income; it hasn't amounted to much yet, but I'm hoping that will change soon." She locked her eyes on mine, raised her eyebrows and flashed me a playful smile. I wondered whether this whole little song and divorce dance was calculated to capitalize her new business venture.

"What do you do for money to run the house and pay your bills? Is there a joint checking account?"

"Yes, we have a joint checking account. Jimmy usually puts five or six thousand in it each month so I can pay the charge accounts and our personal bills. The cars, pool service, liquor and entertainment expenses are all paid by the business."

I nodded my understanding at how they ran their personal affairs. The two brothers were no fools when it came to claiming business expenses. They must have been writing off as much of their personal expenses as they thought they could get away with to stiff the taxman.

"Do the checks to pay house and car expenses come from the mortuary's business account?" Nate interjected.

"Yes, until just recently," Mrs. Simmons replied. "Jimmy has always made the deposit, but something at the mortuary changed that. He gave me a sealed envelope to drop in our bank's night deposit and said it was urgent. Before dropping it in the slot, I opened the envelope to make sure he hadn't made a mistake in the amount he posted in the checking ledger. He was acting so strangely I was afraid he might have bungled the figure and I didn't want to overdraw the account."

"The amount was correct, but I was shocked to see they'd changed banks. The check was drawn on an HSBC Bank in Hong Kong and not our local bank that the business has used for years. With almost all of the mortuary's business coming from the African-American community, it seemed really odd they'd change from a local, black-owned bank to a Chinese bank abroad. I also found it strange that the check was countersigned by a new bookkeeper named Jennifer Wong."

I could tell I was going to like working for Mrs. Simmons.

She was no fool when it came to sniffing out which way the wind was blowing. What were black funeral home owners doing with a Chinese bookkeeper? She'd have access to confidential information about the business affairs of this very private, secretive, highly profitable family enterprise.

"You mentioned something happened at the mortuary recently which changed your husband's pattern of deposits. What did you mean?" I asked.

"I learned that there'd been a fracas in the mortuary's parking lot that shook up Jimmy and his brother. There was some kind of argument and a shooting. Jimmie got a call late at night that I overheard. He thought I was sleeping. They must have asked him what to do with a body because he instructed them to take it inside and stow it in a refrigerated locker until Jimmie could get there."

"Did Jimmy say to call the police?" I asked.

Mrs. Simmons gave a sardonic laugh. "No, he said just the opposite. Jimmy said not to call the police and to get an employee to fire up the cremation furnace and get everyone in the parking lot out of there pronto."

Oh boy, things were getting heavier by the minute. I follow the obits in the *Oakland Tribune* as well as the police blotter. I had no recollection of police responding to a shooting at a funeral home. If Mrs. Simmons' story was accurate, someone was killed in the parking lot and the body crisped in the cooker. This was not going to be a simple find the hidden assets and negotiate a deal divorce case. I was just about to ask Mrs. Simmons if she'd ever met the new bookkeeper, Jennifer Wong, and knew when she was hired, when Nate's phone buzzed loudly.

Saundra had strict instructions not to interrupt Nate during an initial client consultation unless Nate specifically asked her to do so. Nate was so flustered that he pushed the wrong button on the phone console. Instead of Nate hearing Saundra in private, we all got to hear her chide Nate.

"Do you realize that Toni Perkins has been waiting over an hour to see you?" There was a harsh edge to her voice. She was loaded for bear. I knew from experience that if either Nate or I got her on the warpath, we were in for a week or more of hell. Surprisingly, Nate kept his cool even though it was getting to the time in the afternoon when he needed a couple of stiff jolts of Chivas Regal to calm his nerves and maintain his blood alcohol level.

Toni is an unhappy camper. She married a Berkeley switch-hitter in order to conceive a child. The plan was to marry, have the kid and divorce in that order. She and the kid's father, Benny Ross, even drafted a pre-nuptial agreement themselves providing that Toni would get custody of the kid and Benny could walk away from his legal responsibility to pay child support for the next eighteen years.

The problem was that neither Toni nor Benny had thought much about how cute their baby girl was going to be before she arrived or the legality of their pre-nuptial agreement. Now each wanted custody and control. Toni was keeping house with her current lover, Nancy Schwartz, and desperately needed custody of the kid to keep her shaky relationship with Nancy intact. Nancy wanted to adopt the kid as co-parent. She and Toni were fighting because Toni had screwed up the deal with Benny. Benny and his boyfriend also wanted custody of the kid to cement their new partnership. This was not the sort of mess you wanted to deal with after meeting Gloria Simmons.

While we listened to Saundra scold Nate, I remembered that I hadn't completed my investigation of Toni's case. It sounded like Toni's boiler was about to blow and was putting a head of steam in Saundra's sails.

Nate masked his annoyance and stated, "I'm still tied up and probably will be for some time to come. Please tell Toni I'm sorry to inconvenience her. Tell Toni that R.C. can meet with her now or she can reschedule a meeting with me."

We heard muffled noises. Saundra must have put her hand over the phone. Nate interjected, "Tell her R.C. is on his way down and will bring her up to date with the problems we're having getting Benny to go along with the proposed settlement." Nate hung up without waiting for a reply.

This is how you know you're on the bottom rung of the

ladder. I was the fall guy. Toni probably had her lover sitting downstairs egging Toni on. I could imagine Nancy Schwartz' advice over the last hour, "Get tough with these guys. You're payin' them big money and they're playin' footsy with Benny. Maybe we should be suing Nathan Green and R.C. Bean."

Nate nodded for me to put on my fireman's hat. As I got up to leave, he put an arm around my shoulder and said, "I've promised Mrs. Simmons that you and I will personally handle all aspects of her case. That means you will discuss your findings only with me and not with other members of our staff." Nate's tone was conspiratorial and with his face so close to mine he had to register my astonishment. No wonder Saundra and Marcie were as mad as wasps being smoked out of their nest.

Nate continued, "I'm keeping Mrs. Simmons' file locked in my office safe for safekeeping. I'll want to see you first thing in the morning to coordinate a very discreet investigation. Mrs. Simmons fears her movements may be watched, so she may need to meet with you privately, perhaps at her house. I've given her your home phone number along with my own. She doesn't want to call either of us at the office or for us to call her from here. Tidy up whatever outstanding work you're doing on other cases so you can be free to devote your undivided attention to Mrs. Simmons' investigation. She'll call you in a day or so to tell you how and when to meet with her. As she stated, she's very concerned about the strange doings at the mortuary and the shooting she spoke of; she'll tell you more about her concerns when you meet."

As I turned to go, Mrs. Simmons glided in a blur of honey-brown legs to meet me at the door. She extended her hand for me to shake and gave me an intimate smile that started my heart fluttering anew. Her touch sent a jolt of pleasure coursing through my hand and up to my brain. If death by electrocution was anything like this, I was ready to be strapped to the chair.

As we slowly unlocked hands, she locked her eyes with mine and whispered, "I'm really looking forward to meeting with you alone, R.C." She then said in a voice Nate could hear, "Nice to meet you, R.C. I'll look forward to providing you with any information you think may be useful. I'll call you just as soon as I can."

I took my time descending the stairs to meet the angry reception committee waiting to jump me below. Once I unruffled Toni Perkins' feathers, I'd have to deal with Saundra and Marcie's anger. There would be hell to pay when they learned Nate ordered my lips zipped tight and I was to stonewall them regarding all aspects of Mrs. Simmons' case.

To my knowledge, nothing like this had happened before. Nate's infatuation with his new client was jeopardizing years of loyalty and trust from his close-knit staff. I was also worried about my own feelings and involvement. Gloria Simmons fascinated me. She was beautiful and classy but I was clearly out of her league. The shooting incident at the mortuary was worrisome. I was sure Mrs. Simmons expected me to solve it so she could use it to her advantage. She triggered erotic and dangerous impulses which both excited me and scared me to death. Just like Nate, I felt a nagging sense that I was being sucked into something sinister and over my head.

Chapter 2

WHEN I REACHED THE BOTTOM OF THE STAIRS, I noticed Marcie Lynn's door was open and the office empty. I was sorely tempted to duck into my office and do a bunk through my window which opens onto the parking. It would only make matters worse. Better to face the one-three punch and get it over with. The raised voices of the three furies emanated from Saundra's reception area signaled they were waiting for me. No mistaking Toni Perkins' high-pitched cries of indignation over the other voices.

I put on a grin-and-bear-it smile and strode into the room as casually as possible. "Hi Toni. Sorry about the long wait, but I really wanted to explain the problems we're having. Now that Benny's represented by an attorney, we can no longer talk with him directly. All communications have to go through his attorney."

"Just like that two-faced bastard to hide behind the skirts of his pretty-boy attorney. He's that fucker from the Gay Attorneys Alliance, isn't he?" Toni said caustically.

"Yeah, unfortunately, he's hired Archie Fenton. Archie handles lots of cases for the gay community and specializes in child custody and adoption. It's hard to push him because he knows all the ins and outs of the law even if those laws weren't written with your problems in mind." Saundra and Marcie listened to my unconvincing song and dance and just glared at me. They were poised like two lionesses stalking in the high grass waiting for Toni to flush her prey.

"Hey, man, don't give me any of that 'what the law means' shit. Benny knew what he was doing from the get go. He agreed to provide some sperm so I could have my kid and that's the long and short of it. He didn't want a kid. He was just doing me and my daughter a favor by making her legit. The plan all along was for me and Nancy to raise our daughter together; he never ever asked for visitation rights. What we put in writing was what he wanted: to be off the hook for child support. So what's the fuckin' problem?" Toni shrieked.

"I know it's terribly unfair, but the state doesn't recognize agreements it considers bad for public policy. State welfare agencies are plagued with thousands of cases where husbands and boyfriends have abandoned their families and kids. Taxpayers have to pay the freight for raising the kids and they're hopping mad about paying for the offspring of deadbeat dads and screaming in anyone's ear who'll listen. Judges and legislators listen because they have to face these angry folks to get elected. If a judge approved a private agreement between parties that let the father off the hook for child support, every shyster lawyer representing deadbeat clients would be drafting similar agreements. There'd be a taxpayers' revolt worse than when they froze property tax increases."

"That's bullshit and you know it," Toni barked. "What you're talking about is fraud. Male pricks taking advantage of women who don't know any better."

"You got that right, little sister!" Saundra added her grain of salt from her receptionist's desk. Toni was working up a head of steam and Saundra was stoking her boilers. Marcie was still waiting to pick her moment to jump into the fray and badger me.

I rambled on. "In addition to the state's interest to see that men support the kids they father, there's also a requirement in the law that the biological father cannot be deprived of his parental rights which include visitation and often shared custody; it's in the Civil Code." I regretted my words the moment uttered them. But it was too late. Marcie saw her opening to pounce.

"That's really the crux of the matter, isn't it?" Marcie spit her words at me. "The whole damned Code reinforces the paternalistic order and power structure. The male can be a cheat, can be a wife-beater, rape his wife, his daughter and her friends, but he still retains his rights under the law, doesn't he?" Marcie said in a hectoring voice.

I was primed to respond to the way Marcie twisted what I said. A mother could do drugs, beat her kids, sell her body with kids in the house, carve up her husband or boyfriend and act coarsely or lewdly in her kids' presence and she, too, would not lose her presumptive custody rights in most cases under the Civil Code and precedent cases. Still, she was right about the paternalistic bias in the law and its enforcement. I wisely did not contest her conclusions.

"Fuckin' right!" Toni Perkins screamed. "That's what's wrong with the whole stinking system. Nancy and me got no rights 'cause we're lesbians. The whole male patriarchy is against us. We make the kids and the male legislators and judges protect their power and interests by giving superior rights to the kids' fathers."

Toni huffed and puffed and was nearly out of breath when she paused in her diatribe. She had history on her side. The mostly male members of the California legislature had voted consistently not to allow gay couples to marry or adopt kids; this proscription caused all kinds of legal problems for them; in addition to the problems with marriage, kids and custody, they suffered legal inequality in matters of inheritance, medical insurance and taxes and a host of other concerns. I could have pointed out that Benny and his partner suffered the same discrimination vis-à-vis the law and public opinion, but what was the point? Better to let Toni and Marcie blow off steam.

Saundra's head bobbed affirmatively to everything they said. Even though she was much more conservative in her views than the other woman, she was the granddaughter of slaves and could easily identify with racial discrimination and the excesses of paternalistic power. She let me know on my first day of work that she was no woman to mess with. She was real good at using her back-home ways to charm and put Nate's "Berkeley Girls" (BG's to us) at ease, but underneath that veneer lurked a hard-nosed woman with strong views, who brokered no nonsense from anyone and who knew exactly what she wanted.

Saundra has darker skin than me and speaks white folks' talk just as well as or better than me. She's in her early thirties and unmarried. She let me know in the first thirty minutes of my first day of work that she was strictly "off limits" to a no-account upstart like me, who'd completed his law degree but hadn't got around to taking the state's bar exam.

Saundra had a high, prominent derriere that many African-American men find exciting. She wears her form-fitting skirts so they accentuate the bounce of her buns. When she walks her walk, heads turn to notice. She looks as good coming as she does going. Saundra isn't worried about the ticking of any biological clock. She's set her sights on a man with money, brains, and a nineteenth-century belief that marriage is forever.

I knew Saundra would have it out with me, but not in front of others. She'd wait to get me alone and give me a piece of her mind in our own black patois which we don't speak in the presence of whites. She was giving me the evil eye while I was trying to figure a way to get Toni Perkins off my back. Saundra must have been reading my mind.

"Toni, you can see that R.C. hasn't got anything new on your case. I know that for a fact because Mister Green hasn't received a response on our last offer yet from Benny's lawyer. Why don't I make an appointment with the boss for next week when he's sure to have a reply to discuss with you. R.C. still has to see Marcie before he leaves."

Saundra solved the problem of Toni nicely by undercutting my authority and locking me into a showdown with Marcie over the Gloria Simmons case; her deft move was accomplished with wicked smiles exchanged with Marcie. They were both tough cookies and meant to play hardball on the Simmons matter. Toni Perkins was just a warmup act.

Marcie crooked her finger and I followed her to her office. Her face reminded me of a bear trap I'd seen in a Gold Rush museum along Highway 49 in the Sierra Nevada. I could envision its huge metal teeth ready to snap shut on my arm or leg. Gotcha! She pointed to a seat in front of her desk and shut the door.

Marcie was in her late forties, twice divorced and often bitter about her predicament. Who wouldn't be? She saw only the ugly side of men's character day in and day out. Rumor had it that she was one of Nate's BG's years ago, before my time. She was very protective of Nate for reasons only they were privy to. She knew his tastes and quirks better than his wife who spent her mornings puttering in her garden until hitting the sauce in the early afternoon. It was also rumored she and Nate were getting it on every now and then when they could travel out of town together on a case or to a convention. Marcie was clever enough not to leave a trail of smoke and I didn't care to look for a fire. If Nate and Marcie could find a way to get it on together, then "Praise the Lord," as Dad would say.

Marcie was well-preserved for her age with a trim figure; she went to great lengths to dress to de-emphasize her ample bosom. Her dark, wavy hair fell to her shoulders; its natural grey highlights gave her an aura of maturity and authority. She always dressed in pant suits. I'd never seen her wear a dress.

"I'm going to tell you something important, R.C., and I want you to hear me out. I've been working here for sixteen years and I know Nate better than you or anyone else ever will. In this office, relationships have to be based on trust and mutual respect if we're to get our jobs done. You need to get it through your thick head that Nate's in trouble and that you, Saundra and I have to work together to get Nate out of it."

"Marcie, I really don't know what's going on. I never heard of Gloria Simmons before today. As far as I know, it's just a routine divorce case."

"Come off it, R.C. Don't give me that innocent, little boy shit. The Simmons woman's case is no ordinary case and your pecker knows it. She's a high-priced gold digger with a well-earned reputation for blowing her way to the top of the heap. She's got shark's teeth that bite deep and there's a trail of blood and broken dicks everywhere she goes. She's ruthless and extremely dangerous. Nate's way over his head representing her. There's no way he should be handling her case and you know it. If we don't arrive at an understanding and cooperate to help him, he's going to get hurt really bad. And if Nate gets hurt, I'll see that you get hurt too."

Marcie's threats were very direct and troubling. I knew she meant to have me fired if I didn't play her game. She was right, of course. Mrs. Simmons was no ordinary client and Nate was just as infatuated with her as I was. I also wondered why Nate was handling her case when he was clearly out of her league. Marcie had her own sources of information. She'd worked elections for many liberal Democratic candidates in Berkeley and Oakland and had developed sources of inside information in both white and black political circles. I needed to pump her for what she knew before meeting Nate in the morning.

We both heard Nate saying his sweet goodbyes to Gloria Simmons and offering to accompany her to her coal-black E-type Jaguar I'd noticed in the parking lot. Marcie motioned for me to hush. Neither of us wanted Nate to know we were in conference together about him. We waited until we heard Nate's footsteps retreat back upstairs.

"Is Mrs. Simmons connected in some way with the current power struggle to control city hall in Oakland?" I asked.

Marcie paused before replying. "No, but I think Nate got her case through a recommendation from one of the black members on the Oakland City Council."

"Why would a black politician recommend Nate when there are so many up and coming black lawyers in Oakland who'd give an arm and a leg to get her as a client? It doesn't add up."

"I'm glad to see you can still reason with your head, R.C. Saundra and I thought maybe your reasoning powers ended somewhere below your belt when it comes to the Simmons bitch. If you keep asking the right questions, you'll start to see that she's here to use Nate in some twisted power game she's playing with her husband's family and her current lover."

Marcie's last statement surprised me. "Who's her lover?"

Marcie laughed. "That's what our little in-house investigator is supposed to find out."

I was getting the drift of what she expected off me. She was no fool. She must have known Nate would forbid me to share info with my co-workers. If I was reading her correctly, she expected me to unravel Mrs. Simmons' true motives for choosing our office and whatever game she was playing. It was even possible the whole divorce/separation investigation was a ploy to get information she could use for some ulterior purpose. If so, it made sense to use a law firm outside her circle, one that employed a black investigator.

Marcie seemed to be thinking along similar lines. "Find out what's going on inside the funeral home and why the Simmons woman is unable to get the information herself and you'll be well on the way to answering your questions. Try not to lose your objectivity with either Nate or the woman. Nate's already cut Saundra and me out of the loop and he's drooling at the mouth like a fifteen-year-old with his first scent of pussy. He's not capable of objectivity and the Simmons bitch knows it; she has him wrapped around her little finger. That's why you've got to keep your wits about you. Nate's the perfect fall guy for whatever scheme she's hatched. She's got him figured for a menopausal male who hasn't had much action between the sheets; someone who'll die for her if necessary for a good blow job. You, too, better watch your young black ass or she'll take you down with Nate in the bat of an eye."

Marcie's lecture was interrupted by the phone. Marcie listened briefly and hung up abruptly. I could tell from the light on the console Saundra had called. "I gotta go," Marcie muttered. She looked me straight in the eyes. "If you're smart, you won't tell Nate about our little talk, even if he asks you directly. Consider what I've said carefully. When you figure out what the Simmons bitch is up to with Nate, then you'll have a tough decision to make about where your loyalties lie. Both Saundra and I sincerely hope it's a decision you'll be able to make with your head and not your pecker." She paused to let her words sink in.

"Even though you may think you know something about women, you still have a lot to learn when it comes to a real black panther like the Simmons woman. You're going to have to learn to say 'No' and I'm sure it's not going to be easy. You've seen her effect on Nate. He's like a dog on a leash that's got a whiff of a bitch in heat. It's hard to watch because Nate is playing with fire that will burn him. When the time comes, you'd better be smart enough to side with us. Now I gotta go, so scoot out of here before Nate sees us."

I slipped into my office. I needed to make some calls to try and clean up loose ends on cases before Gloria Simmons summoned me. I heard Nate's footsteps on the stairs as he left for the day. I had no time to mull over Marcie's concerns. It was possible that her dire concerns were exaggerated and motivated by jealousy of a young rival.

I also thought Saundra was overreacting. Gloria Simmons was not a woman of color she could respect. Mrs. Simmons traded on her sexuality to get what she wanted while Saundra worked for everything; Saundra owed favors to no one. I was going to have to figure out who was right and suffer the consequences if I was wrong.

Chapter 3

IN MY UNSETTLED DREAMS I WAS BEING VAMPED AND duped by a series of women sirens all of whom presented different faces of Gloria Simmons. The shrill ringing of my phone rudely ended my less-than-sweet dreams; I was relieved to put them behind me.

"The boss expects to see you at 9:00 A.M. sharp, so don't be late," Marcie warned. "You got that through your thick head? Say something so I know you're awake."

"Thanks for the call Marcie. Don't worry. I'll be there. Is there anything else I need to know before meeting Nate?" Marcie's voice didn't sound hostile, but it wasn't super friendly either.

"No, you got the picture. Just remember what I said when the time comes." She rang off without further ado. She'd elected to keep her own counsel and keep the ball in my court. I couldn't expect any sympathy from Saundra either. I was definitely on probation until I came up with the goods on Gloria Simmons and clued them in. I was between a big rock and a nasty, hard place.

I hurriedly shaved, showered and tore into a couple of energy bars from the health food store. I washed them down with gulps of O.J. from the carton. The day was off to a shaky start. Hopefully, it would get better.

Saundra was busy with a new client when I popped through the door. She gave me one of her "you in deep shit" looks as I scooted past her work station and the sad-eyed woman she was tending to. I grabbed the pile of pink message slips and mail from my box that Saundra had sorted and read. I dumped everything on my cluttered desk and headed up the stairs to Nate's office.

His door was open and he was seated behind his desk with his nose in a file folder. He looked like shit. His fleshy face was blotchy and the big bags under his eyes sagged badly. He looked like he'd been on a two-day bender and desperately needed a shot of Scotch to pick him up. I couldn't help thinking of the sorry-eyed waif Saundra was attending to and he would have to interview. Nate was going to have to get sobered up quick and back in the saddle if he was going to get through the morning.

"Sit down, R.C. Did Saundra tell you what happened yesterday with Toni Perkins?"

His words caught me by surprise. "No, Saundra didn't mention anything about the Perkins' case this morning. She was busy with a client. I met with Toni yesterday and everything seemed OK. She seemed more pissed off about Benny's new lawyer than being kept waiting."

Nate didn't appear too interested in probing me about my session with her, so I waited for him to spit out what was on his mind.

"What an ungrateful bitch! I tried to explain to her that the private agreement they made violates public policy and is, therefore, unenforceable. That cocky piece of shit actually threatened me! Can you believe this crap?"

I was surprised by what he said. I thought Saundra had diffused Toni's anger and eased her out the door. It sounded like he'd had a run-in with her. "I thought she'd cooled down after meeting with me. Saundra was going to make her an appointment to see you next week when I left."

"The bitch waylaid me in the parking lot. Can you believe that? I work my butt off all day and when I drag my tired ass outta here to go home, I get jumped by her and her butchy girlfriend." Nate was working himself up to a boil. I needed to redirect his negative energy.

"She was OK when she left. It must have been her girlfriend who pushed her to make a scene. A good row with you probably plays well on the home front."

Nate wasn't about to be mollified. "The bitch gave me an ultimatum. Can you believe this shit? She actually threatened me. She said if I didn't get Benny Ross to drop custody and visitation rights, she was gonna sue me for malpractice and file a complaint with the State Bar. She was screaming in the parking lot, 'if we lose the kid, you're dead meat!' Can you believe it? We bust our balls for these ungrateful bitches and they threaten to cut off our balls if we don't win a case they fucked up from the start. Who needs this crap anyway?"

Nate's boiler was about to blow. His blotchy face had gone from red to purple. He desperately needed a drink to steady his rudder. Better try for a diversion.

"I need to see Mrs. Simmons' file. I've been thinking about the case and I want to kick around some ideas with you. But before I make a fool of myself with her, I need you to fill me in on some of the background missing in our meeting with her. I don't want to look stupid asking her for info she's already provided to you."

The change of subject worked. Nate slammed shut the Toni Perkins file and went over to a bank of locked file cabinets where he keeps his sensitive cases and his stock of Chivas Regal. Nate prides himself on not being an alcoholic by his special criteria. He likes to brag that he never takes a drink before cocktail time, which he roughly defines as starting somewhere between three and five in the afternoon depending on his needs and mood. I know for a fact that he nips throughout the day when he thinks no one is looking. His breath mints may fool his clients, but in our small office, there's no way you can hide much for long.

Nate's broad back was turned to me as he rummaged in the file cabinet. I was sure he was trying to figure out how to sneak a slug of Scotch without me noticing it. He pulled a file and handed it to me. He lingered at the cabinet while I opened the file.

I noted that the plain manila folder had no typed label like all the other files in our office. Nate had written 'Gloria Simmons' in his nearly illegible scrawl. Had Saundra organized the file, the label would have been neatly typed and read "Simmons v. Simmons – divorce." Inside the file, there was no completed office questionnaire with the demographic info Saundra compiles at intake. Instead, Nate had scribbled some nearly indecipherable notes on a sheet from a lined legal pad.

The notes were as follows: "husband – Jimmy Simmons – co-owner of Simmons Family Mortuary w/ brother Tony S. – Gloria (GS) married Las Vegas NV 4 yrs. ago – no childr. – joint checking – GS some separate prop. – royalty residuals from modeling & advertising – community prop? residence? autos? jewelry? Interest in family biz? Believes there's lots of cash and unreported income skimmed from the biz. Value of H's interest before and after 4 yrs marriage? Value of GS career before marriage?"

Nate hadn't been concerned with the usual demographic data: date of birth, date of marriage, reason for breakdown of the marriage, etc. Either Nate knew the info or left it for me to find out. His notes focused solely on evaluating her husband's income and property interests that could be divided in a divorce or legal separation. I jotted a summary of his info and when I looked up, Nate's eye were focused ruefully on his liquor cabinet.

"Where would you like me to start?"

"I want you to dig up financial info on the mortuary for starters. Mrs. Simmons reports that there are currently large amounts of cash washing through the business. As a result, the book value of the business is probably grossly underestimated intentionally. We may have to resort to a court subpoena to flush it out. They're probably keeping two sets of books."

"What makes Mrs. Simmons so sure there's lots of extra cash? Did she provide examples?"

"As she stated yesterday, her husband started giving her

large amounts of cash and putting more in their joint account about six months ago. Before that, he always deposited a business check into the account."

Nate's information seemed to answer how Mrs. Simmons had $5,000.00 cash to pay a retainer. She also must be skimming fat off the monthly budget or else had a sugar daddy on the side. It solved her problem of hiding her hiring a divorce lawyer – no telltale checks or statements for services rendered to trip up her game. Lots of spouses planning to split and run use similar tactics.

"Where does Mrs. Simmons believe the cash is coming from?" I asked boldly

"She doesn't know. She states that her husband likes to gamble and has always carried a big roll of cash on his person."

"Does she think maybe the mortuary gives him two checks as a monthly draw – one to deposit in his joint account and the other to cash for running-around money?" I thought the possibility was dubious but I wanted Nate's take on it.

Nate paused before replying. "I don't think so. Mrs. Simmons believes the cash he gives her every month is just a token of what he carries on him."

Nate was carefully weighing his words. It was not like him to hide and hedge behind "Mrs. Simmons believes." He's usually more open and free-wheeling. I suspected he knew a lot more about the origins of the cash than he was prepared to reveal. I decided to try a different tack.

"Why does Mrs. Simmons want to divorce?"

"She's not sure she does at this point. That's why she insists on discretion and strict confidentiality on our part."

I had to bite my tongue not to point out that's why suspicious wives hire private detectives and not divorce attorneys to get the goods on their spouses. Despite the fact Nate was playing cat and mouse with me, I saw no reason to bite the hand that was feeding us. The legal business is no different from other professions where cash is king. Mrs. Simmons had casually coughed up five grand on word-of-mouth promises and a receipt in Nate's locked file. There'd be lots more cash coming provided we secured and fed her the information she wanted.

I wanted to hit Nate up for a raise in pay. With a couple of well-heeled clients flush with cash like Gloria Simmons, Nate would be able to pay me what I think I'm worth as a junior lawyer and not just as his investigator. But first, I had to produce the goods. I had one more question. "How did Mrs. Simmons get referred to us? I didn't see any mention in your notes."

"That's confidential. When can you get to work on the investigation? I would like to have something concrete to give her as soon as possible in light of her generous retainer."

"It depends on how much work you want me to do on our other cases. There's the final work on Sharon Miller's case as well as Patsy Kline's case to try to settle. Of course, we have Toni Perkins to deal with as well."

"Fuck Toni Perkins! She can kiss my ass. She's gonna stew and bite her nails before she hears from me. If she dares to file a complaint with the State Bar, you will see to it that she never gets sole custody of her kid." Nate's face flushed red again.

Nate's threat to have me sabotage her case was not lost on me. Nate planned to keep my ass in a sling regarding any malpractice complaint. Everyone around me seemed to be hedging their bets and looking for me to take the fall if things went awry or I didn't play their game. I recalled my grandpappy's admonition that "white bosses gonna work your black hide to the bone, then dump you like a broken mule."

Marcie was right; I was going to have to dig up almost all the info on the Simmons case by myself. Nate was stonewalling me. Before I found myself out a limb while someone was sawing it off, I needed to clarify the limits of my authority.

"You want me to restrict my investigation to public sources of information or do you want me to employ my street people to try to get a fix on what's going down at the mortuary?"

"I want you to use all your resources on this case, R.C. Just be discrete and careful. The Simmons brothers won't be amused if they discover you investigating their business." I sensed an uncomfortable edge of danger in Nate's veiled warning. He's not a good liar or actor. He knew much more than he was prepared to reveal. I'd have to snoop around to find out. I needed to know of couple of more things before I started.

"Do you want me to gather the demographic info we need to file a petition for divorce or legal separation that's not in the file?"

"No, leave that to me."

"What about the info I get as I go along? Suppose she asks for it before I can discuss it with you? Do I put her off or give it to her when she demands it? You may be hard to reach if I have to go through Marcie or Saundra; they're sure to listen to anything I say."

Nate rubbed his chin while he pondered what to tell me. "Respond directly and truthfully to her questions, but don't volunteer information. I want a written report on your findings daily. You can write it by hand, but leave no copy in your office computer if you type it. Your reports are to be left in her file in my locked safe."

I was sorely tempted to ask for a notebook computer I could carry with me. I quashed my impulse to demand one. I'd wait until I had some juicy info before insisting I needed an expensive toy to aide my investigation. Nate wanted me to be his good man Friday. He'd be perfectly happy with hand-written reports to have an excuse to meet directly with Gloria Simmons.

Like most infatuated males, Nate didn't want me getting too close to Mrs. Simmons. He expected me to concentrate on the mortuary and leave the more intimate inquiries to him. Nate knows me well enough to know I'd pump Mrs. Simmons for whatever info I needed whether he liked it or not. He also knew I wouldn't reveal how my street contacts worked or what info they developed unless I wanted him to know. He was bound to practice law within the strictures of the California Evidence Code and the Code of Professional Ethics regulating lawyers' conduct; I wasn't yet, so he knew better than press me on my sources or how they got their info.

Nate kept a stash of cash in his safe for me to use to pay my eyes and ears on the street. No receipts and no questions as to how I used the money so long as I got the goods; just as well our client paid cash. There'd be no paper trail in billing records regarding who I paid and for what.

"I'll need $500.00 in pocket money to start. I'll have a written report in your safe by 5 P.M. tomorrow providing I don't have to work on pending cases."

Nate didn't hesitate to swing his safe open and hand me a wad of greenbacks. He knew I only wanted small, well-used bills to pay my "street expenses." I stuffed the pile of 20's, 10's and 5's in my pocket.

"I'm gonna drop Perkins. What about Sharon Miller and Patsy Kline? I'd like to drop them as well."

"I think we have Miller's settlement wrapped up." He rummaged through the files on his desk and pulled one; he removed the top pleading document and handed it to me.

"Make a copy and take it around for her to sign when you have time. Her husband has signed off on the child support and alimony. Tell her I'm sorry I can't meet with her personally. She should be happy with the results. You'll have to meet with the Kline woman. I'm booked solid with depositions. You did the investigation, so you can give her the bad news yourself."

I shrugged. We both knew if Mrs. Simmons called in the meantime, I was expected to drop everything and play run and fetch it for Nate's primetime client. As I left, I was pleased to see Marcie's door was closed. After making a copy of the Sharon Miller settlement, I called her to set up a time to drop by her apartment to sign her settlement agreement. I called Patsy Kline and set up an appointment in my office for later that afternoon.

I hustled out of the office past Saundra who was still with a client. She gave me the evil eye, but held her tongue in front of the woman seated at her desk. I smiled at the woman; she looked to be in her early forties. She regarded me with a sad, doleful expression of bewilderment. Her faded calico dress looked like it came from an old Montgomery Ward mail order catalogue for farm wives. She'd twisted her long, chestnut-colored hair into a flat pigtail and stuffed her still pretty feet into nondescript Birkenstock sandals. No wonder Gloria Simmons could breeze into Nate's office and sweep him off his feet.

I'd work outside the office until my appointment with Patsy Kline to avoid Nate's staff monitoring my moves.

Chapter 4

AFTER SKIPPING OUT OF THE OFFICE, I HEADED TO a funky, little café called "Reggie's Place" on Martin Luther King Way near the Berkeley-Oakland border. I waved to Reggie, who was chopping and dicing vegetables; I slid into a booth at the back where I could watch the door. It's been a habit of mine ever since I read how Malcolm X always kept his back to the wall and an eye on lookout so his enemies couldn't take him by surprise.

As a kid raised in Berkeley, I'd identified with Malcolm X and his red hair and light-colored skin. In spite of Berkeley's reputation for racial tolerance, life was hell for a kid like me growing up in this town. I wasn't accepted by either black or white kids at school. There were few half-breed blacks like me with a black father and white mother to provide a buffer from the insults and taunts from the cliques of both races that dominated high school. Despite my pale milk chocolate-colored skin and frizzy, rather than kinky hair, I was still a nigger to most of the white kids and a pariah to black kids who resented my white liberal mother with her dark, wavy hair and honey-olive skin inherited from her Sephardic ancestors.

They especially resented my father's café-au-lait coloring and Creole good looks. I think kids of both races resented dad most because they thought he'd humped his way into the white man's world where he didn't belong.

I feel at home in Reggie's Place. I come here often to write notes on cases and plan investigations. Reggie and I share first names and black skin. The last time anyone called me Reginald Charles instead of R.C., I was in some kind of trouble.

Reggie tipped his green and white A's baseball cap on my arrival. The lunch special was scrawled on a small chalk board behind the register in large letters, "Fish Gumbo with Corn Bread." My stomach was already responding to the delicious smells coming from the big iron pots on the stove. I pointed to the chalk board and Reggie flashed me a knowing smile.

When he'd finished chopping his veggies, he brought me a steaming mug of black coffee and plopped it down on the Formica table.

"How you doin', R.C.? Mista' Charlie keepin' you on the run?"

"Same as always, Reggie. The Man likes to see his little darkie play step an' fetch it. Otherwise, he don't be too friendly when it's time to cut my pay."

"Yeah, we all's got the same mis'ry, R.C. Them white college folks like to come here an' watch ol' Reggie do some steppin' and fetchin' too. Be along wid' yo' gumbo shortly."

I pulled my daybook out of my backpack and started a list of things to do on the Simmons case. I needed to nose around the mortuary before anyone suspected what I was up to. I planned to pay a visit on my way back from the courthouse in downtown Oakland.

I called my sister, Tiffany, on my cell phone and left her a message to order title, tax and credit reports for the mortuary on the "QT." She's a real estate broker. I signed off with "Catch you later, Miss Gator" which is our code to call me after ten at my cottage.

My next call was to my old buddy, Jeff Banes, at All American Insurance where we used to work together. "Say, Jeff, how you been doin'?"

"Hey, R.C., I was thinking about you, you lucky bastard. I'm commuting two hours a day to the City where I'm chained to my computer terminal while you're running around on the loose spending clients' money on God knows what monkey business. I'm jealous."

"Naw, you got it all wrong, Jeff. I'm the guy running around sweating how to pay the bills and risking his neck on a legal assistant's pay as an independent contractor. You got the paid vacation, the health plan and the company car." Jeff chuckled. We both knew he'd give his eyetooth to be out on his own, but couldn't. He hated the office routine, but with a diabetic kid at home, he couldn't afford to give up his generous medical benefits. If he quit, he'd never get coverage for his sick kid even though he worked in insurance.

"What's up?" Jeff asked.

"I need some info on a case. Need to know who's insuring a black mortuary in Oakland called the Simmons Family Mortuary. I'm especially interested in their liability and malpractice coverage. You know, policy limits and whether they've been nailed for any big claims in the last four years."

"You're not thinking of investing in one of the most lucrative businesses known to man without cutting in your old buddy Jeff, are you?"

"Wish it were so, Jeff. I'm just doing a routine background on a marital property evaluation. I figure there can't be many underwriters for such a specialized business."

"Should be no problem to get the coverage, but it may take a couple of days to track claim records since we don't do this type of underwriting."

"No problem on the time frame. Get me everything you can. Give my love to Polly and the kids."

I had the rest of my plan of attack organized when Reggie whisked a steaming plate of gumbo under my nose and set it on the table. The savory smell of the gumbo along with the three freshly baked pieces of cornbread excited my stomach juices; I couldn't wait to sop up the gumbo with the cornbread. The meal was probably going to be the highlight of my day. I wolfed it down just as fast as I could shovel it in my craw without burning a hole in my throat.

My first stop on my way to the courthouse was at Sharon

Miller's apartment in the University Village where Cal houses its married students in dilapidated four-plexes built for military personnel during WW II.

Sharon was thrilled to sign her divorce agreement which gave her four years of alimony support in addition to child support to complete her undergraduate B.A. degree and earn a Master's degree in business administration. Sharon hugged me and pleaded for me to celebrate her victory over her ex by taking her to dinner. Sharon put her ex through grad school; he rewarded her sacrifices by dumping her and their two kids to start his new career in public planning with a younger wife he'd romanced on Sharon's earnings as a secretary.

I should have said "No" nicely and begged off the temptation. Sharon's a lovely woman with a trim figure, flaming-red hair and an engaging smile. I felt bad to let her down on her moment of triumph which she attributed to my snooping and nailing her ex. I rationalized that a night out dining and dancing would take my mind off Gloria Simmons.

After agreeing to pick up Sharon later, I made my way down San Pablo Avenue to Oakland. The further I penetrated the inner city, the bleaker the tableau became; I passed run-down tenements alongside long-neglected Victorians, their weather-bleached boards raw and screaming for a coat of paint, their windows without glass or papered with cardboard. Bandit liquor stores on most corners had windows barred and mean-looking brothers leaning against doorways, watching who was buying what.

The old courthouse across from the more modern Oakland Museum had barely survived the '89 earthquake. I shuddered to think of the problems if the building had burned. Most of the official records I consult are housed in this antiquated structure.

I stopped first at the Recorder's office. It took twenty minutes working with microfiche to learn that the mortuary's real property was not owned by the Simmons brothers, but by a Nevada corporation called TJS Enterprises, Inc. The deed had been recorded eighteen months earlier. The deed to the Nevada corporation was signed by the Simmons brothers who had gained title from a deed from the probate court at their father's death. I paid to get copies I could pick up before leaving the courthouse.

I stopped next at the "bullpen" where legal actions are filed and stored. While a surly clerk begrudgingly searched for the probate case in the inactive files, I ran the index listing lawsuits filed to see if any were against the mortuary. I was rewarded with one active and two inactive litigation files. When the clerk handed me the probate file, I handed her the requisition slips for the lawsuits and my order and check for copying them. I scooted off to the Vital Records office before the clerk could start bitching and throwing me nasty looks.

I wanted to see if Jimmy Simmons had taken out a marriage license; he hadn't. I had better luck checking the filings for fictitious business name statements. Booker T. Simmons had filed a statement six years ago stating he owned the mortuary as a sole proprietor. I was surprised there was no filing after the father's death and deeding to the Nevada corporation. It might be an innocent oversight by the Nevada attorney unfamiliar with California requirements or it might be an intentional omission to hide ownership by an out-of-state entity. I made a note to check with the Dept. of Corporations in Sacramento to see if the Nevada corporation had registered with the state and designated a local agent for service of process in case of litigation. I wondered also if Gloria Simmons was aware of the Nevada connection to the business.

I picked up the copies I'd ordered and headed back to the office to face Patsy Kline. I got caught in traffic and Patsy was fuming when I arrived. Saundra was smirking behind her word processor and watching Patsy getting ready to take me to task. She'd probably been helping Patsy load her gun for big game for the moment I came into her sights.

Saundra announced, "Mr. Bean can see you now," in a sing-song voice full of sham.

Patsy looked a bit worse for wear; she was in her early thirties and starting to put beef on her thighs. She wore a black cocktail dress that emphasized her buxom features but made her look gaudy. She'd over-rouged her cheeks and lips and wore nail polish that clashed with her hennaed hair worn in a ponytail. Her legs were without hose and her feet were stuffed into scuffed high-heels. She'd worked as a cocktail waitress while her husband took his time getting his M.B.A. degree.

According to Patsy, he started investing her tips in penny gold mining stocks on the unregulated Vancouver Mining Exchange. He claimed they'd be rich by the time he graduated from Cal. My investigation discovered that he'd registered all the mining shares in his name only and had his broker hold them so Patsy couldn't see his deceit. Patsy was sure the stocks must be worth a fortune. Her hubby vanished after getting his master's degree and left her with a five year-old kid and two months worth of unpaid bills and rent. Naturally, Patsy was angry as a disturbed hornet and expected me to find and squeeze money out of her departed spouse.

Patsy lit up a cigarette and blew smoke in the direction of the "Smoke And I'll Croak" sign behind my desk. Working in a smoke-filled bar hadn't helped her complexion or her sense of humor.

"So, have you found the bastard?" Her voice was deepened by years of smoking.

"No, he's still on the move."

"What about all the investments he made with my money?" She took a deep drag on her cigarette and gave me a piercing look.

I tried to avoid her penetrating gaze. "I'm afraid I don't have good news on that front either ..."

"What the fuck! I don't believe this. No way you're gonna sit there and tell me the bastard got away with all my hard-earned money. I'll kill the slick fucker." She had a stranglehold on her cigarette and her other hand pumped up and down in my direction.

"He didn't get away with anything. The stocks are all worthless. They were all highly speculative issues and most of the companies went belly-up."

"You mean he stole my hard-earned money and blew it, don't

you?" Her face was flushed and she was on the edge of her seat.

"That's one way of looking at it. Another way is that he knowingly made high-risk investments and lost."

"The son-of-a-bitch ripped off Katie and me, and didn't have the smarts to turn a profit on what he stole. The loser lived off me to go to business school. What a waste! I want you to see he goes to jail."

"You need to talk to Mr. Green about that. I'll make an appointment for you to see him to discuss your legal remedies," I said with a straight face.

Patsy seemed only somewhat mollified by my shunting her off on Nate. I figured it served him right. She was going to be furious when she learned she had hardly any legal recourse against her husband's actions other than to nail him for unpaid child support. He'd invested community property income and lost it. It might be impossible to collect the child support. We didn't know where he'd skipped to; he was probably in another state busy setting up a new identity. Let Nate take the heat. I made her an appointment to see him in three days. Tit for Tat.

I knew I should cancel my dinner date with Sharon Miller. It wasn't a good idea to date clients. Things tend to get sticky real fast. Instead of cancelling, I rationalized that it would be good for both of us to get our minds off recent troubles.

My plan for our evening was simple: enjoy a nice relaxed dinner so we could get to know each other better, then head off to a club in Emeryville where we could dance our asses off and burn off our dinner. I planned to take Sharon back to her apartment, share a friendly kiss at her door and get to bed at a reasonable hour to be ready for a hectic day tomorrow. I had thought of everything for a nice, uncomplicated evening except for what Sharon Miller wanted.

She greeted me with a big, freckled smile. She was dressed in a sexy, form-fitting, green satin cocktail dress with a scoop-neck bodice and a hem that stopped four inches above her knees. I'd only seen her in jeans and long-sleeved shirts and had no idea until now how physically attractive she was. She'd tamed her mop of carrot-red hair with gold barrettes and wore matching hoop earrings. She let me know she could change her high heels for dancing shoes she'd stuffed in her oversize bag once we got to the club. The lady was dressed to party.

I took her to dinner at a local, mellow seafood restaurant on the Berkeley Marina that caters to a mixed-race crowd. I was reluctant to take her to one of the soul food restaurants I prefer because it could be tricky on a first date with a white lady. Sharon had spent most of her life in a small, conservative, white farming community in the Central Valley. I wasn't sure how comfortable she'd be if we dined on unfamiliar food in a restaurant where she'd probably be the only white person. Once I saw how she'd dressed, there was no way I'd take her to her to dine in a black restaurant.

She might cause a riot.

Sharon took my mind of Gloria Simmons right away. She was real excited to be out on a date after all she'd been through. She was real easy to talk to and we really enjoyed each other's company.

We lingered over our meal to the annoyance of our waiter. Before either of us realized it, we'd sipped through two bottles of Charles Mondavi Chardonnay wine. Sharon's deep hazel eyes kept changing color from brownish to greenish hues as they reflected complex emotions. We talked comfortably about our very different lives growing up. Sharon told me about getting pregnant and dropping out of college to support her husband and the kid. He'd been her high school sweetheart and she'd never slept with anyone before or after she'd married him. She felt betrayed by him; he'd dumped her after ten years so he could start his career with a younger woman.

By the time I paid the bill as the restaurant was closing, we were both a little drunk and in a festive mood. As we made our way to my 1968 Chevy Impala, she slipped her hand in mine and squeezed and I did the same.

Before I could engage the ignition, Sharon was all over me. I'm not used to women I date making the moves, but there was no guile on her part. Her husband hadn't touched her in nine months and she was hungry for a man's touch.

She kissed me with fervor and we explored and probed with our tongues. I slid the palm of my hand slowly across the soft satin fabric molding her breasts. She shivered. Her nipples hardened and stretched to meet my fingertips through her dress as my fingers softly traced their outline through the fabric.

She moaned softly as I moved my fingers slowly inside the bodice of her dress and under her pushup bra. I carefully slipped the dress straps over her shoulders and released her breasts from their restraint. Her moans grew more urgent when I let my fingers move tenderly down her torso to explore her soft but mature body molding her dress. When I reached her thighs, I increased the pressure and moved slowly back up to her breasts. As I reached the swell of her breasts, she arched her back to meet my hand. Her body trembled with anticipation as I gently tugged her erect nipples one by one.

She moaned deeply as she helped me unfasten her bra and slip her dress down to her waist. Sharon's nipples were superb. They were the most erotic and sensitive I've ever touched. They were hard, thick and nearly an inch long when fully erect. I couldn't get enough of either one. They were so responsive that when I stroked one, Sharon guided my hand to her other nipple. Playing doctor as a kid with my female cousins hadn't prepared me adequately for the joys Sharon provided.

We both got pretty steamed up. It had been a long time since I made love in the back seat of an automobile, but that's what we did. We were a couple of happy campers. What a jerk she married not to appreciate how exciting his wife could be once she was turned on. He had an uncut diamond in the rough in his bed for ten years and didn't know it for diddly. Sharon wasted ten years of her life and her college years with a dumb clown who couldn't appreciate her intelligence, kind heart, openness and simmering sexuality. She was so grateful for some good loving that she was crying tears of joy when I finally dropped her back at her apartment in the wee hours of the morning.

I'd flubbed my chance to get a fresh start in the morning, but who cared other than perhaps Nate. Sharon's celebration was a once in a lifetime event for us both.

Chapter 5

I WOKE UP WITH A HEADACHE AND MILD HANGOVER. NOT
the ideal way to start the day, but the memory of last night's
frolic in the back seat of my Impala was worth the price
and more. After showering and loading up on strong coffee,
toasted bagels slathered with butter and heaped with jam, I sat
down to read the mortuary's active litigation file.

The complaint alleged negligent handling of a corpse. It
claimed the Simmons Family Mortuary failed in a timely way
to ship the body of a fifty-six year-old man named Johnnie
Carpenter to Atlanta, Georgia where his relatives awaited its
arrival for burial; they'd shipped it to Las Vegas, Nevada instead.

Mr. Carpenter's wife and daughter claimed the body had
been shipped to the Lone Pine Mortuary in Las Vegas where
it had been "improperly and negligently maintained so as to
accelerate the decomposition of Mr. Carpenter's remains."
They further alleged that the six-day delay to send their loved
one to Atlanta, with no embalming, deprived the plaintiffs and
their relatives the opportunity to bury the decedent in an open
casket and delayed the funeral and burial. They contended that
the sight and smell of their loved one in such a deplorable con-
dition caused them "extreme emotional grief that should be
compensated in an amount in excess of Twenty-Five Thousand
Dollars."

The mortuary answered the complaint by denying "each and every allegation." The mortuary was represented by the local Oakland law firm of Bronson and Bronson, a father and son team. Willard Bronson had served as Judge of the Superior Court, but had to resign his judgeship and return to private practice. There had been allegations of sweetheart investment deals with litigants and unprofessional leaks of information, He'd been pressured by members of the local bar to resign quietly and let the dirty business molder under the rug. It was either that or a grand jury investigation and complaint to the state bar association which could result in disbarment. Judge Bronson had served his stint on the bench long enough to solidify his social standing with the movers and shakers in the African-American community and pave the way for him and his son to mount a very lucrative law practice.

Royce Bronson was a suave ladies' man and cool cat who frequented the local late night club scene. He was the type of attorney I thought Gloria Simmons would choose to handle her business. I'd seen Royce on many occasions around the courthouse. He was tall, dark and handsome and knew it.

I made a note to check out both Bronsons with my legal contacts. To my knowledge, Nate had never had any dealings with either the father or son. I hoped to get some feedback on whether the complaint against the mortuary was merely a nuisance suit designed to get a quick insurance settlement or really had some merit that warranted compensation.

The complaint had been filed by a big-name San Francisco law firm. They wouldn't give me the time of day. But if Jeff Banes could track the adjuster handling the claim, I might get an inside look at the claim records through Jeff's good offices. Insurance pros will share info on a tit-for-tat basis.

It was time to visit the mortuary. As I weaved through the afternoon traffic, I pondered whether Oakland would ever recover from the double whammy of the prolonged recession and the devastating effects of the 1989 Loma Prieta earthquake. Many of the older brick buildings downtown were damaged so severely they remained boarded up. I'd heard through the grapevine that a lot of black merchants grumbled that members of the ever-expanding Chinese community were using Hong Kong money to buy the quake-damaged buildings at fire sale prices.

My sister Tiffany claimed she'd heard of investors arriving from Hong Kong with suitcases stuffed with hundred dollar bills to invest in Bay Area real estate. As San Francisco real estate cost top dollar, smart investors gobbled up Oakland's cheaper properties on spec. The cash might be buying title, but it wasn't doing much rebuilding as far as I could see.

Everywhere I looked, I saw only hard-luck black folks shuffling along in front of boarded up or heavily grilled storefronts. At each corner liquor store, young blacks with no work or prospects waited for a handout, a slug of "gorilla juice" from a malt liquor bottle in a brown-paper bag, or a mark to hit on. Things were not much improved when I arrived at the mortuary at Twenty-Second and Broadway.

The Simmons Family Mortuary stood out from its surroundings primarily because it was nicely landscaped. It was a little oasis in a desert of early twentieth century wood, brick and stucco buildings. The mortuary was situated on a small rise of land and could have been mistaken for one of the many churches sprinkled through the neighborhood if its signs had not been so garish.

The roof of the funeral home looked like a large A-frame structure. The row of French windows upstairs on the left side probably housed the administrative offices. The roof on the right side sloped into a covered breezeway to allow the mortuary's fleet of Cadillac limos and hearses to turn around the building to pick up the casket and the decedent's family from the side door of the chapel.

I parked in the lot to the left near the crematorium and walked back to the front of the building and along the curved brick walkway leading to the front door. I had slipped on a tatty tweed jacket I keep in my car to upgrade my jeans, polo shirt and sneakers. I was wearing my darkest shades to hide my eyes and my role as an aggrieved relative I would play to learn how the mortuary operated.

I was just about to pull the handle of the front door when it suddenly opened as if on command. The dude on the other side must have seen me coming. He was tall, coal-black and slick looking in his double-breasted sharkskin suit. His Fifties'-style threads must have set him back a bundle of C-notes. His designer shades were darker than mine.

"My name's Brother Thomas. What can we do for you in your time of sorrow, Little Brother?"

His sudden appearance caught me off guard and I stammered something unintelligible while I stalled for time. My confusion didn't seem to faze him. He must have been used to soft-pitching scared relatives in the midst of personal grief who were faced with funeral expenses they most likely couldn't afford. Brother Thomas looked more like someone's bodyguard than an undertaker.

"Uh, it's about my Auntie. She's had a bad stroke and the doctor says she ain't about to make it much longer. I gotta see about making some preparations for when she passes. Could be any day now."

"Not to worry, Little Brother. You definitely come to the right place. We gonna take care of all your Auntie's needs in a way she be proud of you. Y'all don't need to do nothin' 'cept decide on which plan you want for yo' special Auntie. We a full service funeral home an' we gotta credit plan for every budget. Juss follow me into the office an' we gonna check out how ta make your Auntie's limited time on earth peaceful an' serene while she waitin' for the Lord to claim her for His own."

I dutifully followed Brother Thomas into a spacious reception room. He sat down behind a big mahogany desk and motioned me to one of several matching blue velour chairs facing him. The chairs looked liked they belonged in a rich man's mansion. They were big, plush and designed to let even the biggest fanny settle right in.

I caught the glint of light from overhead spotlights on the fancy hardware on a row of caskets raised on a special platform encircling the room. The one behind Brother Thomas looked like it had been customized in an auto body shop. It was metallic silver with gold trim; it only needed wheels and some detailing to pass for a street rod. You'd probably need one of those suitcases stuffed with cash to buy one of these boxes.

I could feel Brother Thomas' eyes behind his shades sizing up my reaction to my new surroundings. He'd probably seen me arrive in my old Chevy and knew I couldn't afford anything more than a simple pine box. That wouldn't stop him from trying to sell me a box beyond my means. His next move surprised me.

"Why don't you juss take yo' time, Little Brother. Have a look at our fine selection of caskets and think hard 'bout which one your dear Auntie'd choose for her trip to the Promised Lan'. This here book gotta summary of all our different burial plans and fun'ral services," he said pointing to a large folio on his desk. "An' if yo' Auntie ain't got no burial plot, they's a list of real estate prices at the cemeteries at the end."

I picked up the large, loose-leaf bound book and quickly skimmed through it while Brother Thomas excused himself to let me absorb the shocking cost of being buried in style. "Be back in a few minutes to discuss how we gonna take care of yo' Auntie."

The overhead spots now reflected the glimmer of Brother Thomas' big gold pinkie ring off his spit-and-polish black patent leather shoes as he exited. He must have pressed a hidden button because speakers somewhere in the ceiling now softly murmured the sound of Bobby Bland singing, "Feel So Bad."

As soon as he was gone, I got up and checked the price tags on several of the customized coffins. Prices ranged from $1,500.00 for the simplest one which wasn't much more than the proverbial pine box to twenty-two grand for the most ornate model with gold-plated hardware. A quick glance through the book revealed that the basic plan included pick up at the hospital or morgue, embalming, dressing for the memorial service in the mortuary's chapel, and a trip to a local cemetery. The coffin was extra; so were the services of a preacher for the chapel and graveside service. The mortuary could hire a preacher for a hundred bucks a hit and even provide a church choir to sing your favorite spirituals for an extra grand.

It would take at least $6,000.00 to get my fictional Auntie in and out of the doors of the Simmons Family Mortuary with no extras and a cheap coffin a couple of grades above a pine box; it would have removable handles and cheap velveteen lining. What did poor folks do? Most folks would be shamed into buying a coffin and services well beyond their means. For ten percent down, the mortuary would finance your burial provided you could put up a house, had other valuable collateral, or an acceptable guarantor for the loan. Finance charges were at the going rates for major credit cards.

Up to now, no one had ever clued me in on how expensive dying was going to be. As soon as I got the figures straight, I marked them on a pad and then snuck a look outside the room. Another door not far down the hall was open, so I scampered down the corridor and copped a look. It was a carbon copy of the one I'd just left. They probably watched the newspapers for drive-by shootings and had two salesmen working during busy periods. From my vantage point I saw stairs leading up to another level; a side door to the parking lot, and another door leading to the chapel I'd glimpsed on the way in.

I was tempted to hop up the stairs to confirm where they kept their business records, but knew it would blow my cover. I ducked into the chapel instead.

The chapel was like most local churches except for a big double door on the right. By guessing at the distances to the choir seats and raised platform for the pastor's lectern, I surmised that the cold storage and embalming facilities must be located behind the chapel on the right. That meant the business offices and records were up the stairs on the left overlooking the parking lot.

While I was trying devise a plausible ruse to sneak upstairs, Brother Thomas caught up to me in the chapel. "Sorry to keep you waitin' so long, Little Brother. Had to do some call backs to arrange for this weekend's services. How you comin' along wid yo' plannin' fo' yo' Auntie?"

"I'm startin' to get the big picture. I do got some questions."

"That's what I'm here for, Little Brother. What you need to know?"

"Well, my Auntie come from Louisiana an' she really wanna be buried back home with her people when she pass."

"Ain't nothin' simpler, Little Brother. When da' time come, we gonna take care a' all yo' Auntie's business juss like she want. Everything the same wid' the basic plan 'cept the graveside service an' burial be done down home in Louisiana. She gonna have her memorial service here wid' all her friends an' family, then we gonna ship your Auntie back home first class. Gonna come ta 'bout the same money she buried here. You juss gonna need to order her a fine casket to make shore yo' Auntie and her people back home be proud a' the way you send her off. Where you say yo' Auntie stayin' now?"

I hadn't said anything about where my Auntie was because I didn't have one. Brother Thomas was trying to close a sale and probably had a big, fat commission to make at my expense. I needed to think of an escape without arousing suspicion I was playing him for a fool. I also needed to figure a way to access the mortuary's business records and meet the Chinese bookkeeper.

"Shore is a relief to know y'all can take care of my Auntie when she pass. Uncle Paul shore gonna be relieved, too. He ain't moving too good; he got a real bad problem with stiff joints, a bad ticker an' all. That's why he send me 'round to do some checking. He ain't got a lot of money and he mighty worried about what it all gonna cost. So, could you put down some numbers so maybe he can get some help with financing?"

"No problem, Little Brother. Juss take me minute to do yo' figures. What name you want on yo' papers?"

He caught me by surprise. "Uh, might as well put 'em down in my name; I'm probably gonna have to help Uncle Paul with a credit card. They call me Reggie Jones." I lied hoping the dude wasn't going demand to verify my credit on the spot.

"Then Brother Jones it is." He dropped his jiving when his fingers hit the calculator keys. It was frightening to see how fast he could add up a bunch of figures that would set me back just under $7,000.00 and put me on a fast track to the poor house.

"Say, uh, you think it would be OK if I could bring Uncle Paul down here to one of your chapel services? He be too sickly to go back home when Auntie do pass. Would ease his mind a plenty to know he gonna have a memorial service right here for all they friends."

"No problem, Brother Jones. We havin' special 'morial services Friday an' Saturday evenings. The one on Friday gonna have a full gospel choir from the Ebenezer Church of God. You bring yo' Uncle Paul on down on Friday and he gonna be real happy he doin' business wid' Simmons Family Mortuary."

"Sounds like a winner! See you on Friday."

Brother Thomas gave me a big gold-toothy smile and pumped my hand vigorously. He shoved a sample contract he'd filled out and a credit application in my hand for me to return on Friday. I could almost hear the click, click, click as he mentally rang up his commission from another sucker.

It was just after four thirty in the afternoon as I crossed the parking lot to my car. I decided to pick up an order of barbecued ribs and a six-pack of Bud Light before doubling back to observe the mortuary staff leave for the day. I jotted down the makes and license numbers of all the cars in the lot. I wanted to match faces with each vehicle. I especially wanted to get a good look at the new bookkeeper, Jennifer Wong.

Chapter 6

I MADE IT BACK TO THE MORTUARY WITH ONLY TEN minutes to spare before the first employees started to leave. I watched the door to the parking lot from my car parked across the street. Two middle-aged black men came out together. They were dressed casually and probably worked in embalming or maintenance. They chatted amiably for a bit and then headed for their modest cars and departed.

The next group took its time to appear. It gave me time to wolf down most of my order of barbecued ribs and guzzle a can of Bud Light. I smudged my note book with greasy fingers as I didn't have time to wipe them when three employees burst out in quick order – two black men and a middle-aged black woman in a white blouse and tan slacks. She got into a Honda Civic while the two nattily-dressed men headed for two late model Cadillac El Dorados. By the looks of their highly waxed cars, manner of dress and the ease with which they handled their expensive cars, I pegged them as chauffeurs or detail men in charge of the mortuary's rolling stock.

I had to wait a good twenty minutes for Brother Thomas and his clone to appear. I scrunched down in my seat and hoped Brother Thomas wouldn't recognize my car or me peering over the steering wheel. The two salesmen were dressed alike right down to their designer shades and patent leather shoes. While Brother Thomas's hair was jelled and slicked back in Fifties style, the other Brother wore his short, kinky hair with a part down the center.

They laughed and jived with each other. I could imagine them programming the office CD player with lamenting blues songs sung by Bessie Smith, Muddy Waters and gospel songs by Marianne Anderson; renditions to move the spirit with tearful remembrances of loved ones lost. I marveled at such a cynical business: "Juss sign the contract, Little Brother, an' we gonna take care of everything."

There wasn't much action after Brother Thomas and his buddy left in identical, metallic-black BMW's. I was bored waiting and debated popping the top of another Bud. If I did, I'd have to keep my legs crossed and hope the two remaining lights would be turned off real soon. I have a bladder with a ten-minute timer. What goes in starts pressing for relief ten minutes later. I had no business drinking beer or anything else on a stakeout. The longer I had to wait, the more urgent the need to pee.

Trying to take a leak while parked on a street in Oakland is good way to get noticed fast. Local loungers and the eyes behind the second-storey tattered blinds don't miss much going down on the street. Even if you weren't spotted, you can be sure the moment you ducked behind a tall bush, the mark you've been tailing will choose that moment to slip by you. So, there's really no choice if you're foolish enough to drink on a stakeout; you've got to bake it.

I was about to give in to temptation when a slim, attractive, modestly-dressed Asian woman rushed out the door, looked carefully around the parking lot and made her way quickly to a snazzy, black Toyota Celica at the far end of the lot. I assumed she was Jennifer Wong.

As she quick-stepped to her car in medium heels, one of the two remaining lights upstairs turned off. Ms. Wong slid into the driver's seat of her car just as a handsome black man appeared at the door of the mortuary, scanned the lot and street furtively in all directions before moving hastily to the woman's Celica.

I managed only a fleeting look at the man who had his back to me except for a brief instant when he glanced in my direction where I had ducked. He looked in his mid-thirties, was dressed in an expensive Italian-tailored suit, and had hands the color of the chocolate on a Mars bar that glinted with gold rings. The flash of heavy gold chains dangling from his neck together with the finger rings distracted my view. The man was a walking gold mine. It gave me the macabre thought that perhaps all that gold was custom-crafted from the teeth of his clients.

He slid in beside Ms. Wong and I watched with binoculars as their heads bobbed together for a couple of minutes. As the man exited the car, it looked like he passed a small envelope to Ms. Wong but I couldn't be sure. The man ran his forefinger down the woman's face and her figure as she leaned to pull the door shut.

It was a strange scene. What was an attractive Asian woman in her mid-twenties doing working in a black-owned mortuary? What was one of the mortuary's kingpins doing with the woman in the parking lot? It didn't make sense. Members of Oakland's rival Chinese and Black communities don't socialize or mingle. Was this an office romance – another taboo inter-racial meeting on the sly like the one responsible for bringing me into the world?

I didn't have long to contemplate the unexpected scene. The Celica's motor revved and it raced out of the lot. I ducked my head as it came directly at me. By the time I bobbed back up, the Celica had roared around the corner of the lot and was gone in a flash. I was about to fire up my Chevy and give chase but stopped short. The man who'd met with her was now heading toward me in a shiny, black, late-model Mercedes. I ducked again. The man was probably Jimmy Simmons and I didn't want to follow him home.

I didn't wait for the last person to leave. I'd know which brother I'd seen with Jennifer Wong when I checked license plate registrations with DMV.

I made my way back to Berkeley. I wished now that I hadn't been so quick to agree to provide Nate with a daily report of my activities. I decided not to mention my observations in the mortuary parking lot or my visit to the mortuary invoking my fictitious "Auntie" and plan to return with "Uncle Paul." Nate wasn't being objective about this case and if he shared my report with Mrs. Simmons and she alerted the mortuary, my investigation was dead on arrival.

In addition to the cottage where I stay, I rent a studio apartment in Berkeley. It's on the second floor of a building facing Haste Street. It was stuffy inside, so I opened two windows to coax a cross-breeze and lowered the Murphy bed. I typed out a report on a small PC I keep in the apartment and saved it to a floppy diskette, then erased the report.

I'd print the report later at my cottage on an HP PC and Laser Jet printer. I don't use my office computer for anything other than routine correspondence as Marcie and Saundra routinely access my computer to see what I'm up to.

The red-eye on my answering machine blinked furiously the whole I time I was writing my report. While I'm tempted to retrieve my messages first thing, I've learned the hard way that it's a sure way not to get reports written.

The first message was from Tiffany saying she missed me at the cottage last night. She confirmed ownership of the mortuary was still in the name of the Nevada corporation and that she'd ordered credit reports. She'd call when she had more info.

The second message was from Jeff Banes. He reported the mortuary was insured by All Risk Insurance Co. based in Las Vegas, Nevada. He'd call me again when he had more info. I was surprised at the mortuary's choice of insurers. I'd never handled claims with All Risk, but I knew from other adjustors that they specialized in insuring very uncommon international commercial operations; it was rumored their board of directors served as proxies for offshore foreign interests. So, why was the company insuring a California mortuary? It didn't add up.

The third message was from Mrs. Simmons. She expected me at her house tomorrow at 11:30 A.M. She left an address but no phone number I could call to change the meeting time. She assumed I was hers to command and I was.

My little brother, L.C. Bean, had left a note pinned on the backside of the entry door requesting to use the studio later in the evening. He was a senior at Berkeley High School at a time when it was cool to be of mixed race. L.C. has Dad's suave good looks and light skin. He was very popular with the ladies in high school and at the university. He got more than his share of high school and college girl nooky. As he lived at home, he often borrowed my studio to entertain his lady friends. In return, L.C. ran errands for me and provided me with access to a wide range of young, street-savvy intelligence gatherers from among his peers.

My errands helped finance his expensive lifestyle and wardrobe. Some of his associates had part-time jobs after school, but they were always pressed to come up with enough greenbacks to buy the latest designer jeans, tee-shirts, Air Jordans and rapper cassettes for their ghetto blasters. They all liked working for me as the work was usually interesting, paid cash with no questions asked and gave them special status. L.C. liked it, too; like all contractors, he took his percentage and got to choose the assignments he wanted and farmed out the rest.

Last year, I confided to L.C. that I needed to learn a skill that wasn't included in the bar exam.

L.C. introduced me to B.D., who supplied me with lock picks, pass keys and copies of manuals on makes and models of locks and tumblers.

After a few technical sessions with B.D., whose real name could be Bad Dude for all I know, I could open most conventional doors and padlocks. Since my lessons, I've never felt safe behind a double-deadbolt-locked door. No wonder the flicks show New Yorkers cringing behind armor-plated doors with half a dozen or more locks attached; still, the bad guys get in! Most of the pick jobs I do involve opening locked file cabinets. With B.D.'s passkeys, it's a piece of cake.

I closed the studio and left a note for L.C. to call me at my cottage when he finished his loving business. I had a couple of little jobs for him and his friends. On the way to the cottage, I picked up a spicy pepperoni and sausage pizza. My body needed exercise and not more fatty food. It was too late to shoot buckets in the fading light. I could always run around a track, but I hate jogging.

I was in a funky mood that sometimes occurs when I'm perplexed by a case. I used it as an excuse to pig out on pizza and polish off the six pack of Bud Light while I was at it. I'd have to pay for today's excesses by eating some humble pie tomorrow on the basketball courts.

I was halfway through my pizza when Tiffany called. "Say R.C., what's goin' down with the mortuary?"

"Don't know yet, Tiff, except to say something funny's going on. I'm gonna need you to get me some banking info, too."

"No problem. What you need?"

"I need a fix on the People's Bank of Oakland. Try to find out who's callin' shots on loans and investment capital."

"Hey R.C., that bank is Chinese. What do they got to do with the mortuary business anyway?"

"That's what we got to find out. The mortuary has a new account with the Chinese bank and it doesn't make sense."

"Yeah, you're right about that; but where there's smoke, bound to be some fire. But you know we don't have anything to do with Chinese banks for home or commercial financing. The Chinese banks only finance Chinese ventures and mortgages far as I know."

"That's what I thought. Must be a new strategy to penetrate black-owned businesses. Don't you have some Chinese agents working for your firm in El Cerrito that you could ask?"

"Now you mention it, we do have a couple of Chinese-speaking agents at our El Cerrito office. They're selling homes to Chinese investors and parents of recent Chinese college graduates. They're snapping up most of the reasonably priced real estate now that properties in San Francisco have become so expensive."

"Good, but we gotta keep it on the QT. Something really strange is goin' on and we don't want any tracks leading back to us."

"I hear you loud and clear, R.C. I'll figure out a credible reason to stop by the El Cerrito office and soft peddle for info.

But it's probably gonna take some time. Those agents stick together like birds of a feather. They're not going to give me the time of day if they think I'm tryin' to horn in on their private domain. I'll try to think of something that will fly."

"Thanks, Sis, I know I can count on you."

Tiffany and I are tight. We've been close since we were kids. I can trust her to use her intelligence and discretion to get me needed info in her realm. If that tack doesn't work, she knows how to bat her big brown eyes and turn on the charm as attractive ladies of color know best. Tiff's not shy to show some leg if that's what it takes. She liked my investigating business as much or more than her real estate game. Problem was my business didn't pay anything like what Tiff made in commissions.

My little brother called shortly after I rang off with Tiffany. He planned to take his time romancing his girl tonight so he decided to check with me before taking care of his business.

"What's happenin,' R. C.?"

"Hey, little bro,' I need some info. I want your buddies to put out some feelers with black and Chinese gangs in downtown Oakland. I got a hunch they might be getting together in some kind of joint venture. Just have 'em sniff around. Get 'em braggin' about anything they doing together. May be nothing there, but I need to check it out. Also, put a couple guys watchin' who's coming and going at the Simmons Family Mortuary down on Broadway and 22nd St. I'm 'specially interested to know about Chinese visitors."

"You want me to keep a guy on the mortuary day and night?"

"No, just during business hours and until they close up for the night. They got a Chinese lady working there. I wanna know who she's keeping company with."

"No problem, we can handle it."

As soon as my head hit the pillow, I was out like a light but transferred to the realm of troubled dreams. Gloria Simmons, Jennifer Wong, Marcie Lynn and Saundra Joiner were all conspiring together to make me lose my job.

Chapter 7

I WOKE UP FEELING GROGGY AND HEAVY FROM THE PIZZA splurge. I hopped out of bed, put on my sweats and sneakers, tossed a basketball in my backpack and bicycled to the Berkeley High courts.

I felt stiff and awkward as I warmed up and did a shoot around. I wasn't into my shooting groove when a couple of regulars showed up and challenged me to a game of H-O-R-S-E. It's a simple game in which you have to make the shot your opponent makes or lose a letter. The first to lose the "E" drops out and the last not to lose it wins. The guy doing a cross-over dribble and left-handed lay-ups eliminated me quickly. He noticed I was moving slower than usual and my dribbling was erratic. It's as simple as that. Exploit your opponent's weakness and let him beat himself. By the time more guys showed up and we'd played two, three-on-three half court games to Twenty-one, I was huffing and puffing with the exertion. If I didn't cut down on the beer and fats, I'd soon not be competitive.

I biked back to the cottage, showered, dressed and wolfed down a bowl of granola. I tried to psych myself up to meet Mrs. Simmons.

I stopped at the office to deliver my abridged report to Nate. Saundra gave me her "you still in deep shit" look, but said nothing as she had a client at her desk. She shoved a handful of message slips at me as I scooted by. I snuck into Nate's empty office and dropped my report in his safe as instructed.

I spent most of the morning doing callbacks on cases I'd been ignoring since the meeting with Mrs. Simmons. It's easy to understand why clients get really pissed off when lawyers don't return their phone calls. I put the troublesome cases, like Tony Perkins, at the bottom of the pile. Who knows when or if they'd make it to the top of the heap. I just couldn't deal with Tony's anger, so I ignored it; no wonder she threatened to sue and file complaints. If the State Bar or trial judges ruled in her favor, every attorney in the state was at risk.

I packed it in and left at eleven. I wanted to have ample time to get to Mrs. Simmons' residence and not be late. Since the '89 earthquake collapsed the Cypress Freeway, auto traffic into the Oakland hills remained congested. I considered picking up a bag lunch or Mexican takeout to eat after the meeting as I had no way of knowing how long our meeting would last or whether I'd be offered anything to eat. My tummy growls when it's not fed regularly. I threw caution to the wind and resisted temptation to blow my health kick, which had started only this morning.

The drive through the Oakland Hills reminded me how nice it would be to buckle down, pass the bar exam and earn the kind of money that would put the dog-eat-dog worries of those who live on the bottom of the hills out of my mind. The area was loaded with large ranch-style and imitation colonial mansions on woodsy, oversized lots. Many of the houses featured private parks, ponds, tennis courts and swimming pools.

The entrance to the Simmons estate was marked by two large, square, marble columns that served as plinths for copies of bronze Italian Renaissance sculptures of nude goddesses. The driveway formed a half-circle leading to the entryway of an architect-designed contemporary redwood house in a woodsy setting.

I did a double take at the antique hitching posts setting off the parking area. Each of the cast-iron rings for tethering a horse was set in the mouth of a Negro dressed in bright red livery and black top hat. To me, it was really bad taste. I can understand collecting objects that relate to the history of slavery, but not why one would want to flaunt ostentatiously the symbols associated with Uncle Tom and Aunt Jemima.

The door was opened by a Philippine maid in her thirties. After giving me the once over, she said, "Follow me, Mr. Bean. Madame is waiting for you by the pool."

I followed her down a long corridor. She was wearing a skimpy, fetching little black and white uniform with a white, ruffled cap. I had difficulty concentrating on room layouts and décor. The maid was expert in the art of walking to show off her bouncy little fanny in a uniform that ended mid-thigh. She left a vapor trail of musky scent to tantalize; she smelled of cinnamon, cloves and other exotic spices.

Despite my distraction, I was struck by the rich colors and textures of fabrics and the interior décor. The colors were strong and intense. Whoever decorated the house had a marvelous sense for the juxtaposition of vibrant colors and bold lines. When we arrived at the pool at the back of the house, I knew immediately that Mrs. Simmons was the decorator. She wore a terrycloth robe in the brightest yellow-citron I've ever seen. The contrast of the robe with her deep caramel-hued skin was like looking in a kaleidoscope of richly-tinted mahogany woods in a rain forest. Her Roman-style sandals featured white linen laces that criss-crossed as they wound their way up to her calves. Mrs. Simmons greeted me with a winning smile that would have melted even the hardest-hearted Hannah.

"Nice to see you, R.C. You look all hot and bothered. Why don't you go over to the locker room and change into a swimsuit; have a quick dip in the pool before we settle down to talk. I'll have Maria fix some sandwiches and bring us a drink."

"Thanks. That sounds like a real nice idea." I'm sure I sounded like a starry-eyed teenager, but it was all I could muster out of a dry throat. I appreciated her effort to put me at ease, cool off and collect my wits. I smiled and headed for the gazebo at the far end of the pool.

It was evident Mrs. Simmons had selected or perhaps

designed the swim trunks as well. The colors and lines were fabulous. I selected a royal blue suit that was soft as a new baby's skin. I admired some of the bikini trunks on the visitor's rack, but was afraid to wear something skin-tight; I couldn't afford to embarrass myself in front of her. I settled for a looser-fitting boxer-style swimsuit.

I dove into the pool and did a few laps before climbing out. The water was refreshing, and it relaxed me for our meeting.

Mrs. Simmons was seated by a table laid for lunch as I climbed out of the pool. She'd donned dark, designer sunglasses but I could feel her intense gaze as I made my way towards her; she'd draped a large, multicolored beach towel and blue and white terrycloth lounging robe across a chair opposite hers. It wasn't until I started to dry off that I realized the swimsuit I'd so carefully selected for modesty became transparent when wet. Mrs. Simmons had been appraising my family jewels.

I tried not to show my embarrassment by hiding behind the big beach towel and scrubbing furiously to dry off. Mrs. Simmons slipped off her terrycloth robe, shades and sandals, sauntered over to the diving board and executed a perfect back somersault dive into the deep end of the pool. After exiting at the far end, she shook the water off her hair and strolled slowly toward me. I couldn't keep my eyes off her magnificent body. Her swimsuit, like mine, was diaphanous when wet. She reminded me again of the model, Iman, and she looked every inch Queen of the Nile as she walked her walk. As she approached, I was mesmerized by her full, firm breasts and dark, pert nipples straining to poke through the fabric of her honey-golden bikini top.

I didn't dare look at the bottom of her bikini. Instead, I raised my eyes to meet her gaze and sultry smile. She wore no makeup. Her deep-brown eyes flashed with energy and amusement; they were set off by arched brows and long eyelashes. Her lips were large, pouty and sensuous – the same mocha chocolate hue as her nipples. I remembered Marcie's snide remark that Mrs. Simmons had used her nearly perfect lips to conquer the world around her. The thought of those most sensuous lips on my most imperfect body sent shivers up my spine.

Mrs. Simmons nonchalantly used her beach towel to wipe her body and donned her terrycloth robe. "What do you think of the swimsuits and accessories I designed? I'm hoping to sell my line to a major fashion house."

"I think they're terrific. They're colorful, comfortable and sexy." She smiled broadly at my words of praise.

"You're too easy a sell, R.C. The fashion market is very competitive and often cutthroat for products and models. When a model reaches my age, she's got to start thinking about a different career before the fresh new faces with slim figures push her out."

I'd heard that top models were over the hill by age thirty. Still, it was hard to believe Mrs. Simmons couldn't hold her own in front of a camera against a new crop. Was that why she'd married four years ago? Just to pocket a sugar daddy to finance a new career? Even so, what was the attraction to a playboy-gambler in the mortuary business? On the other hand, she was living a life of leisure and getting a healthy stipend to skim every month.

"I've prepared a portfolio of my designs for you to study along with clippings on my major competitors. I want you to familiarize yourself with the materials so you can discuss contract proposals on my behalf."

Her suggestion caught me by surprise. "I honestly don't know the first thing about either the fashion industry or appropriate marketing contracts for designers. Isn't that a job for a lawyer who specializes in the field?"

She didn't appear concerned by my disclaimer of ignorance.

"I know you don't. I discussed the matter with Mr. Green. He'll provide you with any documentation needed. We have to have a reason for our meetings, and this is the only one Jimmy would understand and not question."

What she said made sense at one level. It would raise suspicions for her to be seen with someone who worked for a lawyer without a credible cover. But why a divorce lawyer's investigator rather than an experienced fashion industry contract lawyer? I decided to play possum for the time being.

"It's OK with me if that's what you and Nate decided."

"Good, then that's settled. Next time we meet I want you to pay more attention to how you're dressed. I want you to wear a stylish suit and tie and look the part of someone who works for the fashion world. There's a folder in the materials with clippings from several French and Italian men's fashion magazines. Maybe you could buy a fashionable suit from the new Emporio Armani in downtown Oakland."

My face flushed with anger and shame. I'd dressed in my usual Dockers jeans and polo shirt. I hate wearing suits. My reaction was uncontrollable. I'm not accustomed to being told how to dress by anyone.

"I'm paid to investigate, not to dress up, Mrs. Simmons." My voice was near cracking as I tried without success to suppress my anger and humiliation at her suggestion.

She kept her cool. "I don't mean to be critical, R.C. You simply need to dress to play a role that will facilitate your investigation. As the dress requirement is part of the job, I expect to be billed for the cost of your new wardrobe."

She had to be aware of my complete confusion. I was both angry and amused. I was pissed at Nate for discussing this aspect of the job with Mrs. Simmons and not mentioning it to me beforehand. I could also see the surprise and anger on Saundra and Marcie's faces when the bill for the new threads and accessories arrived in the mail. Their shocked and jealous reactions would almost be worth the discomfort and indignity off having to dress the way a client dictated. And God forbid, I might even enjoy getting dressed up to the nines if it meant squiring Mrs. Simmons around town to fancy places on her tab. I haven't been stylishly dressed since the senior prom in high school.

Mrs. Simmons didn't give me time to get too discombobulated. "Tell me what you've found in your investigation to date."

"Am I free to speak openly here?"

"Yes, only Maria's here this morning. She's completely trustworthy."

I outlined the information I had put in the report to Nate. Then I showed her a copy of the Nevada deed to the mortuary. "Have you seen this before?"

She quickly scanned the document and handed it back to me. "No, this is news to me. I know Jimmy and his brother, Tony, were talking about restructuring ownership of the business after their father died. I would've expected them to use a California partnership or corporation over one in Nevada. The TJS must stand for Tony and Jimmy Simmons."

She surprised me with her understanding of the legal entities one might use to own a business; each had advantages and disadvantages and different tax consequences. She was no dummy when it came to business. Maybe I did need to get some designer threads to keep pace. Obviously, I had a lot to learn.

Maria appeared with a tray of soft drinks and pitcher of iced tea and set it down next to a platter of tuna sandwiches and a bowl of fruit salad. I was glad I'd passed on the Tex-Mex takeout.

We both watched Maria's practiced wiggle disappear before resuming our conversation.

"Any idea why your husband or his brother would choose Nevada over California to own the business?" I asked.

"Well, there might be a tax advantage, but I really can't say. Jimmy's never mentioned the incorporation to me. He goes to Las Vegas fairly frequently to gamble."

"Has he been recently?"

"He used to go every couple of months, but lately he's been going every couple of weeks."

"Do you go with him?"

"Rarely. I don't really care to be around him when he's gambling heavily." She had hesitated before answering. I sensed she knew more about her husband's activities in Las Vegas than she was going to reveal. I decided to shift to more pressing matters that worried me.

"What about the shootout at the mortuary? Do you think it could have been about a drug deal that went bad?"

She hesitated and crossed her lovely legs slowly, probably

to distract me while she stalled and pondered her answer. "I'm afraid I don't know. Jimmy never mentioned it. I only know what I heard him say over the phone the night it happened."

"What did he say?"

"He was real agitated. He said, 'Get the stiff inside and have James dispose of him.'"

"What do you think he mean by 'dispose of him?'"

"I'm not sure except from what I know of the business, James is in charge of cremations."

"Had it ever happened before? Didn't you find it strange that he'd order the victim cremated and not call the police?"

"Sure, I thought it was strange but Jimmy doesn't discuss his business with me. He's made it quite clear that I'm not to poke my nose into his or his brother's affairs and I don't."

Checkmate on that inquiry. I tried another gambit. "You mentioned he started giving you large sums of cash recently. Do you remember when the change first occurred?"

"It started several months ago. Jimmy's always liked to carry a big roll of cash. He's a generous tipper and likes to show his appreciation for good service. Usually, he'd carry tens and twenties; lately, he's been carrying a big role of mostly hundreds. In addition to Las Vegas, he's also started gambling locally. It's caused some friction with his brother.

"Where does your husband gamble locally?" I would get some of L.C.'s buddies nosing around.

"I know he plays the horses at Bay Meadows and Golden Gate Fields. Both he and Tony also gamble at local card clubs from time to time and Jimmy gambles at friends' houses."

She wasn't giving me much to go on. I decided to try a different tack. "Does your husband do drugs?"

She didn't hesitate to answer. "I know he does coke. He threw a big party here shortly after we married. He provided cocaine to snort for all his guests."

"Do you do drugs with him and his friends?"

"I don't do drugs at all and Jimmy knows it. I don't allow drugs in the house; he does his drugs elsewhere." Could that be related to the shooting in the mortuary parking lot I wondered?

I was pushing sensitive areas that were probably none of my business. But, she wasn't questioning either the subject or its relevancy to my investigation. I decided to keep probing into interpersonal matters until I got resistance.

"Does your husband have girlfriends on the side?"

"I'm sure he must. Jimmy's a handsome guy and never lacked for female admirers. When he's on a roll, he can be a lot of fun."

"And when he's not on a roll?"

"Then he makes me afraid sometimes. He can get real moody, even paranoid. He'll get real angry over nothing important and the next day he doesn't even remember what he got so riled up about."

"Has he ever threatened you?"

"No, not me personally. It's just that I've seen him get so angry that's he's out of control. It's scary. He usually takes out his anger and frustrations on his autos. He's cracked up several expensive cars since we've been married when in his funky moods."

Mrs. Simmons suddenly looked at her wristwatch and exclaimed, "My goodness, I didn't realize it was so late."

I glanced at my watch. It was nearly one-thirty. "Just one more question, Mrs. Simmons. Has your husband mentioned anything about lawsuits affecting the mortuary or him?"

"No, is there something I should know?" She asked a little too quickly.

"No, no. I routinely check out potential business liabilities. I thought you might have heard of something, that's all." I wasn't about to reveal that I was snooping into the mortuary's insurance coverage and negligence claims with a Las Vegas connection. Given the unusual number of events occurring there, it was becoming apparent I'd need to check out the connection without someone looking over my shoulder.

I thanked Mrs. Simmons for lunch and changed back into my street duds. I picked up the portfolio she'd prepared and said my goodbyes. Maria flashed me a big, sultry smile.

It was hard to imagine why Jimmy Simmons would want

to spend his time feeding his nose with coke, gambling and chasing skirts when he had the sexist woman I'd ever seen to warm his bed. I'd have been tempted to share classified info with her in exchange for her charms if she'd been playing Mati Hari when I was in the Navy working as an intelligence officer in the cramped quarters of a 688 attack submarine.

Too many things just didn't add up. Why marry a playboy? Was he really the biggest fish she could land? Hard to believe. Who was her lover and what role did he play in the puzzle I was trying to unravel? My grandpappy Bean once counseled me, "You gonna spend a lifetime studyin' womens an' you ain't ever gonna understand 'em however hard you try." He was probably right, but it wouldn't stop me from trying.

Chapter 8

FROM THE SIMMONS' RESIDENCE I MADE MY WAY DOWN the Oakland hills to the courthouse on Fallon Street. It was sobering to be back in the flatlands where most folks were hustling something or someone to secure their next meal.

While waiting in line to pick up the copies of the two inactive lawsuits on the mortuary that I'd ordered, I reviewed my notes on my meeting with Mrs. Simmons. I was glad I'd not asked what she knew about Jennifer Wong. One of the Simmons brothers was doing more than playing footsy with her and my hunch was it must be her husband. Still, it didn't add up. The funeral home serviced the black community. I could only imagine resentment and even hostility to a Chinese employee when the word got out, and it would, even though she worked in the upstairs office. I needed to meet Miss Wong without Mrs. Simmons breathing down my neck.

I'd wanted to ask Mrs. Simmons who had referred her to Nate. She'd caught me off guard when she mentioned she discussed working on her design portfolio with Nate. It was possible she was bluffing about clearing it with Nate, but I didn't think so. Nate was dancing to her flute and telling me only what she wanted me to know. I was sure she'd hired him because she could throw the stick and he'd fetch it like a good doggie. It was also possible he was getting a bigger reward than a doggie biscuit as Marcie believed.

Whatever her game, I was a pawn on the board hired to gather information for whatever she was up to. Marcie's admonitions were ringing a warning bell loudly and probably worth heeding. For the time being I'd pass on routine information and keep the rest to myself. If I got really stumped, I could always barter with Marcie for info she was also holding back. For now, I'd go it alone.

I scooped up the two litigation files from a surly clerk and ducked into a nearby bar to scan them. The first case involved a slip and fall accident at the mortuary. The complaint alleged that the plaintiff had tripped over an extension cord from a wall socket in the chapel. Royce Clayton had settled the claim. Nothing unusual there. Lots of folks manage to trip and fall in commercial premises in order to pick up some needed change.

The second case was more interesting. A law firm in Santa Fe, New Mexico filed a lawsuit alleging that the mortuary negligently embalmed their client, Reginald Walker, before shipping him to Santa Fe for burial. The complaint claimed that Mr. Walker's body had been allowed to decompose and deteriorate so extensively that he could not be shown or buried in an open casket. The lawsuit was filed ten months ago and the firm of Bronson and Bronson responded to the claims by denying all allegations, which is standard in negligence cases. The last page contained a file-stamped dismissal of the complaint signed by lawyers for both sides. The dismissal indicated the case had been settled.

Two cases for negligent embalming in the space of a year struck me as highly unusual. I made a note to try to locate the decedent's family in both cases. The local telephone company keeps directories of most major U.S. cities in its main Oakland office. The plaintiffs' attorneys wouldn't give me the time of day and would hide behind "confidential information and communications between attorney and client." If I could get a garrulous or disgruntled family member on the line, I might learn something useful.

After my second beer, I felt mellow enough to take on the

slick, snooty salesmen at the upscale men's stores nearby. They'd look at my shoes first and snigger at my sneakers. It'd get their noses out of joint real fast when I insisted on stuffing my street-feet into their sweet-smelling Italian moccasins.

It took two solid hours haggling and squabbling with three over-dressed, highly-perfumed salesmen to assemble my new wardrobe; it consisted of a suit, slacks, sport coat, shirts, ties, foulards, briefs, socks and a pair of snazzy black patent leather dress shoes and soft Italian moccasins. The final bill came to just under fifteen hundred dollars. Mrs. Simmons had suggested Armani and Armani it was. She hadn't imposed a ceiling on cost, so I splurged. I had to admit I was looking mighty spiffy in my new duds. I wouldn't get the suit until next week as the tailor had to make minor alterations. The part I liked best was replying to the question, "And how would you like to pay, Mr. Bean?"

"Please bill the law firm of Nathanial Green," I answered smugly. I tendered Nate's card and added "charge the Simmons' account." These fat-cat salesmen were used to selling to the nouveau riche. They probably thought I'd won a big settlement and wanted to spruce up in designer threads before test-driving a new Cadillac or BMW convertible.

I couldn't wait to hear about Saundra Joiner's reaction when she opened the bill in the mail. I could just see her jaw getting tight. Saundra had pegged me as not being good enough for her even though I had a law degree I'd earned at Golden Gate Law School on the G.I. bill after my military service as a naval intelligence officer. Time for snooty Miss Joiner to eat some humble pie. I was going to be two-stepping around town on behalf of Mrs. Simmons in my stylish new threads while she and Marcie ground their teeth with envy and jealousy. No wonder my dreams were full of angry women wanting to settle scores and bring me down. I certainly wasn't doing anything to warrant their sympathy.

After my shopping spree, I couldn't face dealing with neglected clients or coworkers. I wouldn't be able to keep a smug look off my face either; it would only serve to inflame the hornet's nest when the bill arrived. I didn't want to see Nate either. He'd know I'd been to see Mrs. Simmons and would expect a first-hand report. So instead of facing the music, I headed over to my studio apartment to check messages and see if my private inquiries had resulted in any new leads. I also needed to rehash my plan to use "Uncle Paul" as a smokescreen to get information from the mortuary later this evening.

My answering machine was full of urgent messages from Nate, Saundra and Marcie in that order. Each said it was imperative I call them immediately. I erased them and laughed: No way José. I still had a full night's work ahead of me. Do them good to stew in their juices for awhile.

I dressed in slacks and a sport coat for the evening service at the mortuary.

I packed a small athletic bag with a black tee-shirt, dark denim trousers, black sneakers and shades. I added my lock-picking kit, a flashlight, and sixty feet of sturdy nylon rope with a three-pronged grapple attached to one end and knots at ten-inch intervals to use as hand grips. I remember being impressed in a movie how a cat burglar used a similar grapple to avoid capture. I hadn't had to use it yet, but it made me feel more secure. Whoever says we don't get ideas about how to commit crimes from movies should have to rappel down from the ivory tower.

As one who hopes to practice law one day, I know I risk that career every time I pick a lock or do a bag job. On the other hand, if I'm afraid to do a B and E with a pick, I'll never go far as an investigator. It's a game of cat and mouse. Like stalking subs in the Navy, you got to take risks if you want the thrill of the kill.

I picked up "Uncle Paul" at the shoe repair shop where he hangs out with his shoeshine stand. I briefed him on the role he was to play as we drove to the mortuary. The place was lit up like a 4th of July celebration with colored floodlight from outside spotlights and was jumping with folks dressed in their Sunday best. We had to park over a block away; Uncle Paul had time to perfect his cane-aided hobble as we walked to the mortuary. I helped him up the steps where Brother Thomas was waiting.

"Nice to see you, Mr. Jones. We're so pleased you could bring your uncle to experience how special our evening services are. We'll be here to take care of your dear Auntie when the time comes." I was amused he'd dropped the "little brother" hype; he was seriously eyeing Uncle Paul for his business potential as well. Nothing like a fat commission on a two-for-one deal.

Uncle Paul reacted on cue by coughing and gagging like a terminal lung-cancer patient. Brother Thomas jumped into action and helped seat Uncle Paul on a pew in the back row of the chapel. Several folks up front were wailing over the open casket of their loved one. While Brother Thomas pounded Uncle Paul on the back, I popped into the hallway to fetch a cup of water. I noticed the lights at the top of the stairs leading to the office were lit.

After Uncle Paul managed to stop wheezing, he scrunched down on the bench and closed his eyes with a huge sigh. Brother Thomas watched him intently. When it was clear there'd be no imminent death-rattle, he turned back to me.

"Hope your uncle be alright. I gotta tend to the service. Y'all just holler if you need any little thing." His unctuous tone seemed to indicate he figured he had Uncle Paul in the bag.

I almost blew it by laughing at the scenario. Uncle Paul started to snore. No way he was going to to respond to any questions about his financial means or my dear Auntie's health. I was impressed. It was the first time I'd hired him to act a role and he was giving an Academy Award performance.

Brother Thomas ushered in a church choir and a preacher asked for everyone to take a seat so the service could begin. On cue from the organist, the choir broke into song. By the second hymn, the forty or more mourners were weaving and bobbing heads to the music. Many of the women present were either singing along or providing counterpoint with their cries of "Yes, Sweet Jesus" or "Praise the Lord." As everyone focused on the hymns, I slipped out the door and headed for the offices upstairs.

As I was preparing to bound up the stairs, Brother Thomas' clone appeared at the top of the stairs. We both stopped dead in our tracks. "What you doin' here?" He demanded authoritatively.

"Uh, I was looking for Brother Thomas. See, my Uncle Paul come to see the service for my Auntie, but he doin' real poorly. Need some help gettin' him to the car. Worried to death his ticker gonna give out 'for I get him home."

It was the best I could come up with on the spot. Brother Clone followed me to the rear of the chapel where Uncle Paul was sprawled sideways on the bench and moaning softly. I poked him. "You alright, Uncle Paul?"

He moaned louder and clutched his heart as he struggled to sit up. Brother Clone looked like he bought the act.

"Juss' you lean on me. We gonna have you home in a jiffy. Don't you fret none now. Everything gonna be fine. Easy does it now." Brother Clone managed to get a limp Uncle Paul on his feet where we both held an arm and drag-walked him to the door. I let Brother Clone hold him while I sprinted to get my car which I pulled up by the stairs to the mortuary. We both helped Uncle Paul down to the car and stuffed him into the passenger seat. Uncle Paul slumped down sideways and let his head loll from side to side.

"Bess get your uncle to the hospital fast, young man."

I nodded and gunned the pedal; the car left an acrid smell in its wake. As I careened around a corner, Uncle Paul came back to life.

"You shore wasn't gone long, R.C. You get what you wanted?"

"No, either bad timing or they was on to me. I'll give it another try next week."

I dropped off Uncle Paul at a local bar and gave him forty dollars for his thirty-minute performance. He was worth every penny of it.

I headed over to a funky little restaurant I know in downtown Oakland. I treated myself to a platter of New Orleans-style shrimp and soft-shelled crab smothered in a black bean sauce. I added some homemade Cajun hot sauce on the dish and sopped up what was left with a double order of cornbread. Yummy!

While the spicy dinner gurgled in my stomach, I ordered a bottle of San Miguel beer and pondered how to implement plan "B." I realized my effort to use Uncle Paul as a distraction in order to get to the business records had been too risky and doomed to failure from the start.

The only way I was going to get my nose in their books was to sneak in in the dead of night when everyone was tucked in bed and sawing logs.

I had vaguely entertained the idea of hitting on Jennifer Wong to see if she'd meet me for coffee. That plan also wasn't realistic. She already had one black boyfriend and surely didn't need another. Contacting her directly would probably raise hackles across the board. The boyfriend would be jealous and Mrs. Simmons furious to learn I was hustling the bookkeeper on her tab.

I estimated it would be midnight before all the mortuary staff left and the cleaning crew finished for the night. I needed to kill a couple of hours before doubling back to the funeral home. I was tempted to head down to Jack London Square and hang out at one of the bars that featured live music and lots of foxy ladies looking to dance and find romance. I nixed that idea. If I played the bar or club scene, I'd have to keep drinking and that wasn't a good idea; if I was going to break into the mortuary, I'd need all my wits about me.

I opted for an action movie with lots of blood and gore. I figured I might as well psych myself up by watching some of the top role models in my trade.

Chapter 9

I RETURNED TO THE MORTUARY ABOUT TWELVE-THIRTY; I had purchased a large tub of popcorn and a king-sized container of black coffee from the movie house in case I had a long wait for the lights to go out.

I drove slowly past the mortuary to check the parking lot which contained a lone panel truck. The outside spots were off and only the lights in the chapel and upstairs offices were on. It took another half-hour for the janitorial crew to finish up and shut off the remaining lights. I watched them haul trash sacks to the dumpster at the far end of the parking lot. Their work complete, they both paused to smoke a cigarette before climbing into their truck and easing it out of the lot heading for downtown.

I was parked across the street with my Chevy headed for Berkeley. It had been awhile since I finished the popcorn and coffee and my bladder was sending urgent signals. I had changed into my dark sweats in the men's room of the movie theater; my pockets bulged with my picks and a small Minox camera with a special lens and flash for copying documents.

Earlier, I had surveyed the perimeter of the buildings for security alarms or guard dogs. There could be a motion or heat detecting system I'd missed, but I'd have to determine that once I made it inside.

I waited fifteen minutes after the janitors left in case they'd forgotten something and doubled back. After checking the street for traffic and dawdlers, I quickly crossed the street, staying in the shadows. I halted at the employee's entrance from the parking lot as there was no direct light on the area. The front doors giving on to the street had a nightlight directly over the doors. They'd be easier to pick, but I'd be highlighted like a duck in a shooting gallery. At the side entrance, I could dive for cover in nearby shrubs if a car came into the lot or slowed on the street.

I'd checked the double-keyed door's lock earlier. It was a fairly easy one to pick, that is, if your hands were steady and you had the patience of Job. My heart was pounding and my adrenalin surging. It's like being intentionally fouled in a close basketball game. All you have to do is step up to the free throw line and make two buckets to win the game. It's a matter of good free throw shooting technique and concentration; you've got to ignore the raucous crowd screaming for you to miss. If you blow the shots, you're the goat. Make both free throws and you're the hero. As my lock picking instructor, B.D. said, "If you ain't got strong nerves, better not be pickin' no locks."

It took me longer than B. D. recommended, but I managed to pick both locks in under two minutes and popped through the door; I headed for the stairs to the offices upstairs. I played my flashlight ahead as I slowly mounted the steps. I didn't see any evidence of an alarm system. I guess they were counting on the spook factor. Most folks are scared to go into places that house dead people.

Come to think of it, I never heard of a mortuary robbery that wasn't committed by the morticians themselves. Some employees specialized in collecting gold crowns while others preferred the decedents' wedding bands and rings.

I eased through the door leading to the first office. After a quick glance at the reception station and booths for finalizing contracts, I moved on to the next office; it had three separate work spaces separated by portable partition walls. All the cubicles had IBM clone computers. Each had a shelf with a DOS user's manual, another one for D-Base III, an inventory control program, and a user's instruction book entitled "Using 1-2-3," an accounting program with spread sheets.

It would take only a couple of minutes to get into the computer databases, but an undetermined amount of time to scan the files. I preferred to locate printouts of current financial information and monthly profit and loss statements that I could photograph quickly. If I couldn't find them, I'd have to format diskettes and download files to copy at home. Using the computers risked alerting employees of my illegal entry if the computers had security controls.

Before picking the locks on the bank of file cabinets behind the work stations, I checked out the three remaining doors. Two opened to lushly appointed offices for Jimmy and Tony Simmons. The offices looked like they were used primarily for entertaining. Each had a fully stocked bar, a private bathroom with shower, changing room and clothes closet. Opposite the large antique, walnut desks were modern, comfortable sofabeds which could be used for an afternoon a nap or an after-hours tryst. Nice working conditions if you could get them.

The third door led to toilets for the staff which I used to ease the pain in my bladder. I was tempted to rifle the desks, but figured the forty minutes I'd given myself to get the financial records would be better spent looking for spread sheets and profit and loss statements. I'm superstitious about bag jobs; from the autobiographies I'd read by famous burglars, the longer you stay inside, the greater probability you'll get caught.

A high-speed copy machine stood next to the file cabinets. I turned it on. It would be faster than using my Minox when I found records to copy. I located the general ledger files quickly and scanned them by flashlight before placing them on the copier. I was amazed at how profitable the business was. No wonder these goldmines remained family-owned enterprises and passed on from one generation to the next. If the Simmons brothers ever decided to go public, they'd create a stampede for shares and windfall profits.

I selected the most recent profit and loss statement and the one for the same period the prior year to provide a comparison for business growth and put them with the ledgers to copy. Only one of the metal file cabinets was locked and it sparked my curiosity. I'd been in the building fifteen minutes and hoped to copy the files and get out in the next twenty.

I used a passkey to open the locked file cabinet. The first file drawer held manila file folders with names on the tabs. Each folder contained a contract to embalm a body and ship it out of state. It didn't take long to find the folders for Johnnie Carpenter and Reginald Walker, the two dead men in the lawsuits for negligent embalming. I marked their place in the file drawer and removed them for copying.

The second drawer contained backup diskettes for computer data. It was tempting to take what could be a treasure trove of info, but it would mean returning to replace them and increased the risk of someone noticing they'd been stolen. If noticed, there'd be an unwelcoming reception party waiting to unmask me.

The third file drawer contained more bookkeeping records both in English and Chinese which I pulled out for copying. The bottom file drawer was empty. I looked at my watch; I been inside over twenty-five minutes. Time to copy everything and scram.

I'd copied most of the files and returned them to their proper places when over the whirr of the copy machine, I thought I heard a car motor outside. With my heart ready to jump out of its cage, I raced to the window and parted a blind. A car had pulled into the lot and I caught a glimpse of its rear as it turned the corner of the building and disappeared out of sight. I was startled because the car's lights were off. Shit! It was possible some kids were using the back of the mortuary's breezeway to drink, to neck or do drugs, but I didn't think so. Why would they be driving with no lights?

I caught a flash of red but couldn't see the car which would be hidden from the street. The driver had hit the brakes. All my alarm buttons were going off like firecrackers. My throat was dry and my hands clammy under the surgical gloves I wore. I had to abort my mission immediately. There were only two ways out – down the stairs to the doors or out the second-storey window. The window was out because I'd left my grappling hook and rope in my car. Nothing quite like leaving a dangling rope to advertise the presence of a burglar.

I had to get down the stairs on the double so I could hide and escape by one of the four exit doors. I hastily shoved the ledgers in the file cabinet and depressed the lock. I stuffed all the copies I'd made in the back of my trousers and raced for the stairs. I skidded to a stop as I heard the soft humming of the copy machine I'd forgotten to turn off. I bolted back to the machine, then took off for the stairs again.

I took the stairs two at a time in the dark using the handrail to propel me down. I hit the bottom hard and off balance. I rolled over and came up running the way I used to hustle loose balls for a breakaway on the basketball court. I needed to make it to the chapel where I'd have choices to hide until I could get out a door. As I neared the door to the chapel I heard the roar of an automobile engine and the squeal of tires braking on concrete. Next came the unmistakable rat-tat-tat of an automatic weapon. It's a sound I'd never forget from boot-camp in the Navy. Holy Shit! Somebody was trying to kill me. I dove through the door of the chapel and rolled over and over until I came to rest at the base of a wall and out of the line of fire. Bullets were still flying everywhere, pinging and ricocheting off the walls.

The bullets must have penetrated doors and windows before trying to get me. It sounded like the shooters had a machine gun mounted on an armored car and were going to spray the whole building to get me. I crawled rapidly towards the door to the breezeway. I had to get out before they came at me with bazookas.

I felt like an eternity before I reached up for the bar release mechanisms on the double-doors to the breezeway. I stumbled out the doors and dove behind a line of shrubs to reconnoiter. The shooting had stopped. Suddenly, a motor roared and its tires screeched. I panicked. The shooters were going to come around the building via the breezeway and would have another shot at me. In my haste to escape, I'd put myself right back in the sights of the shooters. I dashed for the short wall on the street side, dove over it and rolled under a hedge as the car swept around the corner of the building and accelerated for the street. I should have tried to get a glimpse of the shooters, but I kept my head down.

The car hit the street hard, spraying metal sparks like a welding torch in its wake as the driver gunned his motor and disappeared toward Oakland. Suddenly, all was quiet. I lay in a crumbled heap. My fist hurt from the death grip I'd put on my flashlight. I could make a dash for my car down the block, but I'd have to do so in front of the nightlights of the mortuary and if the shooters returned, they'd pick me off like a deer frozen in headlights. I pulled myself together and made my way back behind the mortuary using the obscurity of the parking lot to get to my car.

I slipped past a dark-colored Mercedes parked near the garages. It must be the car that startled me when I was upstairs. I didn't stop to examine the license plates. I kept moving on legs that felt like lead pipes; my brain screamed to get out of there before the shooters came back to finish the job or the police arrived to arrest me with my burglar tools in my pocket and stolen financial data on my person.

I stopped in my tracks at the door I'd entered. A body lay crumpled in a heap facing the door that was full of holes and dangling on its hinges with a key still in the lock. I should have kept moving and not give the shooters a two-for-the-price-of-one drive-by night, but I wanted to know who had bought the farm.

Even in the shadowy light, I could see the dead man was shark bait. Most of the bullets had hit his back and legs. It was the kind of overkill some of my high school buddies' dads were still trying to get out of their dreams from Korea and Vietnam. I could tell from the heavy gold chains and finger rings that this was the same guy I'd seen going to the Asian woman's car.

He'd been carrying a small, thick leather pouch, which must have gone flying out of his hand when the bullets started to rip into him. I thought about rifling his pockets for papers but vetoed the idea. They would be full of holes. Instead, I scooped up the leather pouch and scampered for my Chevy parked down the street on the left.

I could see headlights coming down Broadway and hear doors and windows opening as I ran. I got to my car in time but fumbled with the lock as I couldn't get keys out of my pocket to open the locked car.

It was too late to peel out in my Chevy without attracting notice that would be conveyed to the cops whose sirens I could hear. Curious folks were now coming out of doors from second-storey apartments and heading to the crime scene. I slipped off my surgical gloves and placed them, along with my flashlight, lock-pick tools, passkeys and the leather pouch, behind the right front wheel of my car. That done, I slowly ambled back to the scene of the shooting I'd just fled.

By the time I arrived, there was a cluster of black and brown faces surrounding the dead man; with flashlights playing over his body, he looked like a hunk of hamburger in shredded clothes. Some of the onlookers just shook their heads in disbelief; others were providing their grain of salt in high-pitched, excited voices.

"This motherfucker's really full of holes, man."

"Fuckin' 'A,' Bro.' Ain't seen nothing like this since 'Nam."

"Them young punks today ain't got no respect for nothin', man. Done blowed the brother away right in front of the chapel. What's it all comin' to?"

I added my commentary to lay the groundwork for an alibi just in case someone present had seen me flee the scene. "Shit man, my old clunker got hot and cut out on me down the street; them dudes in the drive-by nearly blew me away, too, while I was tryin' to get to a phone."

A grizzled-looking black man with his chin on his chest just sighed and summed it all up, "This here brother done got his in as good a place as any. Won't have to pay no ambulance to get him to his box. Just have to push open what's left of that door and haul him in."

As no one was paying any attention to me, I didn't bother to point out the dead man would be hauled off to the morgue to be cutup, sliced and probed in an autopsy to determine the official cause of death. All this despite the fact everyone could see he'd been gunned down in a drive-by shooting by killers intent to send a message with their overkill. It was obvious the shooters had continued to blast him full of holes when he was already dead and sprawled in front of the mortuary's door.

The police sirens were loud and clear and only seconds away. Oakland's finest would do their crime scene routine and chalk up another drive-by murder for the city. It was only September and the city was over the one hundred mark. This one would get lots of play in the media.

The crowd had swelled to around twenty folks jabbering and milling around. Time for me to slip away before the cops started asking for eyewitnesses and questioning those present. No one paid attention to me. The hangers-on were focused on the body full of holes and the heavy gold jewelry he was wearing. I was sure some folks would snatch some of the gold before the police arrived. The dead man wasn't going to need it anymore.

I moseyed over to my car and retrieved my tools and the pouch, put them in my athletic bag and then eased my car on to the street as police cars surrounded the mortuary. I cut over at Twenty-Third Street and picked up Telegraph Avenue. I was on the way to Berkeley and safety.

Chapter 10

ON MY WAY TO MY STUDIO APARTMENT I NEARLY ran two red lights because my eyes were glued to the speedometer rather than watching the road. Ironically, I could have been pulled over for driving too slowly. By the time I arrived, I was shaking like a leaf. The adrenalin that fired me up during the drive-by shooting had completely worn off and left me unhinged and wobbly.

My feet felt like lead weights as I trudged up the stairs and fumbled the keys to the door again and again. I had to talk to myself. "Chill out, R.C. Get hold of yourself. Just 'ease on in' as Otis Redding says."

It took a while, but I finally unlocked the double deadbolted door. I headed straight for the liquor cabinet and did a chug-a-lug with the bottle of Hennessy's cognac. I felt better immediately as the liquor built a fire from my throat to my gut. I became aware of how my mouth hurt, not from the firewater, but from clenching my teeth on the ride home.

In my struggle to get the door open, I'd dropped my bag with burglar tools in the hall. I checked the empty hallway and snatched the bag. I emptied the bag and unscrewed an electric space heater that I'd modified to serve as a hiding place for money and papers for when my little brother uses the apartment. The heater still works, but the two large side panels are empty. I stuffed the burglar tools in one panel and the pouch in the other and screwed them shut.

The red message light on my answering machine kept winking furiously, but I ignored it. I'd had all the bad news I could handle for the night. I had promised Sharon Miller I'd call her if I couldn't come by her apartment for a late drink when her kids were asleep. It was too late to call and I didn't have the energy to deal with Sharon or anybody else at the moment.

I headed over to our family residence on Carleton Street. It was nearly 2 A.M. when I arrived at the spacious turn-of-the-century house with a big front porch and fenced back yard. If shit was going to hit the fan and implicate me, I knew my family would back my side of the story. Some family members might even be willing to provide me with an alibi, or at least, I would like to think so.

I parked behind the house where my car couldn't be seen from the street. Mom and Dad were sharing a pot of herbal tea in the kitchen after watching a film on the VCR. I joined them and let them know I needed to spend the night. My parents are cool. They know I keep two residences, but they didn't press me about why I chose to sleep at home. They were just happy to see me. When your parents are still holding hands and making eyes at each other after all they've been through, it really helps you take your mind off of your own troubles.

I was just about to turn in when my little brother came in from a late night movie and pizza evening with his friends.

"Hi, R.C. Hey what you doin' here, man?" He asked surprised.

I put my index finger to my lips and pointed to my parents' bedroom. L.C. got the message. "Say, L.C., I had a rough night and I gotta get some shuteye. I need to talk to you first thing in the morning. I'm going to need your help checking out some new problems that have come up with the mortuary."

"Hey, no problem. You really look wiped out, man. I got some news from the guys watching the mortuary, but it can hold 'til tomorrow. Nothing earthshaking. You better get some sleep before you keel over, man. See you in the morning."

I stumbled up the stairs to my old bedroom, plopped into bed and fell into a deep, troubled sleep. I don't know how long I slept like a dead man. I woke up with a jolt. My pajamas were bathed in sweat from tousling with gun-toting demons in dreams. Dad now uses the room as his office. I strained to read the digital clock on his desk. It was seven fifteen. I needed more sleep, but my mind was replaying the previous evening's events like a kaleidoscope. Further sleep would be hopeless.

I showered a long time in an effort to relax my body and get in sync with my racing mind. After dressing, I tiptoed down the creaky stairs to let my family sleep in as they like to do on Saturday mornings. We're all night owls and need the weekend to recharge our batteries. I flipped the switch on the coffeemaker Dad prepares every evening. While it gurgled and snorted, I slipped outside to retrieve the morning paper.

There was no mention of the shooting in the morning *Chronicle,* which had gone to press before the shooting. I'd have to wait for the afternoon papers for an account. I poured myself a mug of coffee and flipped on the TV to catch a local Oakland station. It was nearly eight and time for local news. The shooting was the lead story. Their cameraman panned the scene of the crime to show the zippered bag with the victim being loaded into a coroner's wagon. The entry door to the mortuary from the parking lot looked like a sculpture model of Swiss cheese. It was amazing with all the holes there was enough wood left for it to hang on its hinges. I'd kept the sound low and now strained to catch the voiceover.

"*...authorities were taken by surprise at the ferocity of the attack on the Simmons Family Mortuary that occurred just after midnight last night. Investigating detectives were quoted as saying it was possible that Jimmy Simmons, co-owner of the mortuary, was the victim of mistaken identity. He was gunned down as he made a late evening visit to his office. Authorities have not yet been able to determine why the victim was there at the time of the shooting. A spokesperson for the victim's family said the victim's widow and family are all in a state of shock and unable to comment at this time....*"

The moment I heard the account, warning signals went off in my head. If Jimmy Simmons was not the intended victim, then who was? I shuddered. The shooters only saw Jimmy Simmons' back. Had someone seen me go in, then ordered the drive-by shooting? Did they think they had shot me and not Jimmy Simmons? Or, did they intend to blow away Jimmy Simmons and I just happened to be in the vicinity? Sweat started to pearl down my brow.

I suddenly remembered the leather pouch I'd scooped up at the scene. I figured I'd better get back to the studio apartment and see what it contained. I jotted a note to L.C. and stuffed it in his coffee mug. I let him know I'd call him later to checkout his info. I folded five twenty dollar bills inside the note for payment on account. I left a second note for Mom and Dad apologizing for having to leave without breaking bread with them.

I knew something was wrong the moment I stepped onto the second floor landing. My door was pulled shut but the folks ahead of me hadn't bothered to pick the locks. The door was busted and hung limply from its hinges. I gingerly pushed it open.

The apartment looked like a hurricane had roared through it. Everything was in shambles. My clothes and personal effects were strewn every which way. Every drawer had been removed and the contents dumped on the floor. Bits of mattress stuffing from my Murphy bed were deposited everywhere like someone was feeding chickens with the pieces.

As I took in the scene, a sick feeling hit my stomach. Someone knew I'd been at the mortuary and witnessed the murder. He or they knew where I lived and probably knew I'd taken the leather pouch. I desperately searched for the electric heater with the false panels. I finally found it under a pile of clothes. The panels were still in place. I barricaded what was left of the door with a lounge chair that had been gutted like the Murphy bed.

Using my Swiss Army knife, I unscrewed the panels and removed my stash. I reattached the panels and put the heater exactly as I'd found it. I put the contents from my hiding place in an athletic bag and added a couple of changes of clothing, some toiletries from the bathroom floor and my answering machine which was no longer blinking.

I removed the chair blocking the door and repositioned it as I had found it and pulled the door shut behind me. I drove straight to Nate's law office as it is closed on Saturdays. Before I examined Jimmy Simmons' pouch, I wanted to be able to claim attorney-client privilege, however spurious the claim might be, in case I found Mr. Simmons linked to unsavory activities.

The parking lot was empty and newspapers littered the entrances to nearby establishments. The area wouldn't come to life for another hour or so. I slipped into our building and locked the door to my office. I was sweating again and my mouth was dry. I was scared shitless. Somebody had wanted Jimmy dead and I was probably next on the list.

I struggled to remove the sealed manila envelope stuffed into the pouch. The envelope was bulging and taped shut.I slit it open so the contents would drop directly on my desk. Holy Shit! Bundles of crisp one hundred dollar bills hit the desk. Each was neatly tied with a colorful plastic band. In addition to the money, there were ten small, penny-sized plastic bags containing clear, transparent crystals. At first, I thought they must be quartz crystals. Once I lifted a bag, I realized the contents couldn't be quartz; they were not heavy enough. I opened a bag and smelled; there was no scent. The clear, opaque crystals looked like a clear form of rock candy. I'd seen most types off street drugs, but this stuff was new.

What was Jimmy Simmons doing with all this cash and designer drugs? I counted the packets of money. Fifty bills to each of the six packets. Thirty thousand in new, unmarked bills was a healthy piece of change. Was Jimmy Simmons coming to the mortuary to stash the cash and drugs in his office safe? Had he taken the cash to buy drugs on a deal gone bad? Did the cash come from the sale of drugs or something else? Whatever he'd been up to, he wouldn't be telling me or anyone else why he'd hidden his car and wanted to get the pouch into the mortuary in the dead of the night.

Had he been out on the town or gambling with someone on his arm? Jennifer Wong? Another companion? Was his sexy wife just calmly sitting at home or was she involved with what happened? My heart slowed down as I considered these matters. Like it or not, somebody out there considered me part of the problem. I needed answers to my questions before my unknown pursuers got to me first.

Chapter 11

I T WAS TIME FOR ME TO STOP REACTING TO EVENTS AND go on the offensive. First order of business was to stash the pouch with the drugs and money. Nate's office and my parent's house were out. I didn't want to put anyone I worked with or my family at risk. Since they'd tossed my studio and failed to find the pouch or the documents I'd copied, it was probably the safest place. It wasn't likely they'd search it again given the way they'd torn it apart. They'd figure I'd carry the goods with me or hide them in my cottage residence.

I reviewed the documents I'd copied. I'm not a wiz at interpreting accounting records, but even a dummy could see from the profit and loss statements that the mortuary was doing a nifty sixty thousand a month profit even after the two brothers took a big monthly draw. Interpreting the general ledger for the mortuary was more difficult. I couldn't determine whether they were playing games or not. I needed professional help.

I blocked out the captions identifying the mortuary and copied the data sheets for the general ledger. I wrote a cover note to my sister, Tiffany, asking her to have an accountant analyze the data for a private sale between family members of a funeral home in the Watts area of Los Angeles.

The second set of general ledgers made even less sense to me. The data entries seemed entirely unrelated to the mortuary business when I compared to the mortuary's general ledger. The data appeared to reflect the books of an import/export company importing herbal medicines and remedies from Taiwan and exporting medicines and elixirs made from exotic animals to Taiwan and Hong Kong. Some of the pages were written in Chinese characters. If I was reading the bottom line correctly, the business was realizing a profit of over two hundred thousand dollars a month. I could be wrong, but if not, the Chinese connection was reaping some big-time dividends.

I copied the second set of records and wrote a note to Tiffany to find someone who could read the Chinese writing and figure out what the accounting information was recording. I asked her to find someone "cool," who knew to keep his or her mouth shut and would play ball with me. I would pay cash for the results.

I put both sets of data in separate manila envelopes and sealed them with Scotch tape. I addressed both envelopes to Tiffany at her real estate office; each envelope was marked with a fictitious escrow number. I called one escrow the "J. Carpenter Escrow" and the other the "R. Walker Escrow in honor of the two stiffs the mortuary had errantly shipped to Las Vegas. I put the envelopes in a large folio provided by the title company Tiffany works with. This is the way we handle confidential info related to my investigations. Tiff keeps the folders in a locked file cabinet in her office. My little brother delivers them back and forth.

I reviewed the files for Johnnie Carpenter and Reginald Walker that I'd found in the mortuary. The shipping manifests were both addressed to the Lone Pine Mortuary in Las Vegas, Nevada and not to either dead man's out of state family. Each file contained expensive hotel and restaurant receipts for Jimmy Simmons for the period following each shipment. There were no shipment orders to the dead men's families.

Everything kept coming up – Las Vegas. The decomposing bodies, the mortuary's new incorporation, the lawsuits claiming negligence all involved the Lone Pine Mortuary in Las Vegas. It was a no-brainer; some of the answers to the riddle and perhaps the reason for the murder, the purloined pouch and whoever was after me had a Las Vegas connection. I needed to clean up some loose ends here and make a beeline for the glittering lights in the desert.

I felt better after my decision to blow out of town as soon as possible. A game plan was forming. I might even shake my unknown adversaries off my back for awhile. I needed to buy time to figure out who killed Jimmy Simmons and why. I hoped the answers would lead me to whoever was after me.

I plugged in my answering machine; someone had played all the messages but they had not been erased. The first message was from Marcie and the second from Nate. Both implored me to call them urgently. The third was from Sharon Miller. She was miffed I'd stood her up Friday night. Instead of returning her call, I wrote her a short note telling her I was forced to leave for San Diego on urgent business; I backdated it to Friday and promised to make it up to her as soon as I could return. I penned notes to Marcie and Nate telling them I'd developed some hot leads in the Simmons case and had left for Los Angeles and San Diego. I dated them for Friday and left Marcie's on Saundra's desk to read and distribute.

I left Nate's note on his desk and removed fifteen hundred dollars in tens and twenties in used bills from his safe. I left a receipt for the money in the safe.

The last message on my machine was from Toni Perkins. It was short and to the point. "I'm calling to let you know I'm gonna sue your black ass along with your boss for not working on my case." She was right of course; I continued to ignore her calls and I was not working on her case. I was digging a hole for myself and starting a brush fire that would continue to grow bigger and bigger until I hosed it down with water. Hopefully, it wouldn't intersect with the forest fire I was trying to outrun.

I called my little brother and told him to meet me Reggie's Café in twenty minutes. I called my landlord, Al Johnson next.

"Hi Al, R.C. here. I hope I haven't called too early; I need a favor."

"No problem, R.C. I'm working through a pot of java and

the morning paper. What do you need?"

"I'm in L.A. on some pressing work. I'd hoped to get by the cottage before leaving but didn't make it."

"I was starting to wonder what happened to you. I figured you were holed up with some hot Mama. I can see you'll be shirking your chores this weekend," Al said with good humor.

"No such luck on the romance side. Sorry about this weekend. I'll help you get the new bookcases installed in your study as soon as I'm back. I'll owe you one plus a takeout from Rochester's Bar-B-Cue Ribs."

"Sounds like more than one favor. What's up?"

"Somebody broke into my studio on Fulton Street looking for confidential info on the case that's sent me to Southern California. It's possible they found something to connect me to the cottage. Have you noticed anyone hanging around or casing the property?"

"Not that I've noticed. Do you think they'll try to break in to the cottage?" Al said, concerned.

"They will if they make the connection. They messed things up pretty good at the studio. These guys are heavyweights, Al. Don't try tangling with them. You see anyone suspicious, please just call the police. No heroics!"

Al laughed. "Us old farts in the Ivory Tower need a little action from time to time. I'll set the alarms for my place and the cottage and load my shotgun for two-legged birds. So don't you worry, R.C."

"These guys aren't local B & E crooks looking for TV's and PC's they can flog to the guys selling at the flea markets. They're heavies from out of town and I think there's a major drug connection. They probably have a lot of firepower, so please don't confront them. It's a job for the police Tactical Squad. There's nothing for them in the cottage. If worse comes to worse, they'll toss the place and move on. So promise me you'll stay out of their way."

"It bugs the hell out of me to see these guys get away with these antics. I'll keep the shotgun handy for self-defense in case these punks try to mess with me. You got a phone number where I can reach you?"

"Not yet. Leave any message on the phone in the cottage. I'll pick up from there for the moment and let you know how to reach me directly as soon as I can. Ciao for now."

I planned to have L.C.'s crew watch both the cottage and Al's house on a twenty-four hour basis. I was worried for Al and not my personal effects. I didn't trust him not to try to take on unsavory hoodlums himself. I could see him getting a bead on a couple of dudes from his wheelchair and trying to make a citizen's arrest. Al was that kind of guy. He refused to consider himself handicapped. He hadn't seen what these guys did to Jimmy Simmons, but I had.

On the way to the studio apartment, I mailed the note to Sharon. At the studio, I replaced the pouch and financial info in the panels of the electric heater and dropped off a note to the resident manager demanding that he replace the studio's door with a solid-core door and secure the premises until I returned from L.A. I took the answering machine with me.

My little brother was already seated at the back of Reggie's Place and slurping a Coke when I arrived. Reggie had two king-size hamburger patties frying on the grill. No soul food special for L.C. Bean. He was strictly a hamburger and fries man. Since I was paying, he'd get a double order of everything-- one to eat here and one to take out.

I pointed to the chalk sign special and Reggie nodded and put on more hamburger patties for a group of college kids probably playing hooky from class and slumming in our part of town. Reggie's special was Creole cat-fish with collard greens and black-eyed peas. I figured I should get one good meal under my belt before I hit the road and put my stomach at the mercy of a string of greasy spoons between here and Las Vegas.

"Good to see you, L.C. Sorry about last night. I was too beat to talk. You hear the news this morning about the mortuary?"

"No, I slept in. What happened?"

"Somebody hit the mortuary last night and blew away one of the owners in a drive-by."

"Oh-oh! Sounds like big 'bro' better be watching his rear and coverin' his ass."

"Yeah, and you need to let all your associates know the bad guys are playing for keeps. They gotta stay out of their way."

"Shore do get nasty fast, don't it?"

"Yeah, and they tossed the studio last night looking for my case notes on my investigation. I think they'll try and hit the cottage and I'm worried for Al. I need you to get coverage on Al and the cottage right away."

"We was plannin' on catchin' an A's game but your business comes first. I'll get guys on the cottage. What about the studio?"

"I left a note with the manager to replace the door. Hound him until does it and then clean up the mess." Reggie delivered my catfish and a double cheese burger and fries for my brother. After we finished our meal, I handed L.C. the phony escrow folders to deliver to Tiffany. I also gave him a small envelope containing a sample of the drug from the pouch.

"This envelope contains some kind of designer drug I've never seen before. See if the guys selling drugs downtown can I.D. it for us. I'd like to know where it comes from, who's making it, and what it sells for wholesale and retail. Don't use the guys watching the mortuary for this job. I don't want anybody making a connection between the two."

"I'm hearin' you loud and clear. What else you want me to do?"

"I need to find the Chinese bookkeeper who works at the mortuary. I think she's in danger. When you find her, keep an eye on her until I get back."

"Where you going?" L.C. seemed surprised.

"Can't say for now. If anybody asks, tell 'em to L.A. I'll be checking messages by remote wherever I am on the machine in the cottage, but don't put your reports on the tape. Tell Tiffany to do the same. I'll call you at home after ten at night, so be around the phone."

"I'll be there. By the way, you know the guys watchin' the mortuary say the Chinese lady don't come to work anymore.

They also say two black men in expensive threads had a shouting match in the parking lot on Friday afternoon. One seemed to be hot and bothered about something to do with the Chinese lady."

"Did they see what cars the two were driving?"

"They say they was both drivin' fancy Mercedes and they was real classy with custom pin-stripping and metallic paint."

"That helps. Tell your guys they're doing a good job. You got enough to make your payroll while I'm gone?"

"Doin' just fine for the time bein,' R.C."

"Tell your crew to be cool and stay low. Just observe and report what's happening from a distance. Stay out of their way. These guys are all packing and they're shooters. Later today, go round to bug the manager at the studio. Put some heat on him to fix the door. Don't stay there for the time being. They may come back. I'll call you tonight."

I dropped a twenty on the table. "Gotta go. Pay Reggie when you're done."

"Take care, R.C."

Chapter 12

I T FELT REALLY GOOD TO HIT THE INTERSTATE AND GUN my Chevy to the floorboard. It had been a while since I could blow gunk out of the carburetors. A warm wind was blowing on my face, sun caressed my arm and road speed thrilled my soul. I knew I couldn't keep barreling along at ninety-five for long without attracting attention, but for the moment my demons were behind me and I was buying precious time.

I was trying to sing along to the Coaster's song, "Searchin'" but the squeal of my tires, roar of my motor and whooshing of wind through open windows made it almost impossible to hear the tape even though I had the volume as high as it would go. My head bobbed up and down to the lyrics I know by heart.

I was worrying about Jennifer Wong and how to find her as I screamed the words of the song over the noise of the freeway. I was at the part of the song where they talk about my favorite private eyes: Sam Spade, Sergeant Friday, Charlie Chan and Bulldog Drummond when I caught a glimpse of the black and white CHP cruiser on the shoulder of the road behind a car he'd pulled over. I blazed past him so fast I couldn't see his astonished face, but I could feel the heat of his stare on my back as I instinctively slowed to the speed limit. I knew he'd radio ahead to one of his buddies to intercept me further down the highway to nail me for reckless driving.

The tall road signs advertising service stations and fast food restaurants were a welcome sight. I exited and parked behind the Taco Bell where I couldn't be seen from the freeway. The choice was either Taco Bell or Burger King. I ordered a super burrito with a side order of hot salsa and basket of tortilla chips. I immediately regretted having left a portion of my catfish plate uneaten. I'd have to wait a goodly amount of time before braving the freeway again. There'd be plenty of other speedsters to corral once they tired of looking for me.

I used my forced time-out to draw a list of things to do in Vegas. It would be night before I arrived and all government offices would be closed for the weekend. I planned to check out the casino scene Jimmy Simmons frequented and the Lone Pine Mortuary during the remainder of the weekend. Research could wait until Monday. I hoped to get a lead on what he was doing there when the bodies arrived at the mortuary.

When it was time to resume the game of cat and mouse with the highway patrol, I put on my designer shades and San Francisco Giants baseball cap and blazer; it wouldn't disguise the description of my car, but maybe I could argue it was some other dude they were looking for. There were other vintage Chevys on the road. I put on a tape of Otis Redding singing "Dock of the Bay" and maintained a steady sixty-five along with other drivers trying to avoid a siren and flashing red lights.

It was boring driving through a monotonous desert on a straight road while others raced past to get where they were headed well ahead of me. It was long after sunset when I saw the glare of distant light that indicates the lonely cacti are behind you and a series of hole-in-the-wall way stations for the weary traveler beckoned. Farther on, the garish lights of the desert oasis flashed like strobe lights at a rock concert. I could almost hear the barkers and goodtime girls calling, "Come to me sucker. I've got everything you want and I'll make you a winner."

The lights got brighter as I approached the outskirts of Las Vegas where all roads lead to the Strip which runs from one end to the other of this gambler's paradise. I decided not to stay on the Strip for security reasons. I looked for a cheap motel that wouldn't have a security force watching my comings and goings and willing to reveal my business for a healthy tip. This was not my turf and I needed to be cautious.

I had waited five to ten minutes each time I pulled off the freeway at rest stops to monitor traffic and see if I was being followed. I was confident no one was tailing me, but my pursuers could be waiting for me to show up in Las Vegas.

I pulled in at a nondescript motel advertising itself as "a quiet place of repose for the serious gambler." It was run by a big Mama, who was so corpulent that I had serious doubts whether she could make it through the door moving sideways. She wore her bleached-blonde hair short and shoveled M & M's into her cavernous mouth at a steady clip. Her eyes scanned a black and white TV. She'd managed to squeeze her bulk into a sagging director's chair. She didn't bother to look up as I entered. She waited for me to make the first move.

"I need a quiet room on the second floor with a shower. I'd prefer one on the end with a view of the motel entrance if you've got it."

Her face registered a glimmer of amusement as she pretended to ponder my requests. "You plannin' to rob a casino, Mister?" She said in a husky voice, her double chins bouncing as she spoke. I laughed and so did she.

"Not if I can help it. I'm looking for work and need a place to catch some shuteye during the day and receive messages."

"What do you do?"

I liked her directness. She stopped her assault on the large pack of M & M candy and regarded me with some interest.

"I deal blackjack and seven card poker."

"Who don't in this town. You any good?"

"Never had any complaints and I don't play games for either the house or the clients."

"That why you're lookin' for work in Vegas?"

"Not really. I was working in Tahoe, but the scene was starting to get stale. I like to move around and thought I'd try my luck down here. Hope to save up enough to buy a little farm back home in Louisiana. I want to get out of the game before other people's smoke puts too many nails in my coffin."

She laughed a Gravel Gerty laugh. Her rolls of fat from her chin to abdomen rippled in unison. "I think you might have come to the right place, Mister. We like non-smokers who keep a low profile and a clean nose. You wanna rent by the day or the week? I give a special rate on two weeks."

She hauled herself out of her chair, careful not to spill any candy in her bag and lumbered up to the counter.

"Let's do three days in advance for the time being. After a hard look at the Strip, I may decide to move on. I've several irons in the fire and my messages are important to me. I'd like to hook up my answering machine to the phone in the room, if that's okay."

"Sure, why not? You want me to patch the calls through to your room when you're not in?"

"I'd like you to put through all calls directly to the room without advising the caller whether I'm in or not, if that's not too much trouble. I'd like to screen them all."

"No trouble. It saves me work to just plug 'em in to your room. I can let you have a room with a queen-size bed for twenty-four bucks a night payable in advance."

"That's fine. Could I take a look at what's available, and then settle up?"

"Sure. I've got three rooms on the upper tier that might be suitable."

She shoved a registration form my way while she fumbled under the counter with a box of keys. I suppressed my amusement as she maneuvered her bulk to avoid bending over. I put "Reggie Stewart" on the form and scribbled a phony address in Tahoe City, California on the line requesting a permanent address. She quickly scanned the form and handed me three sets of keys from her bear-sized paw.

"My name is Annie, Mr. Stewart."

"Call me Reggie. Pleased to meet you and I do appreciate your help getting my calls forwarded to my machine."

She extended her fleshy hand which I took in mine. Her grip was surprisingly strong. I scooped up the three sets of keys; each was anchored to a heavy metal plaque that must have weighed a quarter of a pound. Not the sort of key set you'd want to leave in your pocket.

I selected the room with the best view of the entrance and parking lot that could be accessed by stairs both at the front and back. I could beat a hasty retreat by either route. I hooked up my answering machine. The room was clean and sparsely decorated with repros of gambling scenes from the turn of the century. After stowing my bags, I headed back to the motel office to return the unneeded keys and pre-pay my stay with Nate's expense money.

On my return, Annie was back in front of the TV and busy mowing down the bag of M & M's. I plopped the keys on the counter along with my $72.00. Annie struggled out of her chair to get to the cash which she stuffed down her ponderous bosom.

"Everything OK in your room, Reggie?"

"Yeah, everything's just fine, Annie. I was wondering if you know anything about the Dry Tortuga Hotel and Casino in town. I met a dealer in Tahoe who'd worked there and said to try my luck there."

"I know about the place. I had a guy stayin' here who worked there. Eventually, he found a place in town and moved. Nice fellow named Pete Rogers. I think he left a forwarding address for mail. I could try to dig it up if you want to talk to him."

"Yeah, I would like to meet him if you can come up with his address. Do you think he still works there? Put his address and phone on my answer machine if you find it. I appreciate your help."

"He may still work there. He's only been gone from here for about six months. I'm sure I can find his address and I'll put in on your machine."

"Thanks, Annie. I'm going out to get something to eat and then get some shuteye."

I showered, changed into clean clothes and headed into town. I passed a pizza parlor and was sorely tempted to stop for a pepperoni and sausage pizza as an antidote to the burrito and hot salsa that had been talking to me all afternoon. I kept on rolling down the Strip until I spotted the Dry Tortuga Hotel and Casino. It was hard to miss with a huge figure of a tortoise staring down from the top of four metal stanchions. It looked like an over-aged Ninja Turtle with red flashing eyes and a beak that flashed on and off. I sincerely hoped this breed of tortoise was indeed an endangered species on its way to extinction and would not be allowed to propagate beyond the Strip.

I parked my Chevy in a dark corner of the lot and slipped on a tweed jacket to upgrade my casual dress. The Dry Tortuga looked ritzy as if it was trying to attract a higher class of gambler than most of the gambling palaces I'd passed. The two door attendants were nattily dressed in 19th C. livery on a par with any five-star hotel in a major city. The doormen projected a snooty look that said, "Don't bother to come inside chump, unless you got a big wad to play."

As one of the doormen was African-American, I went through his door. He looked to be in his sixties and struck a handsome figure in his red and gold uniform. I smiled my smile while he looked me over starting with my scruffy shoes. He hesitated momentarily before opening the door and I thought he was going to recommend me to a shoeshine stand. Instead, he opened the door gracefully and as I passed through he whispered in my ear, "They crooks at the tables an' wid' they machines, brother. Be careful an' don't play no roulette or high-stakes poker less you wanna get skinned. Bess take yo' chances on the blackjack or craps."

"'Preciate the good advice, brother. I'm juss gonna watch the action for a while. If I think I can do any good, I'll be back another time."

I was surprised and pleased that the doorman would risk his job to warn me about the rigged high-stakes games. I moseyed among the marble columns of the hotel lobby. The big leafy plants in huge ceramic pots reminded me of pictures

I'd seen of North Africa. The potted palm trees and variety of stuffed tortoises hanging from the ceiling, affixed to the walls and hiding in the foliage conjured up a feeling of being in a desert oasis.

I passed through the hotel lobby and entered the casino area. It was standing room only at the blackjack and craps tables. The roulette wheels and poker parlors were set off in alcoves to the right and left. A garish, flashing arrow and sign at the far end signaled the entrance to the banks of one-armed bandits and keno parlor. The layout was smart. Lowball suckers had to walk by the high class salons where the big money games were played to get to the slots and cheap-bet games. They probably had a separate exit for them once they'd lost their stake. The entrance to the Sand Dab Restaurant, where Jimmy Simmons had eaten on several occasions, was located just off the high-stakes gambling alcoves.

The restaurant was fancy and looked expensive. My tummy was rumbling for food, but I passed on the restaurant. Better to be fleeced at the blackjack table than with an overpriced meal. As the restaurant had a large bar, I decided to return to it after I found a more reasonable eatery.

I found a delicatessen-style food service inside the room with the clanging slot machines. I ordered a pair of spicy hot Polish dogs on a bed of sauerkraut and washed them down with a bottle of San Miguel beer. Tummy full, I sauntered over to the poker parlor to watch the action. All the seats for the five- and seven-card poker tables were occupied, so I aroused no curiosity looking on. After fifteen minutes, I noted that all the gamblers but one were losing consistently and that the moment a player's drink was near the one-third mark, it was replaced by a fresh drink on the house.

Drinks were delivered by a pair of very attractive barmaids from the Sand Dab Restaurant across the hall. The barmaids seemed to know exactly when to bring new drinks. Both barmaids were dressed to the nines in stylish cocktail dresses and high heels.

The one that caught my eye was about five feet nine-inches

tall in her shiny black patent leather spike-heel pumps that showed to advantage her slim ankles and nicely turned calves. Her ample figure was poured into a black and white after-five cocktail dress that seemed specially molded to her body. The bodice of the dress was cut in a subtle v-line supported at each side by a thin strap that encircled her neck. My heart skipped a beat when the young lady bent over a player to serve his drink from a tray; her full breasts swelled and stretched against the fabric of her dress as they sought to escape their flimsy bindings.

The guy she served was so intent on his cards and whether to match an upped bet that he didn't even look up at the beautifully rounded globes that nearly brushed his face. I caught her eye as she straightened up and the display was over. I gave a nod of appreciation for the show. She flashed me a steely-eyed rebuke that said "eyes off buster;" but when she registered my amused smile, she reconsidered and threw me a look I took to say, "You can look but not touch."

She walked back to the bar in a slow, measured gait that allowed her buttocks to ride up and down in a tantalizing way in her tight dress; they were like two pistons attached to her long, lanky legs. Her cocktail dress was open at the back and revealed a delectable expanse of creamy, smooth skin the color of mocha coffee that matched my mood perfectly for an after dinner drink.

I spent ten minutes watching the action on the roulette wheel before moseying over to the restaurant. The bar area was nearly empty. I selected a small corner table where I could see inside the restaurant and still watch the gambling from afar. She'd seen me take my seat, but made me wait before coming my way to take my order.

"What can I get you to drink?" She said, with an emphasis on *to drink.*.

I chuckled and broke into a broad-faced grin which helped soften her tough-mama pose.

"I normally drink Hennessy straight-up, but tonight in honor of your beautiful presence, I'll have a Kahlua and cream."

She raised her eyebrows at my implicit reference to the color and texture of her skin. "Will that be straight-up or on the rocks?"

"On the rocks, that'll do me for the moment."

She didn't reply to my innuendo; she just gave me a funny, pouty look before doing a slow pirouette that provided a glimpse of creamy-brown thigh as a slit in her dress sought to catch up with its other half. I told myself, "Go slow, and don't blow it."

She delivered my drink from a tray loaded with others destined for the gamblers. I watched her and her co-worker, a buxom, platinum blond in a fire-red cocktail dress and spike heels, trot back and forth between the bar and the gaming tables on their gambling runs. I worked on my drink slowly. I'm not fond of sweet-tasting liqueurs, but I couldn't very well not drink it given the point I'd tried to make. When I finished my drink I motioned her over to my table.

"I was wondering if you could help me. I'm visiting from Tahoe where I work in a casino like this one. A friend of mine told me to look up a friend of his while I'm here. He's called Peter Rogers, and I think he worked here. Do you know him?"

"Sure, I know Pete. He still works the poker tables and deals blackjack sometimes. I didn't see him tonight, so he may be working tomorrow. Would you like me to find out for sure?"

"Yes, I'd really appreciate your help. I'd save me a lot of time to know when he's due to be here."

I couldn't take my eyes off her expressive face. Her big, brown-eyes were lively and framed by long lashes and a page-boy haircut. Her eyes twinkled as she spoke. Her lips were broad and fleshy and I dared to hope I would have an opportunity to get to know them more intimately.

She was gone in a flash of sheer stockings. I needed to figure out how to get a date without being too forward or presumptuous. She returned shortly.

"Pete'll be working in the morning. He's due to come on the floor at nine."

"That's great news. I'll plan to meet him. Do you know how long he'll have for his lunch break?"

"We only get a thirty minute break for meals. I don't know

for sure what time he'll get a break; it usually depends on how busy the place is."

"No problem. I'll come by late morning and wait until he gets his break. Will you be working tomorrow?"

"As a matter of fact, I have to work the day shift tomorrow from eleven to six."

"I'd really like to invite you to dinner tomorrow if you're free."

"I don't date anyone I meet working here. It looks bad."

"Why don't we meet somewhere after work; we can pretend we met there," I said in a pleading tone.

"I'll think about it. Why don't you check back tomorrow and I'll let you know."

"That's fine with me. By the way, my name is Reggie Stewart. What's yours?"

"I'm called Rita James."

"Nice to meet you, Rita. I'm looking forward to seeing you tomorrow." I extended my hand as I got up to leave and when she gave me hers, I brought it up to my lips and gave it a soft, friendly kiss.

When I looked back, Rita was still standing where I left her. She blew me a kiss and waved. I could hardly restrain myself from shouting out with joy as I contemplated our date.

The motel was quiet on my return. The one message on my machine was from Annie who passed along the address and phone number for Peter Rogers. I called my little brother from the payphone down the hall.

"What's happenin,' R.C.? You OK? The drive-by at the mortuary's been getting' a lot of play on the local news."

"Everything is cool at my end, so not to worry. I'm working some leads that are going to keep me out of town for a couple of more days. Any action at the cottage?"

"No, the guys say there's been a couple of suspicious drive-bys, but nobody stopped. They got it covered, so don't be worryin' about Al. We got his back."

"Thanks, L.C. Any word on what's in those penny bags?"

"Yeah, had two dealers look at the product and they both

came up with the same answer. They call it 'quartz' or 'glass' on the street. White folks and the police call it 'ice.' They say they're surprised to see this form of crank. It's supposed to be worse than crack when they smoke it."

"Did they say what it sells for on the street?

"They say a penny paper gonna go for about fifty, but it's hard to find at any price 'cause local suppliers don't want it on the street competin' with their crack. Something to do wid' how long you stay high. You want I should check it out some more?"

"Yeah, I'm real curious to know who's been handling the ice that' been coming in and whether the homeboys got a contract to keep it out of the hood."

"I see yo' drift. I'll see what I can come up with."

"Thanks, L.C. You're my eyes and ears while I'm out of town. Tell Mom and Dad I'm fine and I'll be home soon for some home cooking. Tell Tiff I'll be in touch tomorrow. Gotta go now. I'm beat and need to catch some zzz's."

I set the alarm for seven and hit the sack. Instead of being chased by demons, I dreamt I was playing poker at the Dry Tortuga Casino and Rita was wearing a topless dress with black straps that criss-crossed under and over her breasts. She kept leaning over my shoulder and dropping her creamy-smooth globes on my cards to signal which one to play.

Chapter 13

THE HIGH-PITCHED METALLIC WHINE IN MY EAR HAD to be an errant mosquito. I rolled over to make it go away, but it just kept making its irritating noise. My body, groggy with sleep, knew it was Sunday, but the alarm on my wristwatch just kept sounding its shrill alarm.

I stumbled out of bed and put on shorts, sneakers and a tee-shirt and headed for a nearby school playground I'd spotted nearby. Three of the four basketball hoops were bent from the local Michael Jordan wannabes hanging on the rim and trying to emulate his dunking moves; all four were missing nets. I had to make do with the hoop the heavy hangers-on hadn't yet bent.

As there was only a wary stray cat and several empty malt liquor cans to watch my moves, I worked on lay-ups and my fall-away jump shot. I chucked it in after about thirty minutes. I'd worked up a good sweat but missed the swish of a net when my shots started to fall with regularity.

Back at the motel, I showered and changed. On the way to a nearby Mexican cafe, I picked up the local newspapers to check ball scores and obituaries to see if the Lone Pine Mortuary had a burial scheduled. By the time I'd finished my order of *huevos rancheros* with a side order of chorizo with flour tortillas, it was time to work the phone.

My first call was to Peter Rogers who I reached before he

left for work. I introduced myself as a friend of Annie who'd given me his number. He eagerly accepted my offer to buy him lunch and talk about work at the casino.

I called my sister, Tiffany, next. She was not amused to be rousted from her sleep before 9:00 A.M. "on her day of rest." I laughed as she chided me.

"Say, Tiff, you know Sunday is an action day for real estate brokers. How come you're giving me such a hard time when I'm out on assignment?"

"Because you're a fool to be up so early. My day doesn't start until eleven and I need my rest. I was partying last night and out late. Damn, it's not even nine o'clock. Are you crazy or what?"

"Un-huh, I do understand, but your brother's bakin' his tail off in the hot desert sand while you're getting your beauty rest."

"Well, you got me awake now. Where are you anyway?"

"I'm in Vegas. I'm trying to get a lead on the mortuary shooting. Did L.C. get in touch?"

"No, he just dropped off some papers, why?"

"His friends I.D.'d some drugs I recovered from the shooting. I think the drive-by was drug-connected and the trail leads through the mortuary somehow. That's what I'm trying to find out here in Suckerville."

"I'm worried for you. Whoever took out Jimmy Simmons could be looking for you. Do they know you were at the mortuary?"

"Somebody does. They tossed the studio apartment looking for something."

"I thought so. I read through the paperwork and it looks like someone's running a money-laundering business. I made an appointment with an accountant friend for Tuesday to give me his take. He's cool. Is that soon enough?"

"It's fine. I'm gonna be stuck here for a couple of days at least. I'll try to call Tuesday evening." I gave her my motel phone number and told her to leave a message if she learned anything else.

My last call was to Al. He confirmed what I'd learned from L.C. No one had yet breached security at the property. He, too, thought someone had been cruising by the neighborhood, probably checking whether I was home. He hadn't picked up L.C.'s surveillance team. He wouldn't be amused to know I was trying to protect him.

After gassing up my Chevy, I headed back into town to pay a visit to the Lone Pine Mortuary. It was located three blocks off the Strip in an area dotted with small businesses and light manufacturing plants. After doing reconnaissance, I decided to park across the street from the mortuary where I could observe both its entry and exit. I eased into the parking lot of a taxidermy shop with a large closed sign in its window. I parked at the far end of the lot near two large dumpsters and under a shade tree.

I raised the hood of my car and set up a protective cloth on the fender and laid out tools. I hoped no one would pay any attention to a guy working on his car on a Sunday morning. From my perch, I could see all the comings and goings at the mortuary. According to the newspaper, there were only three full-service funeral homes in the city and the Lone Pine had a memorial service scheduled for the afternoon.

I set about cleaning and resetting the gaps on my car's sparkplugs. I noted a few cars entering the mortuary's parking which I assumed ferried staff to set up the afternoon service. I did a double-take at the arrival of a shiny black Cadillac hearse. I nearly dropped my jaw when it slowed to turn into the mortuary's lot and I read "Simmons Family Mortuary" in large script on the vehicle's side panel.

I thought better of leaving my spy station to sprint across the street to see who was driving and what they unloaded. I could not afford to blow my cover and alert folks I was in town. Brother Thomas had surely run down my suspicious behavior with Uncle Paul to everyone working for the mortuary. They could be expecting me to show up despite the trail of smoke I tried to leave behind. The fact that they knew to toss my studio for the purloined pouch of money and drugs so soon after the shooting still worried me. They seemed to know a lot more about me than I about them.

It didn't add up to send a hearse from Oakland to Las Vegas just to transport a stiff. It would be much cheaper to transport a body by truck. I couldn't imagine from what I'd seen that business was so slow in Oakland that they didn't need all their hearses on hand, especially after the death of Jimmy Simmons.

My tinkering under the hood of my car was long since finished. I wished I'd had the foresight to bring a thermos of coffee. My mind raced trying to connect the dots to the puzzle. My reverie was interrupted by the sight of the Simmons hearse exiting the parking lot of the Lone Pine Mortuary by way of the breezeway on the right side of the building. I couldn't make out the driver through the heavily-tinted windows. If he was headed back to Oakland, he was going to be mighty tired by the time he got home.

I was tempted to follow the hearse to see whether it headed out of town or not. I would like to know whether it made a stop at the Dry Tortuga Casino. I got an unexpected reward for continuing my patient surveillance. I was packing up my tools and preparing to leave for my meeting with Peter Rogers when a black Lexus roared into the taxidermy parking lot and stopped near the entrance. I pretended to fiddle with my tools and kept my head under the raised hood of my car. The driver paid no attention to me; he hurriedly exited his auto and entered the taxidermy shop.

A short while later, a tall, sandy-haired man exited the mortuary carrying a large briefcase. He cautiously looked up and down the street before dashing across it in a beeline for the taxidermy shop. He must have been expected because the moment he arrived at the door, it opened and he disappeared inside without breaking his stride.

I thought it unwise to keep pretending to work on my car when they finally came out. I was too close to them and they couldn't fail to see my black hide. I threw my tools into the trunk and eased out of the parking lot. I parked up the street where I could watch the door to the taxidermy with my field glasses.

I watched the arrival of several cars that parked in the mortuary's lot. The folks who entered the funeral home were dressed in their Sunday best and I assumed they came for the memorial service. The tow-headed man dashed from the taxidermy shop and scurried to the mortuary about ten minutes after he had entered; he was empty handed. The second man exited the taxidermy cautiously; his eyes scoured the street up and down before he opened the trunk of his Lexus and deposited the briefcase. I got a good look at his face; he was Asian. He gunned his auto out of the lot and was gone in a flash.

I risked being discovered by reentering the taxidermy parking lot and parking my Chevy at an angle to block the view from the street of the store's two dumpsters. I grabbed a box cutter from my tool box and pulled several flattened cardboard boxes from the dumpsters and cut out the shipping and address labels; the cartons were sent from Hong Kong to the taxidermy. Most of the writing was in Chinese characters. I stuffed the cardboard back in the dumpsters so the cut panels were at the bottom.

I was tempted to try to peer into the taxidermy's display windows to see if I could make out items in the shop's interior. There was nothing to suggest the business was run by Asians. All the outside lettering on signs was in English and large stenciled letters on the door advertised, "Professional Taxidermist." I was already late for my meeting with Peter Rogers. I could see stuffed deer and elk heads prominently displayed in the shop's show windows, but nothing more from where I was parked.

I knew I had tarried too long in the lot and I'd have to return in the cover of darkness to satisfy my nagging suspicions about the connection between the mortuary and the taxidermy shop. I hoped that the address panels I'd cutout of the shipping containers might shed some light on the scene involving the transfer of the briefcase I'd witnessed, once the Chinese was translated.

Chapter 14

I ARRIVED AT THE DRY TORTUGA CASINO AT TEN TO 1 P.M.
I avoided the hotel entrance and made for the door to the
slot machine parlor. The place was packed with small-time
gamblers trying to beat the odds to hit a major jackpot.
The clamor of one-armed bandits was deafening. Everywhere
throughout the hall, grim-faced gamblers fed the hungry
mouths of the slots by shoving in small denomination coins
from paper buckets in one hand, and pumped the handles with
the other hand. It reminded me of scenes from leaky Haitian or
Vietnamese refugee boats sinking in rough seas while desperate
hands pumped the bilges and frightened evacuees passed buckets to little avail.

I made my way to the delicatessen. Several employees were
eating lunch, but no one matched the description Annie and
Rita had given me. I moved on to the blackjack tables and
asked a dealer where I might find Peter Rogers. He pointed to
a craps table in the distance.

Peter Rogers was tall and skinny and his face lean and gaunt.
He looked like he'd be more comfortable sitting on a tractor in
Ben Davis overalls and a baseball cap with the name of a local
team or grain silo sewn on the front. He wore a transparent,
green plastic visor while he supervised the bets. He caught my
eye and flashed me a look indicating he'd be with me shortly.

I decided to watch the action while I waited. A big, beefy South Sea Islander in a Hawaiian tie-dye sport shirt and baggy shorts was exhorting the shooter to roll his numbers. The man with the dice was a dark-skinned African-American of medium height dressed modishly in loose-fitting slacks and a colorful shirt unbuttoned to his navel. He was about my age and the heavy gold chains around his neck glistened with perspiration.

I placed a five dollar bet on the shooter's numbers and gave him thumbs up. He commenced to weave and bob his body as he talked to the dice. "Sweet little mamas, come to papa. Papa gonna buy you a gold ring and give yo' sweet asses everything you want. Jess be good to papa this one last time."

He shook the dice furiously in his cupped hands and sweat poured off his brow as he wound up and contorted his body in a tight-fisted ball. Suddenly, he sprang forward and rolled the dice on the green-felt playing surface with a final exhortation, "Come on to papa!" He gasped in disbelief as he crapped out and lost his pile along with my five spot. Peter Rogers suppressed a tell-tale smirk with difficulty at the sucker scene we'd just witnessed. What a way to make a living, I thought.

With a change in shooters, Rogers was free to take his lunch break as his replacement took over. I offered to buy him lunch off the premises, but he declined. He preferred to eat his free meal at the deli to ensure he'd be back at his table in thirty minutes. He ordered a bowl of chowder and a tuna melt sandwich. I ordered a bowl of chili and a hot pastrami sandwich. I followed his lead and tried a domestic non-alcoholic beer. I'd wanted to sample one for taste for a while. It tasted like soapy dishwater, but I said nothing.

We chatted about Annie and life at the motel. Peter babbled on about his trials and tribulations as a card dealer. He, like most I've known in the business, hoped to strike it rich one day, make his pile, and retire to the good life, poolside. He clearly knew the odds for losing but believed he could beat them. He just needed a partner to stake him and his system to a series of high-stakes games with the high rollers. He was a dedicated gambler and couldn't wait to try his "system" on the seven card stud poker tables.

I tried to sound enthused about his passion, but it wasn't easy. He'd hoped I might be the partner he needed to bankroll his dream. He was let down to learn that I was both unemployed and scouting for work. I didn't want to change the story I'd told Annie and Rita. I told him I'd met a lot of high rollers who might be interested in a sure-thing system to win. That brought a glimmer of hope to his steely-blue eyes and a half smile to his thin, bony face. As he was forbidden by his employer to gamble where he worked and in local casinos, he was eager to make contacts with Reno or Stateline gamblers.

I finally got an opening to turn our conversation to my interests. I mentioned I knew Jimmy Simmons and suggested maybe he'd be interested in his betting scheme.

"You ever work the tables when Jimmy was playing for high stakes?"

"Hard to forget him. He was a big tipper when he won, which wasn't all that often. He always flashed a big roll and was prepared to gamble all night until his chick pulled him away."

"Are you sure it was Jimmy Simmons?"

"Sure, everybody here knows Jimmy. He's a regular; comes at least twice a month to gamble. He always stays in the hotel since his suite of rooms is complementary from what I heard."

"Do you recall the last time he was here?"

"I'm not exactly sure, but I think it was about a week or ten days ago. Why?"

"I was just curious. I've met his wife and she doesn't look like the kind of lady one would want to leave at home to go gambling for long periods of time."

"Yeah, everybody knows Gloria. She used to be a chorus girl in some of the big shows on the Strip until she nailed Jimmy."

I tried not to show my surprise. "You mean Jimmy met Gloria Simmons here in Vegas?"

"Yeah, the story I heard was that Gloria was in one of those chorus line shows at Harrah's when Jimmy spotted her. He had a table right in front of the stage and couldn't get his eyes off her long legs and what he'd like to do to her with the feathers in the boa she wore."

"Had she been working on the Strip long before she met him?"

"Long enough to try to nail a number of high-rollers passing through. From what I heard, she put out only for top dogs on a roll. She always dressed real classy when she came here. Rumor had it she was a real man-eater if you could get her in the sack, but she was real fussy about who she bedded. She let everyone know she was interested in money and prestige in that order. Nobody else need bother to apply, if you know what I mean."

"Yeah, that jives with what I've been told. I'm surprised she settled for someone like Jimmy Simmons. Couldn't she do better?"

"Jimmy wasn't such a bad catch for a poor girl like Gloria from what I've heard. She needed money and someone she could control, and Jimmy fit the bill perfectly. He was fun-loving and generous with his women to a fault. The only problem I knew of was when he went into one of his crazy moods or on one his all night benders."

"What do you mean?"

"Jimmy was incredible. Seemed like he was always wired when he played poker or shot craps at my table. I've seen lots of guys play all night, but they get progressively fatigued and start to make mistakes. Not Jimmy. He could play all night and stay focused on his play."

"You said he got moody. What do you mean?"

"Well, sometimes he got real crazy for no apparent reason. One moment he'd be happy and joking even when losing. Then suddenly, he'd lose it. He'd get real angry and jumpy, even paranoid over nothing. Once he yelled at a cocktail waitress without any warning; she was so startled she spilled her tray of drinks all over her dress. Jimmy just kept yelling at her, calling her a dumb, stupid bitch until she took off crying."

"Does she still work here?"

"No, she quit right after that. Jimmy came in to apologize the next day, but she'd already split."

"This happen to anyone else?"

"Not in the same way. He lit into a guy who was just standing by watching the play. Jimmy started yelling and screaming at him without any warning. He accused the guy of spying on him and signaling his cards to other players at the table. He got so angry so fast, it was scary. One moment he could be jovial and joking with the players and the next minute he'd be yelling and threatening to kill a bystander if he didn't get his ass away from the table. Fortunately, the guy moved off. I really thought Jimmy was going to go for him. He completely lost his cool."

"Was he drinking too much or do you think he was high on something?"

"I don't know. He could hold his liquor, and usually paced himself when he gambled. He was more excited by the play than drinking. He never wanted to quit playing."

"Could it have been drugs?"

"It's possible, but I don't think so. He didn't have glassy eyes or seem spaced out like most of the druggies I've seen. We're required to report any gamblers we think are on drugs to the floor manager. It's something to do with liability insurance. I never thought his mood changes were drug related."

I found it strange that they worried about drug use but were perfectly happy to keep pouring complimentary drinks that dulled the memory and affected a gambler's judgment for the benefit of the house. "Did he gamble at your table the last time he was here?" I asked.

"No, I was working a blackjack table and he played poker."

"Was he with his wife?"

"Not Jimmy. He rarely ever brought Gloria here after their marriage. I haven't seen her in over a year.

"Does he have a girlfriend here in Vegas?"

"I don't think so. Jimmy liked variety. He usually had a different babe hanging on his arm each time. Except for the last one. I saw her with him three or four times."

"Do you know who she was?"

"No, but she got a lot of attention on the floor. Always dressed in red. A real knockout for an oriental girl."

"She was Asian?" I could barely mask my surprise.

"Yeah, she was really sexy in her red Chinese dress with slits up the sides and spike heels. She was kinda' slim-hipped but really stacked, if you know what I mean. Never seen an oriental woman like her."

"Catch her name?"

"No, but she was a real live wire. When she got tired gambling, she headed straight for the disco floor in the hotel. She could dance all night waiting for Jimmy. I never saw anyone with such incredible energy. She never seemed to get tired."

Rogers suddenly looked at his wristwatch. He was due back at his work station. We'd both lost track of time. I told him I'd get back to him with the names and numbers of some high rollers I knew in Tahoe and we'd get together again for drinks. I hadn't asked about working the casino, but that was fine with me, as I didn't want to complicate my stay in Vegas by going through the motions to apply for work.

Peter scurried back to his work station and I ambled over to the Sand Dab Restaurant to confirm my date with Rita. She saw me coming and threw me a super-friendly smile. She looked so good in her short black skirt, sheer black stockings, gray suede pumps and pink scoop-neck blouse, I had to suck my breath in to keep from whistling. She waited for me to take a seat before coming to my table.

"Have you been thinking about me?" She said tongue-in-cheek.

"Dreamt about you all night. Can't get you out of my thoughts."

"I'll bet you tell that to all the girls you meet."

"No, Scout's honor. It's true. Reggie, he take one look at de lady movin' last night an' he say, Oo-hee, she got de motion!"

Rita cracked up laughing at my attempt to imitate a Jamaican reggae singer I like. "I sure hope you didn't cut off your dreadlocks just for me," she teased.

It was my turn to laugh. I liked this young lady instantly; she was spunky, liked to banter like me and had a great sense of humor.

"Do you still get off at seven?" I asked.

"Yes, and you're booked, Mr. Stewart. Instead of blowing your wad on a fancy dinner to try to impress me, how would you like to take this girl to a show on the Strip that she's been dying to see?"

"You must've been reading my mind. I'm not much for fancy restaurants, but I do love a show. What's playing?"

"Lou Rawls and Aaron Neville are each doing shows in the cabaret lounges."

"I like 'em both. But if it's a choice between being a "Seventh Son" or "Tell It Like It Is," I'm for Neville and the truth."

"You're right about something, Mister Stewart, in spite of you tryin' to lay a line on this po' girl. We do think alike when it comes to songs. I took the liberty of reserving two tickets in your name to Aaron Neville's nine o'clock show.

"You like pizza, Miss Rita? I have a yearning for a spicy pepperoni and sausage pizza. Could we squeeze it in before the show?"

"You trying to fatten me up? I love pizza."

"Then we're on. Where do I collect you?

"Meet me at the front door to the hotel at seven sharp. What'll you be driving?"

"I'm driving an old burgundy-colored Chevy Impala sedan."

"I gotta go back to work, Mister Stewart. Be sure you're on time."

She quickly bent over me and brushed her lips lightly on my cheek and touched my arm. She smelled of sugar and spice and everything nice. Before I had time to react, she'd turned on her heel and let me watch her do her walk. My-oh-my, did she ever have me glued to "de motion."

I hummed Aaron Neville's tune, "Love, Love, Love" as I skipped out of the bar and headed for my car. I hoped I wouldn't be singing, "She Took You For A Ride," before the night was over.

Chapter 15

OW THAT THE ALLURING RITA JAMES HAD RETURNED to work, I had to take stock of what I'd learned from spying on the Lone Pine Mortuary and what Peter Rogers and my little brother told me. The news that Jimmy Simmons had openly consorted with Jennifer Wong at the casino troubled me. I needed to ask L.C. some questions about Ms. Wong. I pondered the situation while I picked up some supplies I might need later at a local pharmacy.

I called home. No one answered. After listening to Mom's pleasant voice asking the caller to leave a message, I requested my brother to call me at my motel with an update on Jennifer Wong. As all the city libraries would be closed on Sunday, I took a chance and called the listing for the general library at UNLV. I hoped the library at the University of Nevada at Las Vegas would be open on Sunday to assist students cramming for exams and last-minute researching for term papers.

I was surprised to hear a real, pleasant voice at the other end of the line instead of a recorded message requesting I punch a key for the options on a menu. It took me fifteen minutes to get to the library. The friendly lady on the phone turned out to be even more helpful in person. She explained their computerized information retrieval system that indexed journal articles by subject matter. After a few minutes playing with key words related to drugs, I had a list of magazine articles on the drug I was looking for. With the librarian's aid, I soon had a stack of magazines to read.

I was surprised to learn how easy crystal methamphetamine was to fabricate. It could be made from the drug ephedrine, which is found in many drugs sold over-the-counter. All one needed was hot water, a container and a frying mechanism to convert the methamphetamine into "ice." Once converted into crystal form, it was odorless and looked like rock candy. You smoked it through a glass pipe like "crack" and it sold on the street for about fifty dollars in penny-sized bags called a "paper." A "paper" contained about a tenth of a gram of the drug and provided three to four hits.

According to users, one hit produced a high that could last up to fourteen hours compared to the fifteen-to-twenty-minute high with crack cocaine. Some addicts claimed that when they first smoked "ice," they stayed high for a week. They called the sensation "amping" for the amplified euphoria it gave them.

The drug was especially popular with young women in their late teens to early thirties because it suppressed their appetite and helped them lose weight. Apparently, many young women were getting hooked on "ice" because they thought it was safer than other street drugs and because of its long-lasting effects that aided dieting. Others used it at work when required to do fatiguing or repetitive tasks; they claimed it kept them alert for long periods of time and improved their performance of simple manual tasks.

I was particularly interested in the drug's side effects. Addicts reported they often became suddenly aggressive and suffered hallucinations and paranoia. Long-term users reported weight loss, nervousness, irritability, and insomnia and many suffered from severe hypertension, respiratory and cardiac problems. A number of chronic users had died from kidney failure caused by the drug.

Users complained that when they crashed after using the drug, they suffered severe depression and fatigue. One user's testimony really caught my eye: "Once you use ice, you don't want any other drug. It's more potent than crack. Your eyes feel like they are popping out, your ears ring. All your senses are open. Everything is keen and lasts for hours. You don't want to sit down. You feel like doing things. I went to movies, disco dancing and bars. When you crash, it feels like you fell off the tallest building. There's no depression like it. You sit in a corner. You feel suicidal."

The user's description, coupled with what I had learned, had seemed to fit Jimmy Simmons and Jennifer Wong's behavior perfectly on their last visit to the Far Tortuga Casino. Peter Rogers' description of Jimmy Simmons' ability to stay focused on his card playing all night without becoming fatigued or dulled tallied with the accounts I read. So did his aggressive behavior and paranoia. The same was true for Jennifer Wong's ability to dance her ass off most of the night.

What I read confirmed my earlier suspicion that Jimmy Simmons had handed a packet of drugs to Jennifer Wong when I observed them in the mortuary parking lot in Oakland. I had a sinking feeling. Jimmy Simmons had been murdered, so where was Jennifer Wong? Were Jimmy's killers after her too? She hadn't turned up for work. Was she on the lam? I needed to find her before the killers did.

I left the library at closing time and headed for a mail drop business I'd scoped out earlier where I could send faxes. I photographed the writing on the Chinese cardboard panels I'd taken from the taxidermy and faxed it to my sister with a note in code for her to get the writing translated. The guy at the store must have thought I was bonkers; he probably had me pegged for a drug creep and the way things were going, I was starting to feel that way, too.

After sprucing up in a casino restroom, I ducked into a nearby saloon to grab a beer and try to make sense of what I'd learned and decide what to do after my date with Rita. If she turned out to be a live wire, I'd need to take her somewhere other than my motel room unless I wanted her to discover my true identity. It was a dilemma. I risked ruining any chance of seeing more of her the longer I kept up my pretense to be an unemployed card dealer. To level with her might put her at risk from the thugs looking for me. Rita was no fool; I'd have to play it by ear and hope for the best.

I laughed at the thought of the look that would cross Saundra's visage when she tallied my expense vouchers and learned I'd paid for two motel rooms on the same day. She would not be amused. I also wondered how Gloria Simmons would react when she learned how I was spending her expense money. I could try to justify my night out with Rita by claiming she provided me with information and leads in my investigation. It was a pretty hollow claim that wouldn't cut much slack with tough cookies like Saundra and Mrs. Simmons. So far, Mrs. Simmons had paid for an expensive new Armani outfit she hadn't seen me wear. I had to chuckle. She didn't know where I was and how fast I was spending her money. I looked forward to paying tonight's dinner and club tabs with her money.

Chapter 16

W HEN I ARRIVED AT THE FAR TORTUGA CASINO,
I waited in the hotel lobby for Rita. She appeared
right on time, and my oh my, did she ever look
good! She was decked out in a short, black, A-line
skirt, sheer black hose and two-inch black patent leather heels
that were cut low in the back to accentuate her slim ankles. A
form-fitting black top with a v-neck and long sleeves rounded
out her ensemble.

Her top molded her body like a glove and didn't leave
too much to the imagination. She wore three large gold hoop
bracelets on her left wrist and large, thin, golden hoop earrings
that bounced coyly under her pageboy hairdo.

Rita's skirt was something else. At first, I thought it was
sequined. As she approached, what I thought were sequins
were actually shiny, black disks the size of quarters that had
been sewn onto her skirt in an overlapping pattern. The effect
was dazzling. As she strutted, the lights overhead reflected her
movement like ripples of water on a pond. The skirt looked like
a sexy coat of mail.

My big smile and eyes conveyed how good she looked, not
that she needed confirmation. She was fully aware of the effect
she was having on everyone in the lobby. She sashayed up to me
without a word and linked her arm in mine. My chest swelled

like a proud peacock. The doorman must have been watching because the door opened with a flourish and he ushered us out like royalty. He was the same man who'd warned me not to gamble the night before.

"Shore pleased to see you got somethin' on yo' mind 'sides gamblin', young brother. You take good care a' Miz Rita. She's precious."

"Not to worry, brother. I'll protect her like a bodyguard."

He laughed in his deep bass voice. I handed him a five dollar tip but he wouldn't take it. "You spend the fiver on Miz Rita. She works hard an' deserves a night off to have some fun. You two get on outta here an' kick up a leg for me. She looks like she might need some protectin' and then some."

It was my turn to laugh. The way Rita was decked out, I might indeed have to defend her honor in this tinsel town. I hoped the young bloods would be more interested in gambling than hassling us.

"You look so good, you sure you want to eat pizza? We could put on the dog at some nice restaurant," I offered. I was glad I'd replaced my ratty tweed jacket I keep in my car with a smart looking sport coat and despite the desert heat, I'd added a foulard; I wanted to look my best. I could always take off the foulard once we got comfortable with each other.

"Hey, you got money to waste like all those gamblers? I'm happy to be with you, Reggie. I get offers all the time from high-rollers who think any pretty girl working in Vegas is ready to play for a price. I watched you carefully at the casino. I know you're not here to gamble. I dressed up for you. Let's stick with pizza. We'll have time to talk and get to know each other. After the concert, if you want to make Johnny, the doorman, happy, we can go dancing."

While we drove to Rita's favorite pizza parlor, I had more doubts about continuing my ruse to be a card dealer. She was no fool and I risked getting off on the wrong foot with her. She was so levelheaded and down to earth that we hit it off immediately. I was so taken with her intelligence and wit that I could relax and concentrate on her personality and not her eye-distracting body.

Rita made my mind up for me while we laughed at each other's antics trying to corral the long, sinewy globs of cheese with each bite of pizza. We were like a couple of high school kids, oblivious to everything around us and just having fun.

"I've got to tell you something about myself, Rita. I hope you won't be mad with me."

"As long as you're not married or gay, I think I can handle it," she said, eyeing me seriously.

"No. I'm single as the day I was born and not gay. I wasn't telling the truth about being an unemployed card dealer."

"I knew from the start you weren't a card dealer down on his luck. If I'd believed that, I'd have brushed you off. All the dealers I know are foolish gamblers as well. I saw your disdain for the suckers who play and that you don't gamble money foolishly."

"I'm a private investigator here on a case. The dealer story was necessary to meet Peter Rogers. I really like you, and I want to be straight with you and not get off on the wrong foot. Know what I mean?"

"I think so, Reggie. Anyway, I'm not angry now you've decided not to feed me a line. I like you too, or I wouldn't have agreed to go out with you; I'm real fussy about who I see. I hear so many lines that it was refreshing you didn't try to hustle me out the door like most men. I hoped you'd turn out to be a breath of fresh air; that's what I want to find out."

As she spoke, I pulled out my business card with Nate's address and handed it to her. After glancing at it, she laughed. "I'm glad to see that you're really called Reggie. I like the name. So what brings you all the way to Vegas?"

"I'm investigating an Oakland mortician named Jimmy Simmons. Remember him? I hear he was a fixture here at the casino tables."

"Sure. Jimmy had an eye for every pretty girl to cross his path and roving hands if you got too close. He also had a nasty side and mean temper; he could be very insulting if crossed. He got the message straight from me the first time. I told him,

'You can look but not touch.' He didn't like it, but he learned to keep his hands to himself and his mouth shut when it came to me."

"Peter said he insulted one of the barmaids not too long ago and she left in tears. Were you working that evening?"

"No, but I heard about it the next day. Julie was so upset, she quit. She shouldn't have to put up with that kind of abuse."

"Did you see him with an Asian girlfriend?"

"Sure. The same woman was with him the last few times he gambled at the casino. She was real pretty – tall for an Asian woman and real slim. She seemed more interested in dancing than gambling. They dined together a few times in The Sand Dab. She could get really animated and spacey at times. I was surprised because she was not at all like most Asian women who gamble here, who tend to be quiet and demure."

"Do you think she was high on drugs?"

"I don't know. She seemed more nervous and jittery than drugged. She couldn't sit still even at dinner; she was constantly fidgeting. Is this related to your investigation?" Rita asked, giving me a hard look.

"Yeah, she worked at the mortuary and Jimmy Simmons was her boss."

"You must be kidding. She didn't act like an employee. She was real assertive; I was surprised to see her boss him around and he took it. I was rooting for her all the way. She could pull his chain and he just sat there and had to grin and bear it." Rita paused and gave me a strange look. "Am I part of your investigation, too?"

"Yes, to the extent that you can provide info about Jimmy Simmons' activities. But I didn't ask you out just to pump you for information. You made my heart jump the moment I first saw you and it's never stopped racing," I said sheepishly.

"You liked what you saw hanging over the table, right?"

I laughed. "Yeah, I liked that, too. But that's not reason enough alone to ask you out," I lied. "There are lots of very attractive women in this town and where I live in Berkeley. I was attracted to you immediately by the way you reacted to me. I liked your spunk and sassy ways. I knew you were a live-wire and would be fun to know and be with. So far, my intuition is spot on."

"So, it wasn't love at first sight?" Rita said, tongue-in-cheek.

We both laughed. "You sure know how to put a guy on the spot."

"That's because I'm a serious person, Reggie. I don't like working as a barmaid. It's just a means to an end. I make enough money in tips in six months to pay my college tuition and expenses for a year and then some. I've been working at the Far Tortuga for almost a year, and I plan to quit in a few months and finish my degree at UNLV."

"I wondered why you'd put up with having to serve guys like Jimmy Simmons night after night. Did you know his wife?"

"No, but I heard plenty about her. She was like a lot of women here in Vegas, looking for good times and a sugar daddy. From what I heard, she and Jimmy deserved each other. Are you working for her?"

"My boss is. I'm supposed to dig into her hubby's finances."

Rita glanced at her wristwatch. "Hey, we better finish this pizza or we're going to be late for the show, Mr. Gumshoe."

We gobbled the rest of our pizza and laughed at each other's antics. Rita passed me her pocket mirror so I could see my light-chocolate-colored mug strung like a Christmas tree with thin streamers of pizza cheese and bits of topping. I made her look at her own face; we looked like a funny variant of the Bobbsey Twins. It took two trips each to the washroom before we were ready to face the crowd at the show.

I felt proud and special to walk to our table near the stage through the haze of smoke, buzz of voices and curious gaze of the club-goers with Rita on my arm. While Rita wasn't the only classy woman dressed to kill, all eyes were riveted on her dress and what rippled under it.

I ordered a Hennessy straight up and Rita had a vodka gimlet. We were both excited to catch the show. I couldn't get over the irony of being in Las Vegas among hardened gamblers and losers trying to score a killing against a stacked deck only to hear the four Neville Brothers dedicate their music to the poor and disenfranchised of the world – to Saint Jude and to Jah God, the Great Spirit.

I heard them sing "Sister Rosa" for the first time. I was thrilled to hear their rendition of how Sister Rosa Parks refused to take a seat on the back of the bus in Montgomery, Alabama on December 1, 1955 and became the shining spirit and symbol for justice in the Civil Rights Movement – the same struggle that brought my Mom and Dad together. It was like listening to the story of my birth. My eyes were tearing by the time the last chorus finished with, "So we dedicate this song to thee, For being a symbol of our dignity. Thank you Sister Rosa."

There was no time to get maudlin. Aaron Neville followed with a song about a Voo Doo Woman, and Rita and I were swaying to the beat of the music and tapping fingers during the rest of the show. We were feeling really good by the time they sang their last encore to the enthusiastic crowd.

We'd been making goo-goo eyes at each other throughout the show and beaming at each other with looks that conveyed an understanding of how excited we were to have found each other and share this special concert experience together. As the music vibrated through our bodies and put all our senses in motion, I could feel us coming together. There was so much high-charged electrical energy passing between us that I felt high just being in her presence.

As we left the club, I put my arm around her shoulders and hugged. She slipped her arm around my waist and squeezed back. When we got to my car, instead of getting in the passenger side, she turned to meet my eyes and without a word, she put her arms around me and we kissed. It wasn't a sweet little "Thank you for a nice time" kiss you get at the door on a first date from a lady who wants to go slow.

Rita's kiss was passionate and energetic. Her full lips sucked on mine and as we probed with our tongues, she pressed her full, ripe body against me and we started to move in sync. We probably looked like a honeymoon couple who couldn't wait to get to their hotel room. We were both oblivious to the rest of the world as we started our mating dance in the parking lot. Our bodies did all the talking. She slipped her thigh between my legs and slowly moved against my hardness.

Our dance was rudely interrupted by a cat call from a drunken reveler, "Hey, I want the next dance with the hot mama!"

I looked around to see a small crowd of leering males watching us and miming our movements. I flashed on the doorman's warning and quickly hustled Rita into the car and laid down rubber getting out of the lot. I was furious at myself for the close call I'd subjected Rita to.

"Take it easy, Reggie. We've got all night. I don't have to be at work tomorrow until eleven," Rita said soothingly.

I slowed the car down and she slid over to me, put an arm around me and snuggled her head on my chest. I had difficulty concentrating on the road as Rita let her other hand rest lightly on my thigh.

I ignored the light in the manager's office of my motel and escorted Rita up the back stairs to my room. The red eye of my answering machine was blinking furiously. I ignored it. Pleasure before business. We started our kiss where we'd left off. We were both pretty steamed up when the telephone started to clang like a burglar alarm. It became evident the caller was not going to give up. Rita finally said, "You better answer it, Reggie, before it wakes up the whole neighborhood."

I shuffled over to the phone trying to mask the hardness in my loins. I didn't dare look at Rita. I did hear her chuckle at the ridiculous sight of me crab-walking to the phone. She said, "Go ahead, Reggie, answer the phone; I'll still be here when you finish dealing with the call."

I picked up the receiver and Annie announced I had an urgent call that was too important for the answering machine. "It's okay, Annie, put it through."

"That you, R.C.? It's your brother. I've been waitin' for you to return my earlier call. You O.K.?"

"I just walked in the door. What's so urgent it can't wait?"

"Your boss called the house today. He sounded really pissed. He's figured out that you ain't in L.A. and he's loaded for bear. He ordered me to get a message through to you to 'get your black ass home on the double if you valued your job.' I thought you'd better know."

Chapter 17

WHILE RITA HAD HEARD ONLY MY SIDE OF THE conversation with my brother, she'd heard more than enough to be alarmed and wasted no time getting on my case. "Are you in some kind of danger, Reggie?"

"I'd hoped not to worry you. Jennifer Wong's been missing since Friday. She's either on the run or even worse, in the hands of people who want to harm her."

"Why would anyone want to harm her?" Rita asked perplexed.

"I'm not sure, but I don't think the Chinese in Oakland think too highly of her personal relationship with Jimmy Simmons."

"What was she doing working in a black-owned mortuary, anyway? So he could do his hanky-panky on the job? It doesn't make any sense to me," Rita said.

"I think it's more complicated than that. I'm pretty sure the two of them were doing drugs together and he was involved in drug trafficking with Chinese drug gangs. They probably placed her in the mortuary as a bookkeeper to monitor their interests and serve as an informant. If I'm right about this, Jennifer Wong got hooked both on drugs and Jimmy Simmons."

"If that's the case, she's really in danger, isn't she?" Rita said with a worried look.

I hesitated. I was debating whether to level with Rita completely or stick with only part of the story. My instinct said to trust her completely. I needed to listen to the other messages on my machine and Rita would hear them as well. She waited patiently and expectantly, sensing my dilemma.

"I'd hoped to avoid involving you in this ugly business, Rita, but I see I can't. Jimmy Simmons was murdered Friday night and Jennifer Wong disappeared the same day. I'm worried that the same people who took out Simmons may have caught up with her as well. I think she's here in Vegas."

Rita stared at me perplexed and worried. "Reggie, this is a matter for the police. If she's here in Vegas and you're trying to find her, you are courting danger. I just found you; I don't want to lose you!" Rita's voice and eyes pleaded.

"I don't have any proof to take to the police and I'm not authorized to report my suspicions by my lawyer boss who's bound by rules of confidentiality which I'm supposed to follow. It's complicated. I need to verify my suspicions before blowing the whistle on anybody. So far, I'm only guessing at what's going on. I have to verify a couple of critical pieces for the puzzle to be complete. If I reveal my presence here, even to the police, I may create more danger and risk, putting you in harm's way as well. I'm going to clear the rest of my messages and then take you home."

Rita gave me a hard look. "No you're not! I'm going to stick to you like hot molasses. You're not going to drop me off so I can worry myself to death all night about what you're doing. You booked me for the night Mister Gumshoe and you're stuck with me. So you better get that through your thick head!" Rita's big brown eyes blazed with fire and determination.

"I can't do that, Rita, however much I'd like to be with you. What I have to do may be dangerous. I want you home for your own safety. It's part of my job to take risks in order to get information. I've always worked alone. That way I never expose others I care about to risks ..."

Rita cut me off before I could get up a head of steam.

She was having none of my little sermon. "Sounds like your brother is also up to his neck in this affair, Reggie. So, don't go trying to lay down a line of caution and bull to this girl. You're not going anywhere alone tonight, so you might as well tell me what you're planning to do so we can figure out the best way to do it together. And don't give me that hangdog look either! I'm serious. You try to dump me off when the going gets tough, then you better start looking for another girl because when I like someone, it's all or nothing. You hear?"

"Yeah, I hear you loud and clear. I'm worried you're going to get into something over your head and I'll get you into serious trouble. You could get arrested or even shot. I can't risk that."

"Well, you can just stop worrying. I'm a big girl and I'm not afraid of trouble. Why don't you listen to your messages and tell me what's going on from the beginning. This is my town and I can help you do anything that needs doing here. Just loan me one of your warmup outfits and I'll be your boy Friday or even your Miss Rosa Parks."

I couldn't suppress a chuckle. Rita was too much. I'd never met anyone like her. One minute she was prepared to be my lover and the next my sidekick and buddy in crime. I pointed to my wardrobe hanging in the closet and while she picked through it, I rewound my message tape.

The first message was from my brother repeating what he'd told me. The second call was from my sister who reported that the address labels I'd faxed her came from import/export companies in Hong Kong and Taiwan. Her accountant friend thought the second set of books I'd copied from the mortuary was a record detailing a drug-related money laundering scheme. The message ended with a plea to be careful and not to do anything foolish as Jimmy Simmons' killers were still on the loose. I heard a "I told you so" behind me and I turned in time to see a pair of creamy brown thighs disappear into one of my basketball warmup suits. Rita's face broke into a big smile as she carefully laid out her short, dazzling dress, top and sexy shoes on a chair. She was now busy stuffing newspaper into a pair of my sneakers.

"Was that your girlfriend back home? I see I'm not the only one worried about you and your nefarious activities," she said mischievously.

It was my turn to smile and wag my finger. "You got it all wrong Miss Gumshoe wannabe. That was my sister, Tiffany. The two of you have a lot in common. She helps me check information through her real estate connections. And as for your insinuation, I don't have a steady girlfriend back home."

Even though my warm up suit was three inches too long, Rita still looked gorgeous to me. My oversized sneakers peeked out from under rolled up pants legs. Rita looked like a cross between a high school bobby-soxer and a circus clown. I couldn't get an amused smile off my mug.

"You like what you see, Buster, or you wanna complain?"

I laughed at her tongue-in-cheek mocking. I was tempted to tease her about how funny she looked, but she beat me to the punch. She took a flying leap that caught me by surprise and we tumbled onto the bed with Rita on top. She wasted no time proving she was a world class tickler. She was much stronger than I suspected. By the time I wrestled out from under her and got in some serious tickling of my own, we were both laughing uncontrollably. Before long we were both bent over double and out of breath from our activity. We just fell in each other's arms, too breathless to kiss, so we just hugged.

When we finally recovered from our fun, Rita cuddled in my arms and asked me to tell her what I knew about Jennifer Wong and why I thought she was in Vegas. I told her about what I saw in the parking lot between Jennifer and Jimmy Simmons and what I'd seen in the lot of the taxidermy shop. I told her everything except about my bag job at the mortuary the night Simmons was pumped full of holes.

"You think they drugged her and transported her to the Lone Pine Mortuary in that hearse, don't you?" Rita said when I finished.

"Yes, I think she's held captive in the mortuary or the taxidermy. She's in grave danger because she knows too much about the drug smuggling scheme and the hit on Jimmy Simmons for her own good. They can't trust her anymore."

"Will they kill her?" Rita said, worried.

"Probably, if I don't find her and stop them."

"How are we going to stop them?"

"That's why I want to take you home. I have to pay a late night visit to the mortuary and find out if she's being held there or across the street."

"Reggie, that's dangerous and illegal. Suppose they are waiting for you and call the police to arrest you for burglary? Or even worse, they want to harm you?"

"That's a chance I have to take and two reasons why I need to take you home. You could be charged as an accessory to my illegal entry."

"Well, at least you'll be in jail in Vegas. That ought to cool the heels of your girlfriends back home. On the other hand, I'd prefer you on the outside. I don't like kissing through jail plexiglass and I'm not going to let anyone harm you," she said with conviction.

"Stick with me and I'm afraid you won't be on the outside looking in."

"That settles it then, doesn't it? We'll just have to be smarter than our adversaries and not get caught. Two heads are better than one and you need a backup and you got her," Rita said in no uncertain terms.

I got off the bed reluctantly and removed a small athletic bag from the floor of the clothes closet. I removed a number of items I'd bought earlier. By the time I'd arranged almost all the items from the bag neatly on the bed, I had Rita's full attention. When I pulled the last items out, Rita, who was resting on her elbow said, "Wow!" I'd added my lock picking tools, master keys, gloves and black ski mask to the pile.

I handed Rita a pair of rubber gloves, a flashlight, and a highly potent canister of Mace and another of pepper spray. I put the lock picking tools and keys in the small pocket of a fanny pack and placed the syringes, cotton swabs, small spoons, duct tape and laboratory vials I'd purchased earlier in the day in the larger pocket and zipped it shut. I changed into a dark-colored warmup suit and sneakers and clipped another pair of canisters onto my belt.

"I wasn't exaggerating when I said I hoped you'd turn out to be a serious young man. Little did I know I'd be teaming up with a cat burglar. You are something else!" Rita exclaimed.

"The anti-dog pepper spray gave me away, didn't it?"

Rita laughed.

Chapter 18

WE DROVE BACK TO TOWN AND MADE A BEELINE for the mortuary. As we drove past it, I asked Rita to observe the taxidermy for signs of life while I looked for vital signs at the Lone Pine. Both parking lots were vacant and only a lighted sign for the mortuary and one in the display window of the taxidermy pierced the night sky and winked at the street lamp down the block. After driving around the block, I parked behind a pickup truck in front of a residence that gave us a good view of the entryways to both establishments. One advantage of having Rita along on a stakeout was that I wouldn't look suspicious sitting alone in my car this time of night. We managed a fair amount of serious necking while monitoring the street.

I had to move the car closer to the mortuary once we'd fogged up the windows and could hardly see out. While both parking lots looked empty, I was concerned there might be a live-in watchman whose car was parked in the large hangar housing the mortuary's rolling fleet. I had noticed a small room over an outbuilding near the hanger on my first visit. It was possible Jennifer Wong was held there; if so, there'd be armed guards. Rita tensed up the moment I advanced my Chevy. It was almost one in the morning when I moved to make my reconnaissance of the mortuary's perimeter. I instructed Rita to honk my car horn if she spotted any sign of danger. I tried to assure her that I'd be playing the role of a lover taking a leak.

After checking the windows all around the building's perimeters for signs of alarm taping, I studied the locks. Surprisingly, there was no evidence of an alarm system and the locks were the kind you could buy in any hardware store and easy to pick. The Lone Pine Mortuary, like the one in Oakland, appeared to rely on the spook factor for security. After my tour of the premises, I signaled Rita I was going in. She would be my lookout.

I unlocked the double back door using my passkeys. I figured it was the pathway to the coffins and would lead to the workshops and body storage areas where Jennifer Wong most likely would be held. My heart beat furiously as I stepped into the dark void behind the door. While I'm not normally superstitious, this was the second mortuary I'd broken into in three days. It wasn't a habit I wanted to continue. After waiting for my eyes to adjust to the gloom, I advanced slowing down the hallway feeling my way along the wall. There were a series of doors on the left and one double door on the right that must lead to the chapel and connect to the breezeway in front.

I opened the first door on the left; it opened smoothly and led to a small room with windows looking on to the parking lot that let in just enough light to see it was a small lunch room for the staff. I checked inside the refrigerator but found only cans of soda pop and stale sweet rolls.

The second door was much wider and locked. My passkey opened it easily. My hands were clammy inside the surgical gloves I wore. My apprehension was mounting along with my pulse at what I might find. The first thing that hit me was the pungent smell of formaldehyde and other embalming chemicals.

As the room had no windows, I flicked on my small, pinpoint flashlight. The room was laid out like a college chemistry lab except for the special morgue slab in the center of the room. The slab table had gutters around its edges to capture body fluids and visceral matter removed by the morticians. Along one wall, there were two large double sinks with shelves of chemicals and glass jars above.

As I played my light over the jars, I noticed several bore labels with Chinese characters. The contents were murky but looked like body organs preserved in fluids. I shivered involuntarily. My mind raced at the possibilities. I hoped I wasn't seeing Jennifer Wong's vital organs in neatly labeled jars. I snapped a series of flash photos of the jars and the room with my Minox camera. I also photographed the many murderous-looking instruments laid out on a side table. I'd watched Navy butchers dissect meat carcasses, but I'd never seen such a formidable collection of hacking and cutting tools assembled on the table. The collection would do justice to a medieval torture chamber.

The door leading to the next room was locked. I was sweating profusely now as I feared what I might find behind the locked door. After picking the lock, I crouched and jerked the door open. I let out a big sigh of relief to see the room was empty except for a number of refrigerated pull-drawers that dominated the chamber. I was both disappointed and relieved to see no sign of Jennifer Wong. It was more likely she would be kept in the Chinese taxidermy across the street.

Several of the twelve metal drawers were labeled. Four bore names of individuals, three were labeled in Chinese and the remaining ones were unlabelled. I pulled out one of the unlabeled drawers first; it was empty. All the labeled drawers were locked. I recognized the names of some of the individuals I'd seen in the obituary columns. I glanced at my watch. I'd been inside for close to fifteen minutes. I needed to speed up my work and get out of the mortuary as quickly as possible. I'd told Rita I'd be out in no more than twenty minutes. But I couldn't leave before picking the locks on the three Chinese-labeled drawers. I debated briefly whether to return outside to tell Rita, but decided it would take even more time and add risk. Better to finish up here as quickly as possible and bolt out of here.

It took more than a minute to pick the lock of the first Chinese-labeled drawer. I cautiously pulled it open and gasped. Staring back at me with big, glassy, black eyes was a baby black bear cub. I could hardly believe my eyes. My mind raced back to the collection of cutting tools and jars of pickled organs with Chinese labels in the adjacent room. It all started to make sense at last.

The Chinese across the street were using the mortuary's facilities to butcher animals on the endangered species list. It was clever. The mortuary regularly disposed of blood and visceral matter. The bear's head and pelt would be removed, cured and sold to collectors. The bear paws and organs would be pickled or dried and shipped to clients in Asia where they were prized and commanded exorbitant prices for their alleged medicinal properties. Here the animals could be poached in their natural habitat, transported to the mortuary, and butchered in a safe, secure and private facility the local Department of Fish and Game would never suspect.

The scheme made me hopping mad. The bear cub had probably been lured away from its dead mother that I expected to find in the next drawer. I photographed the little bear before closing the drawer. I would submit my photos anonymously to the proper regulatory authorities once my investigation was over. If I was lucky, I might nail both the morticians and taxidermists and get their licenses yanked.

The second drawer revealed another eye-popping surprise. A sleek, glassy-eyed puma with barred fangs stared at me. The dead cougar was medium sized and its pelt was a rich tawny brown; it was probably destined to adorn the shoulders of a rich Asian client. I'd read somewhere that Asian herbalists ground the bones of Bengal and African tigers so their clients could literally drink the animals' essence to gain the beasts' strength and ferocity in fighting and lovemaking.

I'd never seen such a beautiful animal at close range. Even in its mild state of rigor mortis, the six-foot puma was lithe and supple. I ran my hand gently down the animal's soft fur. I was incensed that such a magnificent creature had been killed to harvest its pelt and body parts.

Both animals must have been shot recently and transported directly to the mortuary. They'd probably had to store them because of the weekend services; they'd be butchered in between regular funerals. I photographed the cougar and moved on to the third drawer, expecting to find another bear or puma.

My heart caught in my throat at the sight of the young Asian woman. She was completely naked and still beautiful in spite of her pale skin in her cold resting place. It was sobering to know this slim, attractive young woman would smile and dance no more. Someone had closed Jennifer Wong's eyes.

I saw no evidence of gunshot wounds or trauma to suggest a violent death or evidence anyone had started an embalming process. She must have died very recently like the animals and awaited a calm moment for the disposal of her remains and evidence of her death. Transporting her in the Simmons' hearse made sense: no compromising shipping records with an inter-state carrier. They could drug or kill someone, transport the body out of state, and dispose of it without suspicion and in a manner that would not cause a ripple of interest.

The obituaries I'd checked in the library indicated no young woman had died in Las Vegas in the last two weeks. Jennifer Wong had been murdered because of her association with Jimmy Simmons. Another piece of the puzzle fell into place, but I still had no proof of who had actually ordered and carried out the two killings. I still needed to establish proof.

Careful inspection of Jennifer Wong's upper torso revealed a couple of small needle marks on her left arm. I removed a syringe and two empty blood vials from my fanny pack. I care-fully worked the needle into one of the needle holes in her arm and soon thick blood filled the syringe. I repeated the opera-tion in the other needle hole. I transferred the blood from the syringes to the vials and placed the syringes and vials against Jennifer Wong's still-pert breasts and took photos with and without the blood samples.

I was shocked when I glanced at my watch. I'd been in the building for just under forty-five minutes. I wanted to look inside the remaining storage drawers, but it would take too long. I still needed to search for shipping and drug-related records connecting the two mortuaries.

I was bent over Jennifer Wong's drawer taking a last photo when the room flooded with light and a deep bass voice yelled, "Freeze or you're dead meat!"

The shock of the light and the command sent cold shivers up my spine. I slowly raised my arms over my head and turned to face my captor. He was the same Asian man I'd seen enter the taxidermy to meet the tow-headed guy from the mortuary. He didn't look any happier to see me than I to see him. He was pointing a mean-looking automatic pistol at me and I didn't have any trouble imagining the series of holes it would make if he squeezed the trigger. He seemed confused and unsure about what to do with me. As he was dressed in blood-stained overalls, I decided to gamble for my life.

"Hey man, why are you pointing that shooter at me? Ain't you with the taxidermy folks across the street?

"Who are you and what're you doing in here?" He demanded menacingly.

"The same as you, my man. I'm Brother Charles from the Simmons Family Mortuary in Oakland. I brought her on the body run last night." I said pointing to Jennifer Wong. "We was on our way back to Oakland when I realized we forgot to take the blood samples. So, we had to come back," I said, showing him the syringes and blood vials.

"Blood samples?" He said with a bewildered look.

"Yeah, on this chick." I said pointing a syringe at Wong's corpse. Our doctor can't sign off on the death certificate unless he has samples of her blood to verify she overdosed on drugs. I had to come back to take the samples. I'm gonna catch hell for being late."

I watched his reaction closely to my cock-and-bull story. He still looked unsure about what to do. Nothing like a ray of hope for a condemned man. I was sure from his bloody smock that he'd come to butcher the animals and not deal with Jennifer Wong. While he pondered what to do, I lowered my hands, replaced the vials in my fanny pack, winked and waved a syringe.

"Where's the other guy and the hearse?" He demanded.

"He dropped me off to get the samples and went to a

Colonel Sanders to get us a bucket of fried chicken and some biscuits to eat on the long ride home. He'll be along any minute to fetch me."

"How did you get in here?" He said suspiciously.

"They gave us keys in Oakland so we could put her in cold storage if we arrived when the mortuary was closed."

"Why are you wearing plastic gloves?" He was staring at my surgical gloves. I hoped he wasn't thinking I was doing a bag job. I forced a little laugh and put a nonchalant grin on my mug.

"I always wear gloves when I have to touch them bodies, man. When I heard the chick in the drawer was doing drugs, I was afraid she might have AIDS, man. No way I wanna get no disease handling her blood. I always wear gloves when working on druggies. How about puttin' that shooter away so we can both get on with our work?"

He hesitated but did lower his weapon so it pointed at the floor. I was trying to figure my next move when he jumped at a loud noise in the next room and he turned to check it out. If it was the blond-haired man, I'd be dead meat and soon be lying in a drawer alongside Jennifer Wong. I had to make a move. I let out an ear-piercing scream and with a rush and flying leap I was on the Asian guy with fury. He'd frozen at my bloodcurdling scream and given me just enough time to grapple for his gun with one hand as we both hit the floor. With my other hand, I jabbed the syringe into his cheek just as hard as I could.

My AIDS story must have got to him because he dropped the shooter and clawed at his face to extract the deeply imbedded syringe. I rolled over and snatched the automatic pistol and braced myself on my elbows to mow down whoever came through the door to help him. To my surprise, I heard, "Reggie, I'm coming to help you!"

Rita burst through the door in a blur of motion. She was swinging a vicious looking hatchet she'd snatched from the instrument table in the adjacent room.

The Asian guy sat in the corner of the room trying to stem the flow of blood from his face with his shirt. He looked first at me covering him with his pistol and then at Rita poised to strike with her menacing hatchet. Rita and I looked at each other and burst into laughter at how ridiculous we appeared. She looked like an armed Amazon from a circus and I looked like a refugee from the movie *M.A.S.H.* with my weapon clutched tightly in surgical gloves.

"What are you waiting for, Reggie?" Rita asked.

"For Jim Dandy to the rescue, who else?" I said tongue-in-cheek with a big sigh of relief.

Rita laughed at my illusion to the Coasters' rock and roll song. "I saw him go in and I was worried he might have caught you off guard when you didn't come right out," Rita said, pointing to the Asian guy still fussing with his wound.

"You're one hell of a sidekick, Miz Terrorist. While I keep him covered, bind him up," I said, flipping her a roll of duct tape from my fanny pack. Rita deftly taped his hands to his sides and his ankles together. I opened an empty storage drawer and we bundled him in face up. I stuffed his bloody shirt in his mouth and taped it in. I decided to give him some food for thought while he waited to be rescued. "By the way," I said addressing his bulging eyes, "I heard the chick died from AIDS, man. I hope you don't get it. Better have yourself tested the moment you get out of here."

I had frisked him and removed his wallet and keys. His driver's license identified him as Larry Chin. I placed the license on his throat and photographed it and his face in the drawer. After taking several other photos, I dropped his wallet on his chest, turned off the air conditioning and closed his drawer so as to let in only a small amount of air.

I decided to forget about searching the office for compromising financial records. Since Larry Chin hadn't questioned my story about working for the Oakland mortuary, he'd confirmed my suspicions of their working relationship. I didn't like the idea of sticking around to check out the taxidermy across the street, but I needed to verify the role the animals played in the drug smuggling operation before Larry Chin turned up missing and the shit hit the fan.

Chapter 19

RITA SAID, "NO WAY!" DEFIANTLY TO MY SUGGESTION she resume her post as lookout in the car while I poked my nose in the taxidermy store. She'd risked her life to save mine and she knew she'd earned her stripes. We traversed the still deadly quiet, spooky street together. I'd been on the job over an hour and all my heightened senses counseled me to get gone as fast as I could.

Larry Chin's associates were going to be hopping mad when he failed to show in the morning without having butchered the animals. They'd find him quickly and be furious at the hand scrawled message left on his chest saying, "Here Lies Larry Chin – May He Turn Into A Fat Worm To Be Devoured By Crows In His Next Life For Murdering A Baby Brown Bear And A Cougar. If The Killing Of These Endangered Wild Animals Does Not Stop, We Will Skin You Alive And Hang You As A Trophy In Our Underground Trophy Room." It was signed, "Eco Terrorist Cell No. 13."

To add a macabre touch, I'd added a skull and crossbones to the note using Jennifer Wong's and Chin's blood still left in the syringe I'd used to stab Chin. Who knows? Maybe she did have AIDS and he would get what he deserved.

My note would not deflect attention from me for long. Once Larry Chin recounted his story of my impersonation of

Brother Charles from Oakland and he explained his syringe wound, I would be directly in their gun sights. I had to act fast and get out of town quickly.

The taxidermy had an activated alarm system that I deactivated easily with Larry Chin's alarm key. It only took a few seconds to shut off the alarm in the store. Rita followed me in and we headed for the rear of the shop that was curtained off from the front. In the gloom, our noses confirmed what our flashlights illuminated – we were in the middle of an animal parts processing center.

As our eyes adjusted to our dim surroundings, I could make out the stuffed and mounted heads of bears, pumas, wildcats, Big Horn sheep, grey wolves and other animals. Bald eagles and other rare raptors perched on a work bench.

I was appalled as we traipsed through the large workshop. I'd read about African poachers who kill elephants and rhinos in the wild for their horns and big cats for skins and body parts, but I had no idea similar activity was going on under our noses here and on such a large scale. Rita had been silent until she bumped into a clothesline strung with bear parts. There looked to be more than twenty pairs of paws and as many gall bladders pegged to the line.

"God damn bastards! I'm gonna tear out their hearts with my bare hands and feed them to the sharks!" Rita was pissed big time.

I understood her outrage. I was getting nauseous from the rancid smells and ghoulish sights.

I spotted a door on the left side of the room and made for it in haste. Instead of the restrooms I expected, I found myself in a soundproof drug-packaging laboratory. I was thankful for my brother's quick identification of the methamphetamine hydrochloride crystals I'd found in Jimmy Simmons' pouch.

Piles of sheet-like transparent crystals were stacked on work benches. One bench contained a cutting and weighing machine and boxes of penny-size plastic bags for stuffing the one-tenth of a gram papers for sale on the street. There was no mystery why the drug was variously called "quartz," "freeze," or "glass."

I photographed the drug lab, the endangered animals and the animal parts. I had Rita pose with the string of bear claws for the record. I planned to give her a framed, jumbo-sized print when this ugly business was over. I had Rita photograph me holding bear claws in front of the clothesline full of animal parts to prove the lab's existence in case the bad guys tried to dismantle or sanitize it.

I reset the alarm and locked the entry door as we left. I hoped our surreptitious entry would go unnoticed in the morning and give me time to alert the proper authorities to raid it before the bad guys could shut it down.

I gave Rita the keys to my Chevy and I drove Larry Chin's expensive Lexus down to the Strip where I parked it in the lot of one of the biggest casinos. I rolled down the windows and left the car keys in the ignition. It wouldn't take too long for a loser to discover the unlocked car. I was betting he'd be unable to look a gift horse in the mouth.

Rita liked the idea of recycling Larry Chin's expensive auto she was sure had been bought with the proceeds of illegal animal slaughter and drugs. Larry Chin should consider himself lucky that Rita hadn't visited the taxidermy before we left him in the storage drawer. Rita probably would have removed his crown jewels with her butcher's hatchet and stuffed them in the cougar's mouth had she known his role in the animal poaching ring. She had firmly established herself as a charter member and activist in my underground Eco-terrorist commando unit.

It was nearly three in the morning by the time we finally returned to the motel. We showered together and before the adrenalin wore off, we tumbled into bed, made love and were soon asleep in each other's arms. It had been an exciting night with the prospect of more to come.

****

I had set the alarm for eight and unplugged the answering machine before we crashed for the night. We both slept through the alarm. The phone wouldn't stop ringing. Rita pulled a pillow over her head and disappeared under the covers. I had to shake my groggy head and force myself up. I felt like pulling the phone cord out of the wall, but knew it would only make matters worse.

The caller was Annie who laughed at my confusion and warned me that the wages of sin were worse than death. To that, I had to agree. My head felt like a scooped-out Halloween pumpkin the day after the kids hauled away their loot. I was no match for Annie or anyone else with my leaden head until I could get a pot of coffee. Annie had two messages for me and the callers had left callback numbers saying I needed to speak with them urgently.

I asked Annie to make me a fresh pot of coffee. I wanted to let Rita sleep undisturbed. As last night's events started register in my foggy head, I knew I needed to work the phone to set the rest of my investigation in motion. Annie was busy stuffing her face with a gooey jelly donut that was dripping its lifeblood down her chin. She flashed me a devilish grin and pointed to a box of donuts and the coffee machine and beckoned me to help myself.

I poured a cup of over-brewed coffee and selected the last chocolate-covered donut. Best not to be shy about food around Annie. When she finally gobbled the last of her donut and reached for another, she laughed at me. "You sure look like something the cat dragged in during the night. You should be careful not to burn the candle at both ends. Las Vegas women are known to wear a man down in no time," she said playfully.

I looked at myself in the office mirror and had to agree. I looked as tired and rumpled as I felt. My eyes were baggy and bloodshot. I chuckled to myself. Annie must think I'd been chasing women all night. I could see her point. Why bring a woman home from the Strip and only spend half an hour with her unless you were looking for another one. Annie probably thought I trying to carve notches on a gold-handled cane.

"Your lady friend really looked a lot better going up the stairs in her short skirt than she did coming down in your jogging suit. We gotta a rule here about single guests not entertaining members of the opposite sex, but we don't enforce it unless it looks like a business proposition," Annie said, gobbling the last jelly donut.

"Me and my girlfriend, Rita, are friends from our college days. She's helping me with some of my business here in Vegas." I decided to level with Annie. She probably knew from my phone callers that I wasn't job hunting.

"I appreciate your help and discretion, Annie. I lunched with Peter Rogers and gave him your regards. I have to go back on the road for a few days. I'd like to keep my room while I'm gone and have you keep taking my messages if you don't mind. I'll call you once a day to check my messages and leave instructions for my girlfriend who's working with me."

The sugar and coffee were starting to defog my head and a plan of action was taking shape. I would need both Annie's and Rita's help. I wanted to be sure I could count on Annie.

"I could tell you weren't no card dealer the moment you walked in the door. Are you involved in something dangerous?" Annie queried as she reached for the last donut.

I hesitated momentarily. "Yes, Annie, it's dangerous. I'm investigating a double murder with a drug connection. I don't think anyone will trace my movements to your motel, but there's always a chance the bad guys will come looking for me here. I could check out if you're worried."

"You must be kidding. I love a little excitement. It gets real boring around here tending to gamblers down on their luck. I'm stuck here in the office. Just me, the phone and the boob tube. How can I help?"

I handed her one of my business cards. "Let me know if anyone comes snooping around asking questions about me. If they know my movements, then my girlfriend, Rita, is in real danger. You'll need to warn her as they will go for her to get to me."

"She's real cute. I understand why you're worried about her falling into the wrong hands."

"I can't call her at work, so I need you to be my central switchboard for messages as well as our early warning system in case of trouble."

"Sounds exciting. When do I get to find out what it's all about?"

"The less you know about the details for now, the safer you'll be. When it's all over, I'll hire a replacement for you for a night and you, me, and Rita will pay a visit to the best steak house in Vegas. I'll tell you all about it over prime rib and baked potatoes smothered in gobs of butter and sour cream."

"You're on! Do I know you as Reggie Stewart or Reggie Bean?"

"To strangers, I'm Reggie Stewart—just another drifter passing through and trying to change his luck at the tables. My friends all know me as R.C. Don't leave my business card lying around. My brother, L.C. Bean and my sister, Tiffany Bean, will be calling me here to pass on info. You'll be our message exchange service."

"While I think of it, you had two messages this morning," she remembered.

I was glad I had not tried to bullshit her. She knew where my calls were coming from and had figured out I was up to something not related to my alibi. A smart lady lurked underneath all that blubber. She'd make a good ally.

She handed me a message slip from L.C. It said, "No sign of the Chinese lady. You better call the office." The second message was from my insurance buddy, Jeff Banes, who must have gotten the motel number from Tiffany. His message was marked "call me – urgent." I handed Annie a five spot and asked if she could change it for quarters so I could work the pay phone. She offered to let me use her office phone, but I told her I didn't want any record of my outgoing calls traceable to her phone.

It was eight-twenty. I decided to try to reach Jeff Banes at home. I pumped quarters into the slot until the robotic voice finally gave me a dial tone.

"Jeff Banes here."

"It's R.C., Jeff. I just got your message. What's up?"

"I've been following the shooting in the paper, R.C. The scuttlebutt is that it was a wipeout for a drug rip-off. I'm not so sure. I thought you'd like to know that Jimmy Simmons' brother, Tony, took out a one point five mil policy on Jimmy's life two months ago. He insured him as a key employee through the mortuary. I can't find any evidence of malpractice insurance."

"Who wrote the policy?"

"American Star Insurance Associates. They also carry liability coverage on the mortuary."

"Has a claim on the life insurance policy been filed yet?"

"Too early. They just dropped him in the hole yesterday."

"Do me a favor and see who's carrying the insurance on the Lone Pine Mortuary here in Las Vegas. Both mortuaries are working together. I've got some guys on my trail here, so I may have to boogie out of here to shake them. It's likely I'll arrive late at the cottage."

"I'll get the info today. Where do I leave it?"

"With my sister. Thanks for your help. I owe you another one."

"Dinner on your boss's tab will do for the moment. My choice of watering hole and restaurant when the dust settles. You pick up the babysitter's tab. You putting the moves on a special lady? Let's make it dinner for four."

"You're on for dinner, Jeff. The fourth wheel's a little complicated at the moment. It's not like choosing a partner to play bridge."

"Be careful, R.C. Whoever snuffed Jimmy Simmons won't be shy to take out anyone who gets too close to the truth. Don't you think it's time to go to the police?"

"It's getting close, Jeff. I don't think it's about the insurance. It's more like Tony Simmons knew his brother was playing with fire and stood to get bumped if he got too involved in the operation. Tony was probably just making a side bet. If he's right, he cashes in big. If not, he's got a business expense at tax time. I may be wrong, but I don't see him as a player in his brother's death."

"I hope you're right. Take care. You could be out of your league with these guys. They impress me as enforcers who shoot first and ask questions later."

After hanging up, I got a sheet of paper from Annie and started a list of additional calls to make and things to do while I loaded up on more coffee. My investigation was at a critical point. I wasn't sure how Jeff's information about the life insurance policy fit into the puzzle. I'd have to figure it out on the road. I needed to buy time, finish my investigation in Vegas and hit the road to get the heat off me.

I plugged more quarters into the slot and called Detective Johnny Walker of the Berkeley Police Department. Walker had gone to school with Mom in the old days. He was fair, honest and old school; he believed in doing favors tit-for-tat even though he didn't like working with private investigators. I had passed him some leads from my little brother that enabled him to bust a nasty gang of drug dealers terrorizing high school students. He owed me one. It was time to collect.

It took a while to get him on the line. I had to plead it was a matter of life and death to the duty officer before he plugged me through to Walker.

I could hear Walker sucking on his cigar as I explained what I was doing in Vegas on the Jimmy Simmons case. He was all ears at my account of the stakeout of the Lone Pine Mortuary and the taxidermy. When I recounted the arrival of the Simmons' hearse, I could tell he was hooked.

"You wanna hear the rest?" I paused in my tale.

"Damn straight. It's the best lead we got so far."

"You know my problem with confidentiality and lawyer/client privilege. Can you get the Vegas police to bust the bad guys and keep me out of it?"

"If it's not a cover for a homicide or a forcible felony and the tip solves an important crime, they'll wink unless you left prints or witnesses at the scene."

"You've got to cover two unauthorized entries and physical evidence to prove a murder and a major drug distribution center. You got your info from a reliable informant you've used in the past, but my accomplice and I must stay out of it. You'll have to make the case for probable cause without our testimony. We left no prints or tangible evidence and there were no witnesses except the perp we immobilized whom the Vegas police will find trussed up like a mummy in a compromising environment."

"We can handle the two B & E's. The D.A.'s on both ends won't like the 'reliable tipster' source for probable cause to make the bust, so the bust needs to be dynamic enough to catch the front page."

"It's gonna create some major headlines, especially in Berkeley." I went on to detail my foray into the mortuary. I heard him suck hard on his cigar when I told him how I discovered Jennifer Wong. He actually laughed when I described how we'd left Larry Chin taped up with the Eco-Terrorist placard.

"I like the Eco-Terrorist touch. It's gonna play big time here in Berkeley. I'll make sure they send a crime lab photographer along on the bust. If we get lucky, the noon TV news is gonna be filled with the exploits of some new environmental terrorist group and you're gonna have better cover than we could give you." Walker was laughing so hard now that he sucked his cigar too hard and the smoke went down the wrong channel, and he wound up choking and gasping for breath.

Walker was so excited to get the Vegas police on the scene that he let me off the hook for the moment. We both understood that the Vegas police needed to get to Larry Chin and Jennifer Wong's body before the bad guys did. The same was true for the animal parts and drug lab in the taxidermy. Both sites needed to be raided by a commando team as fast as they could scramble their personnel. The raid would keep the Vegas bad guys hopping and fast stepping. No time to worry about me.

The local criminal attorneys were about to get a lot of good-paying business.

My next call was to my little brother before he left for school. I told him to forget about trying to track Jennifer Wong and to watch the evening news for a new twist in the case. He likes to connect the dots on his own. I alerted him that I would be coming home to my cottage soon and to redeploy his street troopers to assure no one was waiting to ambush me when I arrived.

My list of things to do in Vegas was still long, but I knew I needed to get some rest if I was going to stay awake on the long, monotonous road home. I gave Annie Rita's work number and asked her to call Rita in sick with food poisoning and that she wouldn't be able to report for work before the dinner shift, if at all. I told Annie to hold all my calls and wake me up at noon. She gave me a knowing wink which seemed to say, "Hope Rita's not having morning sickness so soon!" She couldn't imagine me climbing in the sack with Rita just to catch up on my zzz's.

Rita was sleeping peacefully on her side. I undressed and climbed in beside her. The next thing I knew, the phone was ringing nonstop. I looked at my watch and stumbled out of bed to answer Annie's wakeup call. She reminded me it was time for me to get to work on my case. I mumbled my displeasure and she saucily replied that she was only following my orders. I could see Rita move and stretch out of the corner of my eye. She was lying on her side with her back to me and the sheet tucked around her shoulders.

I hung up the phone and watched her move. As she slowly turned onto her back, she stretched lazily like a calico cat my parents had when I was a kid; the sheet gradually slipped down to expose her breasts. The friction of the cotton fabric moving against her skin aroused her nipples and my imagination.

Rita must have been reading my thoughts because she slowly peeled the sheet down over her thighs to show me by the light of day what I had so hurriedly explored in our passionate coupling in the dark.

Rita slowly stretched her sexy torso. My juices were ready to bubble over. Any resolve to get to work dissipated completely as I watched Rita's voluptuous body open like the unfolding of flower petals in the first warming rays of the sun.

Rita's offer to make love was irresistible. We made love slowly and tenderly. It was the perfect thing for the moment. To hell with watching the news at noon to see if the bad guys had gotten busted. Making love is such a nice way to start the day.

Chapter 20

I T WAS PAST 2 P.M. WHEN RITA AND I RELUCTANTLY
finished our lovemaking and cleared out of my motel room.
The grin on Annie's mug would have put a Cheshire cat
to shame as she contemplated her two lovebirds. Annie
offered us coffee, but I demurred. The box of donuts was long
gone; Annie was now stuffing her face with Nacho chips and
slurping a Coke as I introduced Rita. Rita managed a sheepish,
embarrassed, "Hello Annie," before lowering her eyes.

Rita was famished; she'd missed both breakfast and lunch
due to our escapade last night and our romantic interlude this
morning. I stopped at the Mexican restaurant up the road from
the motel. Rita went for the combination plate with a taco,
enchilada and tamale. I ordered *enchiladas giganticas* which
came with cheese, beef and pork enchiladas. We played footsy
and fed each other tortilla chips dipped in homemade chili
sauces while we waited for our orders. We pounced on our
spicy food like hungry wolves who hadn't eaten in a week.

Rita cracked up laughing at my attempt to cool an oversized mouthful of hot cheese enchilada by bouncing it from
one side of my mouth to another. The inside of my mouth was
still tender from similar antics with our pizza from the night
before. Once we'd stuffed our tummies, we slowed down to
dawdle. We knew we'd soon be parted. I'd explained my need

to finish my investigation which I could do only by returning to Berkeley as soon as possible.

"Will you call me when you get to Berkeley tonight?" Rita pleaded.

"I'll probably be quite late. Why don't I call you in the morning before you go to work?"

"No, I need to know you got home safely. I'm not going to rest easy until I know whoever killed Jimmy Simmons and his girlfriend are behind bars. You promise you'll work with the Berkeley homicide detective?"

I nodded affirmatively, but Rita suspected I'd do my own thing as long as I could and that worried her. I took her home so she could bathe and change clothes before dragging in to work. We kissed and hugged for several minutes outside her door. As we parted, she stuffed something into my pocket and murmured about it keeping me safe until we were together again.

The only way to get her out of mind and avoid moping around was to get back to work. I hustled over to the county office buildings to do research I should have done instead of dallying with Rita. It took only fifteen minutes to learn that the Lone Pine Mortuary had been owned by the AJS Corporation for more than eighteen months. The Simmons brothers had bought the Las Vegas funeral home shortly after receiving their father's inheritance. I wondered whether they had the drug scheme in mind before their father kicked the bucket.

It occurred to me that they may have had the scheme in mind all along and helped dear old Dad to an untimely death to further their plans. I made a note to check the death certificate in the Oakland probate clerk's office to see who certified the cause of death. If their father had opposed their plans, would they eliminate him? I wouldn't be surprised.

My stop at city hall confirmed that the AJS Corporation was doing business as the Lone Pine Mortuary. It listed its corporate headquarters on a street a few blocks away from the mortuary. I arrived at the address to find it was just a mail drop.

I presented myself as a client needing to rent a mail box. The counter clerk was busy feeding a stack of documents into a fax machine one by one. He was a big, burly guy with short-cropped brown hair and girly tattoos crawling up his arm. He looked to be about six feet seven and should have been playing power forward for coach Tarkanian's Runnin' Rebels at UNLV. He looked up when I came through the door, but paused only long enough to take my measure before returning to his task.

"Be with you in a minute, just as soon as I finish with this gentleman's order." He pointed to a short, dark-featured man who was dressed like a card shark. His pinkie ring flashed a diamond big enough to pass for some two-bit monarch's crown jewel. It would make a real dent in someone's jaw if the guy was provoked to fight.

"Take your time. I'm just inquiring about renting a box," I said.

"The contract's on the counter by the register. You can look it over while I finish up this transmission," he said with his back to me. I watched him feed each page into the machine before the sheet in the machine finished its transmission to avoid breaking the phone connection. It's what one has to do with a cheap machine that can't process a stack of paper.

I moseyed over to the counter and picked up a copy of the rental contract. I kept one eye on the clerk and his client who were both engrossed in faxing the stack of documents, and with the other I scanned the row of mailboxes. The locks were just like the ones in the older post offices. I fingered my lock picks and calculated the odds I could open a box unseen. To my surprise, the fax machine shrieked its electronic displeasure and abruptly terminated its transmission. The clerk cussed up a storm while he had to restart the process.

With the clerk and client preoccupied with the machine, it was a piece of cake to open the AJS Corporation's box. I snatched the one letter inside and slipped it in my pocket. Royce Bronson's business card was taped to the bottom of the box with a note to forward mail to the attorney's office. It was no surprise he was still handling the mortuaries' legal business.

I tried to shut the box door gently, but had to wince at the loud clicking noise it made as it snapped shut. Fortunately, the two guys huddled over the whirring fax machine were too absorbed with their task to notice. I chuckled at my good luck as I exited the store with the unread contract and the purloined letter in my pocket,

I drove down the Strip to a gas station and while the attendant checked the oil and filled the tank for the trip home, I used their phone book to find a private drug testing lab. The nearest lab was in a medical building a few blocks away. The ad in the Yellow Pages offered several plans for testing employees on and off at the workplace and elsewhere.

I was glad I'd slipped on my tweed jacket when I walked into the lab's reception area. It looked more like the offices of an upscale advertising firm than a laboratory. The décor featured large, expensive looking oil paintings of desert scenes and the plush leather chairs and settees had a "made in Brazil" look; their dark mahogany frames and smooth leather smelled of pungent musk and exotic oils and waxes.

My musings as to what the setup must have cost were interrupted by a cheery-voiced woman who arrived through a door marked "private." As there was no receptionist, they must have had a buzzer on the door to alert the presence of a client.

"May I help you?" The young woman asked. She looked to be about twenty-five and was smartly dressed in a brown leather skirt and matching vest with a stylish cut. Her designer glasses with large tortoiseshell frames were perched coyly on her pug nose. She was real cute and knew it. The way she balanced herself on her back leg and thrust the other leg forward attested to what she'd learned in charm school.

"Hi, I'm a private investigator working on a very sensitive drug case for a group of defense attorneys. We need some blood analyzed for drug content. Is this something your firm can handle?"

"Yes, of course. We specialize in testing employees on and off the work site. Who referred you to us?"

"A local attorney who defends employers against invasion of privacy lawsuits from disgruntled employees." I said, trying to be as general as possible. I'd missed the local noon news and didn't want to give these folks cause to associate my blood testing with what might have been discovered at the mortuary and be blaring away on the local news. I could invoke a claim of confidentiality of sources if pressed. She didn't push for it.

"What sort of testing did you have in mind?"

"Well, we believe our client's employees have been selling coke and speed to others on the job. The employer markets upscale women's ready-to-wear cocktail and party dresses and uses fashion models at trade shows to model new lines. Some of the models have got themselves hooked on a new form of speed that's smoked like crack cocaine. Are you familiar with it?"

"Of course, it goes by a variety of street names, 'ice,' 'quartz,' or 'glass.' It's methamphetamine hydrochloride. It's very addictive but relatively uncommon here in Las Vegas." She seemed surprised I proposed testing for the drug here.

"One of the models who got hooked on it is from here. Apparently, she started smoking the stuff to stay hyped and alert for runway performances and to stay thin. Does it have that effect?"

"Yes, it's become very popular among certain professional women concerned about retaining their figures and staying alert for long periods of time on the job. Do you want us to test the entire work force?"

"Eventually. For the moment we are defending a wrongful assault case. One of the models went crazy on the job. She'd been getting progressively paranoid. She attacked another model who she accused of trying to stab her in the back to get her fired. She even bit her manager who tried to pull her off the woman she attacked. She collapsed and an attending doctor, a friend of the employer, was able to take some blood samples. He's afraid of being sued, so I have been called in to secure the test results."

"Did the woman give her consent to the sampling?"

"I can't answer that. It's what the lawsuit is all about. What I'm telling you is off the record, right?"

"You can count on our discretion. We're used to helping clients prevail against malicious litigation by substance abusers and their families who blame employers for their own mistakes. We take pride in winning," she said self-righteously.

Her face beamed as she crowed about her lab's biases. I was glad I hadn't stumbled on a lab that worked for disgruntled employees and their heirs. They probably would have cooked the results or leaked them to the press. I wondered about the woman's lack of objectivity and obvious loyalty to her clients and if she and her staff also weren't above cooking the test results for a healthy fee. It was a scary thought!

"I'm really glad I found the right lab to do our testing. I'll need a copy of your testing protocol for our attorneys."

She motioned for me to follow her. We jogged around a corner and entered her office. I could smell the chemicals but couldn't see the lab further down the hallway. I handed her a vial of Jennifer Wong's blood that I'd labeled "Ms. XJW." The X was in honor of Malcolm X.

The woman's office door bore a name placard stating "Betsy Arnold, B.S., M.B.A., Director of Marketing." I picked up her business card on her desk and slipped it in my pocket.

I tried to look nonplussed when she handed me a receipt for the blood sample and a demand for $250.00 prepayment for testing it. It's really hard not to push back against being robbed in broad daylight. Ms. Arnold's business training must have emphasized billing practice theory. Get the client to pay up front before performing any tests. I peeled off twelve twenties and a ten spot from my dwindling wad of expense money. I left Annie's motel exchange number and said my assistant, Rita James, would stop by to pick up the test results in a day or two. I gave her my business card and smiled at the thought of Miz Rita and Miz Betsy sizing each other up. Betsy Arnold was in for a big surprise.

I looked forward to the ride home. It would give me time to devise a battle plan for the challenges ahead. I stopped at a café and had the waitress prepare a takeout order of sandwiches and fill my thermos with strong coffee. While I waited, I called my office to set up appointments with Marcie and Nate. Saundra's pleasant voice changed tone immediately upon hearing me.

"You in some deep shit 'round here, R.C. You hear me, boy? Ain't nobody buyin' your cock an' bull story 'bout goin' down to L.A. Nate's in a dither an' Marcie's ready to have you tarred an' feathered. An' I'll give her a hand pourin' on the tar. You got no idea how many times I had to make excuses for yo' sorry ass. So, you better get straight wid me and quick. You keep jivin' wid me an' what's left of yo' black hide's gonna feed them gators over in the Steinhart Aquarium. You hear?"

"I've been dodgin' bullets from Jimmy Simmons' hit men and the situation is still dangerous. You and Marcie gotta help me," I replied in a serious but humble tone.

"It's about time you came to your senses, young man." Saundra's change in diction and tone signaled she was no longer able to speak freely.

"I need to speak with Marcie before I see Nate. Can you set it up between ten and eleven tomorrow? It's urgent."

"It'll take some schedule shuffling, but I'll put you down for ten-thirty. Be sure to be on time. Mr. Green's assistant is currently out of the office. Is there a number where she can reach you in an hour or two?"

"No, I'll be on the road. Tell Marcie I'll call her from a rest stop."

"Yes, I understand. I'll be sure to leave your message. Mr. Green's assistant will be expecting your call."

Nate must have come into the office. Saundra would make the arrangements despite her threat to offer my sweet ass at feeding time to the alligators in the aquarium in the park in San Francisco. I should have called her first thing in the morning, but my dalliance with Rita had preempted thoughts of paying the piper on the home front. Nate and my two office mates were going to put me on a short leash no matter what.

I also needed to meet with Mrs. Simmons, but not before Marcie helped me put my plan of action in motion.

I paid for my order of two turkey club sandwiches and coffee and headed for the interstate. I hoped the bland sandwiches would give my sore mouth a rest from all the hot sauce punishment it had received lately.

It felt good to see the cacti whooshing by as I kept a close eye on the rearview mirror. I needed to make good time without picking up a ticket. I stayed mostly in the slow lane doing seventy-five through the desert stretches leading to Barstow and Needles and on to Bakersfield.

Three hours down the road I stopped to rest, fill the tank and call Marcie. She picked up immediately. I leveled with her about what I was doing and pleaded with her to keep Nate out of the picture until I could ensnare the persons I was seeking to trap.

Marcie was surprised to learn that I was behind the events at the Lone Pine Mortuary and the taxidermy raid. Both had received extensive media coverage in the Bay Area. The poaching revelations had created a sensation among the ecology advocates in Berkeley. The discovery of Jennifer Wong's body had been relegated to a short by-line near the obits. A photo of Larry Chin trussed up like a mummy in a morgue drawer next to the dead animals and my placard claiming his capture by my Eco-Terrorist group had fired up the animal rights activists, according to Marcie. They were already hawking tee-shirts celebrating the bust to students and eco-freaks on Telegraph Avenue the evening the story broke. I asked Marcie to leave a message for my brother to buy me a selection of tee-shirts and to meet me after school the next day.

Marcie audibly sucked in her breath when I related my discovery of Jennifer Wong's body. I scared her by asserting the killers would do the same thing to me and then take out Nate if he didn't play along with their illegal schemes. Marcie was pleased to hear that Jennifer Wong had been cavorting openly with Jimmy Simmons in Las Vegas as it put horns on Mrs. Simmons, whom she detested. She'd have something to crow about later to Marcie.

I asked Marcie to tell me who was Mrs. Simmons' lover. She hesitated but finally told me she had been seen on several occasions in the company of Royce Bronson. The pair had been spotted most recently in the seaside town of Carmel holding hands and sharing a romantic candlelit dinner at a restaurant catering to newlyweds. Marcie also told me that Royce Bronson kept a bungalow overlooking a beach near Monterey that he used for his trysts.

According to Marcie, the two got together when Jimmy Simmons headed to Las Vegas to gamble. I asked Marcie whether it was possible that Mrs. Simmons was just playing a game of tit-for-tat to get even with her husband for cavorting with Jennifer Wong. She hesitated before saying, "I don't think so."

I didn't want to push Marcie too far. She was still mad about my disappearing act and it would take time to earn back her complete trust. I needed her to do something for me that only she could do, but would entail a big degree of risk should Nate learn of it. I was sure Nate had more information on Mrs. Simmons that he hadn't wanted me to see and which had been removed from the file he'd shown me. I explained my suspicion to Marcie and suggested the information he was hiding might be the key to forcing Nate off the case. That was all the bait needed for her to agree to my request. I gave her the combination to Nate's safe and told her about a secret compartment and how to open it. It had been empty when I'd taken my travel expense money, but I suspected it might now contain what I was looking for.

Marcie believed my claim that it might be a matter of life and death for Nate and agreed to do my bidding. She, like me, knew she risked her job and relationship with Nate if he learned of our collusion. My last request was that she have Saundra to set up an appointment for me with Mrs. Simmons as soon as possible after I met with Nate.

I spent most of the long drive home mulling over how to smoke out the murderers without winding up in a refrigerator drawer like Jennifer Wong and Jimmy Simmons.

Chapter 21

MY BLEARY EYES FINALLY FOCUSED ON THE ALARM clock that wouldn't stop clanging and whose hands had moved past 9 A.M. I had a vague recollection of saying "Hello" to my landlord and briefly telling Rita I had arrived home safely. Everything else was hazy except I knew I had an appointment to see Nate.

I was tired, stiff and sore from the trip. I took a long, hot shower instead of heading for the basketball courts and exercising. I gave a long look at my answering machine and decided to ignore the backlog of messages. I had no time to listen or do anything about them in any case.

I called Annie in Las Vegas to check for messages; there were none. I knew I should call Rita before she left for work and clue her in about the need for the blood test results; instead, I asked Annie to do it for me. Rita deserved a chance to talk, but I didn't have the time or energy. I needed to get a pot of strong coffee in my system and some breakfast in my stomach to face my critical meeting with Nate.

I stopped at Reggie's Place and let him scramble some eggs and fry two thick slices of honey-cured ham for me. His breakfast plate was garnished with fried sweet potatoes and hominy grits and served with a basket of freshly baked corn muffins. I added the better part of a small bottle of Creole hot sauce and used the muffins to soak up the juices. After my fork attack on the delicious food was over and the coffee pot empty, I was ready to face the music at the office head on.

In between gobbles of food and slurps of coffee, I glanced at the front page of the morning newspapers published in Oakland and San Francisco. Photos of the interior of the taxidermy depicting the clothesline with bear claws and dried gall bladders headed the lead stories in each paper.

I almost choked and sputtered my coffee when I read how two separate groups of self-professed radical ecologists each claimed responsibility and credit for the coup. I was secretly pleased. Let the honchos in the movement fight for the glory and free publicity for their causes. The more they jostled each other publicly, the less interest there'd be in Rita's and my involvement.

I got to the office shortly after ten. I said "Hi" to Saundra who was helping a client fill out forms. She glared at me but held her tongue. She handed me a large, sealed manila envelope and an inch stack of pink message slips with a Post-It in her hand on top saying "Knock on Nate's door at ten thirty-five sharp!"

I scurried down the hall, darted into my office and locked the door. I quickly sifted through the message slips and put them aside; they'd all have to wait. I tore open the large manila envelope and extracted copies of three legal documents and a note from Marcie. The note instructed me to destroy the documents after I'd read them. She confirmed my brother would meet me after school and Mrs. Simmons insisted I meet her at her home at nine-thirty that evening. I was instructed to take a cab to her house, come alone and not have the cab wait for me; she would arrange to take me home.

I wondered why all the cat-and-mouse antics. But, by the time I'd read the documents, Mrs. Simmons' precautions were on the backburner. I needed to see her and the sooner the better.

The three legal documents Marcie found had not been in the divorce file. I organized them in chronological order. The first was a prenuptial agreement between Jimmy and Gloria Simmons dated over four years ago. It provided that each party's earnings would remain their separate property as well as assets owned by each prior to the marriage. Should the marriage produce children, each child would become an heir of the father and share equally with other surviving children in the father's separate property assets at his death. In case of divorce or death of the husband, the wife would be entitled to a monthly support allowance of $3,500 for a period not to exceed ten years so long as she remained unmarried. By signing the agreement, Gloria Simmons explicitly renounced any further claim on the husband's separate property or additional support. The agreement had been prepared by Judge Bronson.

The second document was a will signed by Jimmy Simmons dated shortly after the prenuptial agreement and referenced and reincorporated the terms of the pre-marital agreement. The will capitalized a trust fund to provide the $3,500.00 per mo. maintenance for Mrs. Simmons. Any remainder of the trust was left to Jimmy Simmons' surviving children, and if none, to his father, Booker T. Simmons, and his brother, Tony Simmons in equal shares. The will provided that Judge Bronson was nominated as executor with his son, Royce Bronson, to serve in his place if the judge could not serve for any reason.

The third document provided the big surprise. It was a codicil to the will dated just two months ago. This amendment to Jimmy Simmons' will revoked the terms of the pre-nuptial agreement incorporated in the will. It provided that Jimmy Simmons' property would go in equal shares to any surviving children of the marriage and if none, then one half to his brother, Tony, and one half to his wife, Gloria. She was nominated executrix of the will and codicil and brother Tony as her backup.

The codicil had my mind buzzing with questions. Why had Jimmy Simmons changed his will so radically in favor of his wife? Had she blackmailed him over his liaison with Jennifer Wong and threatened to leave him or expose the affair? Was she aware of the drug activity and insisting on a cut? What about Tony Simmons? Under the will he stood to inherit all of his brother's interest in the mortuary and drug business. Under the codicil, he'd have to share his brother's interests with his sister-in-law.

Tony Simmons had plenty of reason to be unhappy with Gloria Simmons. She was in the driver's seat as executrix of the will and codicil. She could claim her husband's assets were community property and she should inherit the lion's share as his surviving spouse. She also had Tony over a barrel regarding the significant cash being reaped through the mortuary's drug and animal parts business. She could name her price or blow the whistle.

I compared the signatures on all three documents which Jimmy Simmons had signed.

They all looked the same to my eyes, but I'm no expert. All the documents had been signed in the presence of witnesses. This is a requirement to prevent fraud. The original will was witnessed by Judge Bronson and a woman who listed her address as the judge's law office; she was probably an employee, which is common. The codicil was witnessed by a woman named Maria Benevides, who gave her address as Gloria Simmons' residence. The second witness was a woman named Alice Brown, who listed her address as the mortuary.

Maria Benevides must be the same Maria who worked as Mrs. Simmons' housemaid. The other woman must work at the mortuary I'd burgled. Where had the codicil been executed? Had it been signed at the Simmons' residence? At the mortuary? At Judge Bronson's office? I didn't believe the witnesses had been transported to the judge's law office. Had it been signed separately? The California Probate Code provides that the witnesses to a will or codicil have to sign the document in the presence of each other and the testator. Was the codicil a fraudulent attempt to cut down Tony Simmons' share by Mrs. Simmons and let her highjack her husband's estate?

What was Nate doing with the documents, anyway? Marcie had copied original documents which Mrs. Simmons must have provided him. Why weren't they in the Bronson's law office? If Marcie was correct about Royce Bronson and Gloria Simmons being lovers, why would she have Nate handling the probate instead of Royce Bronson?

The documents provided more questions than answers and

they didn't neatly fit my theory of the crimes. My cogitating was rudely interrupted by the shrill ringing of my phone. The light on the console indicated the call was intra-office.

"Yes?" I answered.

"It's ten-forty five and, if you don't get your butt up to Nate's office on the double, I'm going to send my client up who's been patiently waiting!"

"I'm sorry, Saundra. I've been studying the file Marcie left for me and I've lost track of time. I'll pop right up the stairs." I heard an "Un-huh" and the line went dead.

I gathered the stack of message slips and Marie's documents and stuffed them into my briefcase. I felt like a sneak-thief as I eased out of my office, climbed the stairs and rapped on Nate's door. Nate beckoned me in. Probate attorney, Mort Goldsmith, was seated in front of Nate's desk; he had a big grin on his face. I nodded to "Goldy," as he's known to his associates. I wondered at the coincidence. Was Nate consulting with Goldy about probating Jimmy Simmons' will and codicil?

As Goldy got up to leave, he handed Nate a bundle of papers which Nate slipped into a file on his cluttered desk. Goldy winked at me on the way out. I plopped into the vacant chair which was close enough to the file to read the file tag penned "Gloria Simmons Probate." There was also a probate handbook on his desk.

I was apprehensive. I expected Nate to chew me out big time for my disappearance and the false trail I'd left. To my astonishment, Nate greeted me warmly and asked how I was doing as if nothing out of the ordinary had happened. I had planned to brief him on most of my exploits, but I changed my mind. Let Nate carry the ball.

"What did you find out about Jimmy Simmons' assets while you were out of town?"

"The trail led to Las Vegas where he gambled heavily in the company of a girlfriend who worked as a bookkeeper at the mortuary. Public records in Las Vegas revealed that the Simmons brothers own the Lone Pine Mortuary in that city." I paused to let Nate pick up on what I'd said.

"How big an operation is the Lone Pine?"

"About the same size as the one in Oakland. There're only three funeral homes in the city, so they must be doing pretty well."

"Did you locate the girlfriend?"

"Yeah, she was found dead in the Lone Pine's morgue when the police raided the premises and found her and the dead animals in cold storage, as well as the animal and drug lab across the street. Jimmy Simmons was involved in the drug trade which used the mortuary as a cover for distribution."

"That doesn't concern us. It's a police matter," Nate replied too hastily. I tried to keep my jaw from falling open. "We're only concerned with locating Jimmy Simmons' assets and min-imizing his liabilities. We'll be handling the probate of his will. His wife is nominated executrix and has retained our office to represent the estate and determine its assets. In effect, we'll be continuing the job we started with the divorce. Now we'll be able to compel direct access to the financial records of the businesses we were denied while the husband was alive. I want you to meet with Mrs. Simmons and continue your work to discover hidden assets," Nate added.

It was a clever arrangement. With Mrs. Simmons now in the driver's seat as executrix of the will and codicil, she would determine which assets were included in the estate and filed with the probate court. She'd have no incentive to list the cash from drug and animal trafficking being laundered through the mortuaries. She'd declare only the legitimate activities of the mortuaries in which she'd share ownership with her brother-in-law. He could contest the codicil, but to do so would risk exposure of his illegal activities and income. She had him over a barrel.

"I don't know much about probate procedure," I replied. "I'm surprised the will is not being probated by the attorney who drafted it or a probate specialist, like Goldy." I was fishing to see how much Nate was willing to reveal about why he was handling the probate estate. He had done some probate work for members of his family, but he routinely farmed out clients' probate matters to Goldy and took a finder's fee.

"The paperwork is very routine. The only tricky part is marshalling all the estate assets and defending the estate against interlopers."

"Are we expecting someone to contest Mrs. Simmons' interest and authority?"

"I'm not sure at this point. There may be a problem with Mrs. Simmons' brother-in-law who may be unhappy to see her inherit an interest in the family business. He may try to hide assets or profits and he'll probably be uncooperative. That's why Mrs. Simmons has engaged me to handle the probate. She continues to rely on our ability to probe discretely for hidden assets."

"I'm confused." I decided to play the fool. "My research in Las Vegas shows that the two mortuaries are owned by a Nevada corporate shell entity that is wholly owned by the Simmons brothers. Mrs. Simmons would only get whatever shares in the corporation her husband left her in his will. Tony Simmons should still be able to control both businesses and all the income as he owns half of the shares outright plus whatever he may inherit from his brother," I said without revealing what I knew was in the will and codicil.

"It's more complicated than that, R.C. The business has been family owned and operated from the start. It's often hard to accept loss of control or to have others suddenly involved in management decisions when you've been used to running the show."

"But Mrs. Simmons is a family member. It's not like his brother left his interest to his Chinese girlfriend. Don't Tony and Gloria Simmons get along?" I was trolling for as much info as Nate would give up prior to my meeting with Mrs. Simmons.

Nate replied, "Let's just say relations may be strained by the probate proceedings." He wasn't giving me much to chew on. Things could get ugly when the police started probing Jennifer Wong's death and the mortuaries' drug connections. It was clear Nate would continue to protect his client blindly.

"I've made an appointment to see Mrs. Simmons later today. What should I do for her?" I asked.

"I want you to arrange with her to meet Tony Simmons to gather copies of the business general ledgers and financial statements for both mortuaries. We need to know especially what the Las Vegas holding company owns and controls."

"The corporate attorney for the Nevada holding company that owns the two mortuaries is Royce Bronson. Wouldn't it be simpler to meet with him and get the records from him?"

"No, I don't want you to contact Royce or his father. I want you to get the info we need from other sources. I will contact Royce Bronson when I'm ready," Nate said emphatically.

I was surprised at Nate's position regarding Royce Bronson. I couldn't see any reason, given what Marcie'd told me about his relations with Mrs. Simmons, to suspect he would not cooperate fully with any requests that helped his lover become financially independent. It was possible he would be pissed at Nate for handling the probate as he'd lose the fat statutory fee based on the size of the estate, but that was a onetime deal. He was still corporate attorney for the mortuaries, and the Lone Pine Mortuary would have to be probated in Nevada by Nevada attorneys of his choice.

He'd still be raking in plenty of fees as corporate counsel for the AJS Corporation. Every phone call to the executrix, Mrs. Simmons, could be billed for top dollar. It was also possible that Nate knew of the intimate relationship between the two and was jealous. There were lots of new questions to sort out.

"I have a shitload of messages screaming for attention on other matters. You still want me to drop everything in favor of the probate investigation?" I asked for the record.

"It's your top priority. The rest will have to wait."

"Okay, I'll get right to work on it. Do you still want me to write up a report of what I discovered on the road since my last report?"

"No, I prefer you to report your findings to me orally. If there's a will contest, I don't want written investigation reports we'd have to reveal to the contestants."

I left Nate's office with another five hundred dollars of Mrs. Simmons' expense money. I dashed off a quick note to Marcie telling her where and when to meet with me to discuss developments. I dropped the note off with Saundra and scooted for the door before the glares of Saundra and Nate's client could burn holes in my back.

Chapter 22

MY HEAD WAS READY TO BURST FROM OVERLOAD and my body was out of sync from the stress and fatigue of the last few days. Despite feeling lethargic, I needed physical activity to get back in balance. I changed into sweats and sneakers and bicycled to the Berkeley High courts where several pickup basketball games were in progress. I joined a team playing a game of Twenty-One and an hour later, I felt hot, tired and rejuvenated.

After showering, I checked out my studio apartment to see if the landlord had repaired the door and changed the locks. The manager handed me a new set of keys and gave me a sour look. He probably figured I'd brought the damage on myself and he was right. I was pleased to see my brother had cleaned up the mess. He'd even had the mattress of the Murphy bed repaired. The lack of a bed would have put a serious crimp in his love life.

I installed myself in a back booth at Reggie's Place for the afternoon. I'd asked Marcie to join me for a late lunch or snack when she could slip out of the office. I also left a message for Detective Johnny Walker to drop by to compare notes on the Jennifer Wong case. I left him a teaser claiming I had some valuable information for him.

While waiting for Marcie, I spread my notes out and tried

to make sense of what I learned from the will and codicil. Prior to this morning, my theory was that two sets of players wanted Jimmy Simmons and Jennifer Wong dead: the first group was the Chinese drug gang working with the mortuaries as partners.

My research on the drug "ice" indicated drug traffickers sought to move the new street drug to the U.S. from Taiwan, Hong Kong and probably Hawaii, where it was already the designer drug of choice. Since ice would have to compete with crack cocaine on the streets, its introduction by a new set of players would be resisted by local wholesalers, middlemen and street vendors of crack who'd carved out their turf block by block in Oakland and nearby towns; they'd fight to defend their territory.

Much of the new investment capital flowing into Oakland passed through Hong Kong and other places in Asia. The Chinese community in San Francisco lived mostly in cramped quarters and couldn't absorb the continual flow of immigrants seeking economic betterment, political freedom or the lure of joining more prosperous family members settled here. Oakland, with its Chinese population in the center of town from Gold Rush times, served as an ideal place for expansion. Commercial and residential properties were cheap compared to San Francisco and the Silicon Valley. Much of the inner-city property was dilapidated and needed repair or replacement. Much of the Chinese expansion in Oakland came at the expense of poor blacks who were forced out to make way for an ever growing Chinese community. Tensions between the two groups were inevitable.

With the insecurity caused by the Chinese takeover of Hong Kong from the British, many wealthy Chinese were hedging their bets by buying up Oakland's residential and commercial properties and exploiting cheap immigrant labor in Chinese-American enclaves. Organized Chinese gangs and criminal groups joined the migration. The Oakland police were not equipped or prepared to deal with this new development. They were already undermanned and lacked the firepower to deal with existing gangs and drug dealers.

The Chinese gangs and criminals preyed primarily on their own people and most police couldn't tell the bad guys from the good guys, even if they wanted to. So long as the Chinese confined their activities to their own community, as they have done in San Francisco's Chinatown since Gold Rush days, the police have been willing to look the other way, especially when someone slips them an envelope full of cash.

Any attempt by Chinese gangs to supplant the lucrative cocaine trade would require black partners. A local mortuary would be an ideal medium for moving dope to central distribution points like Las Vegas. Who's going to stop and search a hearse carrying a dead man or woman and drugs, with grieving family members in the trailing limo?

A mortuary also has the advantage that the bodies of victims in fratricidal drug wars could be neatly disposed of by burial or cremation. As long as folks were willing to grease the palms of the right officials and obliging doctors with a hefty-bribe, they would sign off on death certificates attesting that heart attacks and natural causes struck down the deceased, so there'd be little flak and no inquiry.

It looked like the Ice Merchants were trying to do an end run around the local crack trade. They targeted the upscale recreational drug user who had plenty of money to spend on designer drugs and all the cute gadgets sold in the local head shops. Once the high-end users were hooked, the suppliers could move into the trenches to fight it out in turf wars on the street.

Ice provided attractive features competing drugs lacked; ice could be rationalized by users as an aid to dieting, a way to stay slim and trim, a way to stay alert on the job, and a way to get a longer-lasting high. It had the potential to open up new, lucrative markets: housewives and white collar workers who didn't have to rob or steal to support their habit. It didn't take a lot of imagination to visualize the upscale diet and exercise freaks easing off treadmill machines and forsaking gyms and spas in order to slim down by smoking a pipe of ice while listening to Eric Clapton and Bonnie Raitt singing the virtues of cocaine. The drug had the potential to hook teenagers and college students as well. It could serve as a cheap, long-lasting high to replace Ecstasy at their raves. With ice, they could dance their asses off all night long.

The Las Vegas connection was ideal. Organized crime families already had a monopoly on gambling and prostitution. Ice would provide them with a new horse for their stables. The Lone Pine Mortuary provided excellent cover and a transshipment point for drugs. Las Vegas casinos attracted gamblers from all states and from abroad; the high-rollers arrived with money burning holes in their pockets and looking for fun, good-time girls and the thrill of watching a ball on the roulette wheel stopping on a winning number. The Simmons brothers' mortuary in Oakland was ideally located near the Port of Oakland to receive drug shipments from Asia and good cover to transport the drugs to Las Vegas. Jennifer Wong must have been placed inside the Oakland mortuary to assure the Chinese importers that their black partners weren't cheating or cooking the books. She would spy for her masters. They hadn't reckoned that she would fall for Jimmy Simmons and his glamorous lifestyle.

Once her masters realized she was hooked on drugs and Jimmy Simmons, she would be viewed as liability, a disloyal and untrustworthy turncoat. She could be controlled and blackmailed by her drug dependence. She'd also not win any Brownie points with the conservative Chinese community by openly cavorting with a married black man. They wouldn't tolerate a woman who knew too much and who they could not control.

The obvious solution to the embarrassing situation and potential double-cross was for the Chinese to eliminate her and Jimmy Simmons. That's where the second part of my theory came into play. Both Gloria and Tony Simmons also had reason to want Jimmy Simmons dead. He gambled heavily, cavorted openly with Jennifer Wong and both were hooked on the drugs they marketed. In addition to souring their relationship with their Chinese partners, Jimmy was a big risk to start dipping into the till. He had to support his playboy lifestyle and his and his girlfriend's drug habits. His constant and ever-growing need for cash to gamble and support his lavish lifestyle could come from only one of three sources: skimming cash from the partnerships, skimming drugs to use and sell on the side, or taking advances from the partnerships.

Tony and Gloria Simmons and their Chinese partners had to be angry as wasps if they determined Jimmy was skimming drugs or cash. The pouch with drugs and cash I recovered from the drive-by shooting of Jimmy seemed to support my theories.

Was Tony Simmons callous enough to take out his own brother in the drive-by? Somehow, I didn't think so. He'd taken out a two-million dollar life insurance policy on his brother's life. The policy would more than makeup any loss of inheritance due to the codicil in favor of Gloria Simmons or retaliation against his brother by his Chinese partners or drug competitors. He seemed to have carefully hedged his bets.

From what I'd seen of the two brothers, Jimmy was the glad-hander who mixed, socialized, worked the clubs and pushed the mortuary's interests in the black community. Tony was more reclusive and ran the funeral home's business.

That left Gloria Simmons and her lover, Royce Bronson, as my prime suspects in her husband's death. I couldn't imagine that she was jealous of Jennifer Wong. She'd married for money and status and knew he would always be a gambler and play-boy. If she wanted to carry on openly with Royce Bronson, she might be tempted to do him in but why Jennifer Wong? If she arranged the hit on her husband, it would be for the money. There was no financial incentive to see Jimmy dead until she had the codicil which would leave her a rich widow and in control of her husband's assets.

She'd hired us to find hidden assets. As executrix of her hus-band's estate, she would control the discovery and declaration to the court of all assets. She wouldn't declare the bundles of cash her husband might have skimmed and stashed away. Would she work out a deal with her brother-in-law to hide the cash from the tax man or their partners? The possibilities were endless.

As for the codicil, had her husband really signed it in front of witnesses or was it a clever fraud? Tony Simmons only stood to lose if he contested the codicil; she could expose his connection to the drug partnership and let him and the Chinese slug it out in criminal court while she took over the legitimate functions of the mortuaries. I'd made copies of the signature pages of the will and codicil and other documents with Jimmy Simmons' signature to give to Detective Walker. I hoped his crime lab experts would determine the validity of the signings. It was unethical to ask him to do so, but without a juicy item to trade, Walker wouldn't give me diddly.

I was troubled by the witnesses to the codicil—Mrs. Simmons' housemaid and a female employee, Alice Brown, at the Oakland mortuary. Did someone transport both witnesses to a lawyer's office? Was Alice Brown driven to Mrs. Simmons' residence and the codicil signed there? Neither were likely scenarios. Normally, wills and codicils are signed in lawyers' offices where disinterested witnesses are readily available.

I learned from Nate that only one of the two witnesses to the signing of a will or codicil had to make the declaration to the probate court that it had been executed in front of both witnesses to prove its authenticity. That meant Nate could have Mrs. Simmons' maid sign the declaration and never contact Alice Brown. In fact, Nate or Mrs. Simmons might order me not to contact Ms. Brown. I realized I needed to contact Alice Brown before meeting with Mrs. Simmons this evening.

I needed to know who had drafted the codicil. The pleading paper did not bear the imprint of the lawyer or draftsperson. Anyone, including Mrs. Simmons, could buy pleading paper in a stationery store. The language used in the codicil was lawyerlike. I was pretty sure Nate hadn't drafted it. The logical person was Royce Bronson. While the Bronsons stood to lose two hefty statutory commissions if no longer executor or probate attorney, it was normal to nominate a spouse as executor.

It also made sense for Royce Bronson not to do the probate. It might create a conflict of interest or animosity if Tony Simmons knew they were lovers and he was corporate attorney for the TJS holding company. But why use Nate? He wasn't a probate specialist. Mrs. Simmons and Royce Bronson may have picked Nate because he wasn't a probate attorney and outside the circle of folks who knew the lovers' business. Why was Mrs. Simmons putting the make on Nate? Did she and her lover want Nate and me handling a phony divorce asset investigation before they killed Jimmy Simmons so what we learned couldn't be used against them later?

Both Nate and I were bound by lawyer/client rules of confidentiality. If we learned of illegal activity by our clients, we could withdraw from representing them, but we couldn't finger them. If we slipped compromising evidence to the police showing commission of a crime, the evidence, when traced to us, could be suppressed at trial and jeopardize our licenses to practice law. We'd look like turkeys and I'd be unemployed and guaranteed never to be admitted to the bar based on moral turpitude.

I was taking a big risk by enlisting Detective Walker's support, but I couldn't trust Nate when Mrs. Simmons had him in thrall. I hoped to pass the bar exam soon and work for Nate or another attorney on a contract basis. Nate made more money than me on every hour I billed.

With Walker, it was strictly tit-for-tat. If I messed up, Walker would cut bait and leave me hanging out to dry. It was like I was back in the Navy involved in submarine war games again. Let the enemy lock its targeting radar on you and you could wind up dead.

With the codicil, I now knew Mrs. Simmons never intended to separate from or divorce her husband. No way she'd settle for thirty-five hundred a month. She'd get nothing more no matter how many assets I found. The moment she announced her intention to separate or divorce, Jimmy Simmons would revoke the codicil if he'd written it, which I didn't believe.

Mrs. Simmons had everything to lose and nothing to gain in a divorce action. She'd hired me to get the goods on her husband while she figured out how to become his heir by way of the codicil and the convenient drive-by shooting. Whatever my investigation turned up could only help her cause.

Nate would earn a nice fat fee based on the value of the estate; he wouldn't bite the hand that was feeding him and perhaps stroking him.

Royce Bronson had to keep his distance from Nate's probate action. Nate would push her interests and the codicil against Tony Simmons. Tony would be defended by Royce Bronson who would appear to defend the will against the codicil. It looked very much like an agreement by both boxers to throw the fight.

Chapter 23

MARCIE TAPPED ME ON THE SHOULDER. I'D BEEN so absorbed in my musings that I'd not seen her enter the eatery. So much for following Malcolm X's advice about keeping your back to the wall and an eye on the door in a public place.

I briefed Marcie on what I'd learned in Las Vegas. I also told her about my studio being tossed and why I felt I had to cover my trail by putting out the story to one and all that I had headed for Los Angeles and not Las Vegas. She still glared and looked dubious, so I admitted I was doing surveillance of the Oakland mortuary when Jimmy Simmons got hit. I asserted that whoever did the drive-by must have noticed me and followed me to my studio. I suggested they must have been concerned that I could identify the shooters' car. Marcie's face now registered surprise and interest.

I didn't tell Marcie that I suspected Mrs. Simmons was involved in the plot to murder her husband. "I can't protect Nate without your help, Marcie," I pleaded.

"What do you need to know?" Marcie asked guardedly.

"Did Nate draft the codicil to Jimmy Simmons' will?"

"No, I'm sure he didn't. And I was angry as hell to learn he'd agreed to probate the will and codicil for that bitch. Normally, I do all the accounting of assets and liabilities for all the divorce cases we handle. It's the same for probate schedules which are similar, yet he didn't even tell me he had the estate documents and intended to probate them. He's kept up the charade that we're working on a divorce case." Marcie's voice was hard and tight and she was struggling to keep her excitable temper under control.

"Why do you think he cut you out of the loop?" I decided to go to the heart of the matter.

"I'm sure the Simmons bitch insisted he keep me in the dark."

"It doesn't add up, Marcie. Nate's no good at figures and he doesn't do the schedules and routine paperwork. So, don't stonewall me, Marcie. I need to know." Marcie's eyes glowered at me as I continued, "I think the codicil's phony and she planned all along to use our office as a clever cover to get control of her husband's assets. If Tony Simmons contests the codicil and wins, Mrs. Simmons could sue Nate for malpractice as he's not a probate attorney. She could even blackmail him by claiming he wrote it …" I didn't need to continue my scare tactics. Marcie bought my speculative scenario hook, line and sinker.

"Over my dead body! That conniving bitch! She's not going to get away with it. I knew all along she was playing with Nate. He's such a fool!" Marcie was clearly upset.

"Calm down, Marcie. Just tell me what's going on with Nate and Mrs. Simmons."

Marcie pulled several Kleenex out of her purse and blew her nose. "I'm sorry, R.C. I'm so damn mad. I could thrash that whore. It's probably all my fault Nate fell for the setup."

"What happened?"

Marcie paused to wipe a tear that trickled down her cheek. Her face was flushed and livid with rage. I've seen her rip-roaring mad, but never like this.

"You've gotta promise me you'll not tell anyone … especially Nate?" She was struggling to hold back tears.

"Of course." It wasn't the moment to say, "Scout's honor," but it crossed my mind.

"You probably suspected it. Nate and I have been in a relationship for some time now."

"I figured as much. But it's none of my business," I said sympathetically.

"We've tried to be discreet. It's been really hard, especially working together every day, always on our guard, then sneaking around like thieves to have any private time together." She paused to blow her nose again and dab the tears that she hadn't been able to hold back.

"Does Nate's wife know about the affair?"

"I don't think so. Not that she'd really care. She and Nate have grown apart. They live in the same house, but that's about all they have in common. She gardens and talks to her plants. She's pretty well smashed by dinner time on the martinis she nurses all afternoon. After dinner, she toddles off to bed to watch TV and finish her pitcher of martinis until she nods off."

It sounded like a self-serving tale of a frustrated mistress to me. Time to cut to the chase. "How did Mrs. Simmons come between you?"

Marcie gave me a hard look before softening it. "I had a spat with Nate. After fifteen years of playing second fiddle, I got fed up with Nate's dilly-dallying. He'd promised for years that he'd separate from his wife so we could live together. You know him; he's a master procrastinator." Marcie's voice trailed off and she poked at her face with more tissues.

"How did Mrs. Simmons learn about your rift?"

"She must've got wind of it through Royce Bronson who picked it up from his father. Nate was on a State Bar Committee Judge Bronson chaired. You know Nate and his big mouth when he's feeling his Chivas Regal."

"Why would he discuss his personal life with Judge Bronson? It doesn't make sense." I gave Marcie a disbelieving look. She gave a little sigh and took a deep breath before answering.

"Nate used to take me to his bar association meetings out of town. It was our chance for a long weekend together away from the fishbowl we live in here in Berkeley." Marcie paused and I motioned her to continue.

"We never stayed at the convention hotel because one of Nate's loose-lipped colleagues might spot us together. Four years ago we attended a State Bar meeting in Santa Barbara and we stayed in a cozy little bed-and-breakfast inn a few miles out of town. Unfortunately, Judge Bronson had the same idea. He'd booked the same B and B with a goodtime girl. I was scared shitless and pleaded with Nate to move elsewhere. Nate said it was too late to skip out and pretend we didn't know each other or what was up. So, we all had to just laugh at the coincidence and make the best of it. He was right. We were like four teenagers on a lark after the senior ball. We became co-conspirators. We even went out dining and dancing together like kids double dating. It was stupid but exciting at the time.

"Was Judge Bronson married at the time?"

Marcie put aside her tissues and laughed heartily. "You betcha. Married thirty-five years to a real classy woman who's a pillar of respectability with the Oakland Hills crowd. She's a society babe on everyone's charitable fundraising list. That's part of what made the weekend so much fun. Judge Bronson had a lot more to lose from wagging tongues given his wife's social visibility and reputation if Willard's weekend tryst hit the *Tribune's* gossip columns."

"Was his companion from his office?"

"No way was Willard going to get involved in-house, like Nate. She was thirty years younger than him and strictly a goodtime party girl. She knew she was booked just for the weekend and set about to make the most of it with the judge footing the bills generously. We spent the whole weekend partying. Neither Nate or Willard made it to a convention meeting in Santa Barbara."

This hidden side of Marcie and Nate surprised me. I had a hard time imagining Marcie letting down her hair with a party girl. I guess it shows how little I know about women. Marcie's escapade raised new concerns and I needed to find a delicate way to broach the next line of inquiry.

"Did either Judge Bronson or his date do any drugs together during the weekend?"

"Why did you ask me that, R.C.?" Her tone was harsh and defensive. We both knew that an admission of illegal drug use was a violation of California's Rules of Professional Conduct that could lead to suspension of a lawyer's license or even to disbarment.

"Because I think the murders are related to the Simmons brothers' drug activities and their attorneys might also be involved. It's hard to believe that Mrs. Simmons didn't know about the mortuary's extensive drug involvement either. You said the weekend occurred about four years ago. Was Gloria married to Jimmy Simmons when you spent the weekend with the judge?"

"Now that you mention it, Judge Bronson couldn't stop talking about what a hot number she was and how she'd made a spectacular debut on the social scene."

"Was Royce Bronson involved with her at this time?"

"I don't think so. He was just one of the dogs in the pack running after the bitch in heat."

"Did father and son know her personally?"

"They had to. She was a provocative dresser. She really knows how to strut her stuff. The judge couldn't stop talking about a black tie benefit party for the Oakland Museum's black artists' collection. According to the judge, she arrived at the private viewing champagne reception on Jimmy Simmons' arm wearing a slinky little dress that would have been too short even on a tennis court. Great legs are one thing. What really got eyes popping and tongues wagging was her see-through top. There were a lot of upset ladies the next day when the *Oakland Tribune's* society columnists ignored all the ladies wearing expensive designer dresses and lavished all their attention on the impression the bitch made pushing her tits in everyone's face." Marcie's description dripped venom and she was back on her high horse.

I had already seen Mrs. Simmons in a see-through bathing suit and could imagine the effect she could make at a stuffy fundraising party with lots of bored old geezers in attendance. She was a Las Vegas showgirl who knew how to walk her walk and strut her stuff. I had to suppress a laugh at the thought of all those Oakland patriarchs swishing the tails of their tuxedos like tom cats craning their necks to get a closer look at those magnificent titties.

"Marcie, I asked you whether Judge Bronson did any drugs that weekend. I'm not interested in anyone else."

Marcie paused a long moment before replying. "The two of them did lines of coke with rolled fifty dollars bills that the judge tucked into his girl's bra just like he was tipping a belly dancer."

I would have loved to ask how she could witness this intimate scene as an uninvolved observer, but passed on the thought to keep her talking. "Did the judge mention how he'd scored the coke?"

"No, and I wasn't about to ask." Marcie said defensively.

"Could he have gotten it from his son, Royce?"

"Sure, but he didn't talk about it. He might be stupid to do coke in front of others, but not so stupid to talk about it. No way either Nate or I was going to say 'Boo' about it either, and he knew it. No one would believe the party girl over the judge's denial if she tried to shake him or us down. So, it wasn't really a big thing to any of us as it was done in private."

"So long as no one got busted for driving under the influence," I added too quickly without thinking.

"We took cabs. I still don't see what this has to do with the Simmons bitch," Marcie said testily.

"Have you heard any scuttlebutt around town linking Royce Bronson or Mrs. Simmons to drugs?"

"No, but I wouldn't put it past them."

"What about the judge? Was there anything about drug activity or abuse in the charges that lead to his resignation from the bench?"

"No, it was more a corruption thing. Something to do with taking perks for favorable rulings. Both the Bronsons work on criminal cases that often involve drug transactions. You know how easy it is to get all the drugs you want from drug clients."

Marcie's observation was so obvious I wondered why it

hadn't occurred to me. Criminal defense attorneys demand most of their fees upfront in cash or kind. As much of the criminal defense work in the Bay Area is drug-related, attorneys could easily score drugs in exchange for work with no questions asked.

I should have investigated who the Bronsons had represented locally in criminal matters. Maybe there was a link to their Asian partners. I'd ask Detective Walker to look into it. I still had to pin down Marcie for more info and get over to the mortuary to speak with Alice Brown before she slipped out of my grasp after she finished work.

Reggie waved to me and pointed to the phone next to his fry grill. I shook him off and signaled him to take a message. I didn't want to give Marcie time to finesse my questions or skip back to the office. This was probably the only time I'd get her to talk about Nate and his relations with Mrs. Simmons.

"I'm still not clear why Nate would cut you out of the Gloria Simmons' case."

"Nate got pissed at me for pressuring him about his wife. We had a really big row over it. I was stupid to believe he'd dump his wife for me. He's had me on his own terms for fifteen years. Why the hell should he change now? He knows I love him and don't have anyone else in my life. Judge Bronson asked Nate personally to handle the Gloria Simmons case. He said his son had a conflict of interest. He tantalized Nate by saying the bitch was a real hot number who likes to work closely with her associates and rewards them with special favors." Marcie was oozing venom again.

"Judge Bronson actually told Nate she'd play footsie with him if she liked his legal work?" I said incredulously. My jaw was about to drop off.

"Nate told me in a moment of pique that the bitch gives terrific head and that she told him herself not to be shy about asking for it if he got off on it. The sleazy slut has a track record of blowing anyone who'll advance her interests."

I was stunned by what Marcie told me. From what I'd seen, she didn't need to give blow jobs to men to get them to do what she wanted. Marcie must have let her jealousy get the better of her reasoning on this in order to slander her rival. Marcie picked up on my doubts.

"You know very little about predatory women, R.C. She knows how weak and vain most men are and how easy it is to get a man to do her bidding. To her, it's like what other women do when they flirt. She gains her power by using men's weaknesses and vanity to give them something they think is taboo and sexually liberating. Why do you think all those white, middle class johns cruise MacArthur Boulevard to get a blow job?"

"You're right. I don't understand," I said shaking my head.

"Girls learn early that the boys they date only want one thing – to go all the way. If she gives in to the constant pressure, the guy most likely will brag to his buddies or in the locker room that she's an easy lay. She gets an instant reputation as a slut and guys she hardly knows now want to date her to screw her and expect her to put out. She will be compromised whether she accedes to their demands or spurns them; she may lose the guy she wants to marry because she's no longer a virgin and she's used goods with an unsavory reputation. It's a cruel double standard, but it's a fact of life." Marcie gave me a tough look before continuing.

"So, teenage girls learn to make accommodations to protect their virginity and reputations. Some ease the pressure to go all the way by jerking off their boyfriend, while others will give a blow job to the lucky guy. It's a compromise that preserves their jewel and doesn't hurt their reputation or popularity because the other girls in their peer group do the same."

"But how does that relate to Nate and Mrs. Simmons?"

Marcie gave me a look that said, "How could you be so naive?" "Many women are taught that oral sex is a dirty practice only offered by prostitutes. Many women won't do it even with their husbands. Some women actually prefer getting oral sex to conventional sex and can't achieve orgasm without it. So, women like Gloria Simmons know it can be a real source of power over men. The bitch uses it to get what she wants from certain men. She learned of Nate's rift with me and decided to use her fangs on him. He's such a dumb lump when it comes to women's motives that he fell for her sweet sugar lips hook, line and sinker." Marcie was ready to bite someone as she spit her words out.

"Wouldn't Royce or her husband be furious with her?"

"Why should they? They own the prize. Nobody she manipulates gets in her pants. Everyone wants her, and she gives them a taste but no more."

"You're sure she got to Nate this way?" I was still doubtful.

"Yeah Buster, I'm sure. He threw it up in my face. It's his way of saying our relationship stays on his terms or else. A great kick in the butt after fifteen years being the loyal mistress."

I didn't reply to Marcie's angry denunciation. I'd learned all I could from Marcie for the moment. I told her I had to interview an important witness regarding the codicil to the will. Marcie took her leave growling about how she was going to get even with Mrs. Simmons and how I was obligated to help her. She wanted me to find a way to destroy her rival, but I didn't have a clue how I might bring it off. So far, I was full of theories and suspicions, but short on any proof.

After Marcie left, Reggie informed me that Detective Johnny Walker had called to say he was stuck at the office and couldn't get away. He asked me to stop by and see him later as he would be working late.

Events seemed to be accelerating and headed for a show-down with Mrs. Simmons over the codicil. I felt both excited and fearful about our upcoming meeting. Would she try to envelope me in her web as she'd done with Nate? The thought sent worrisome shivers down my spine.

Chapter 24

MY NEXT MOVE WAS TO CALL THE SIMMONS Family Mortuary. I asked to speak with Alice Brown. The voice of the other end asked my name and put me on hold. After a long wait, I heard a click and faint breathing at the other end.

"Hello. Alice Brown?" I asked into the void.

"Uh-huh."

"My name is R.C. Bean and I work for the lawyers who are handling Mr. Jimmy Simmons' estate. We need you to sign a paper so his will can be filed with the court." I paused to get a reaction. Nothing but silence at the other end. "You still there?" I demanded.

"Uh-huh."

"According to our records, you were a witness a couple of months ago to a codicil to his will. The judge requires you sign a paper verifying your signature. When can I meet with you to get the paper signed?" I said assertively. I was getting annoyed at her silence. Time to stop being nice. "The judge wants this matter taken care of today and so does Mrs. Simmons. What time this afternoon can you meet me to sign the paper?"

"Uh, I don't know. It's not really convenient today. Could you call back tomorrow?"

"No, Mrs. Simmons has to file the paper with the court

tomorrow morning. The judge is going to be mad at you if you don't cooperate. No telling what he might do. He's been known to issue arrest warrants for contempt of court and have the Sheriff haul folks into court to appear before him. Sometimes he lets them cool their heels overnight in jail if he's in a bad mood."

"I sure don't wanna do no jail time. I gotta pick up my daughter from daycare after work," she said in a trembling voice.

"What time do you get off work? I'll meet you and it won't take more than ten minutes." She was stalling for time, probably hoping to cue Tony Simmons to my request. I couldn't let her off the hook.

"Uh, I get off of work at five but I can't meet you at the mortuary."

That suited me fine. I couldn't risk Brother Thomas seeing me in my new role as a legal investigator and putting two and two together after my charade with "Uncle Paul." "Name a place not far from the mortuary and I'll meet you there right after work. It won't take but a minute."

"Uh, I guess it'd be the Farside Café, uh Broadway and 19th."

"Okay. What'll you be driving?

"I'm in an eighty-four Cutlass."

"Good. I'll meet you there at five-fifteen. Park in front of the café and wait for me inside." I didn't wait for a response. I skipped out of Reggie's Place and hauled ass for downtown Oakland. I needed to get to the mortuary before she left work so I could follow her to the café without her giving me the slip.

I left a message for my brother to treat himself to a hamburger on my tab and to meet me at the cottage at 8:30 sharp with someone driving a late model car as I would need their help later.

I nearly missed catching up to Alice Brown. I was bombing down Telegraph Ave. doing fifty plus in a thirty-five mile an hour zone and running through yellow lights turning red when a police cruiser swung out of a side street and locked onto my tail. I moved over to the right lane to prepare to stop. He hit his siren as I pulled over, then whipped to the left of me and took off like a bat out of hell. He must've gotten a call about an officer in distress or something worse just as he was about to nail my tail.

Sometimes you just get lucky. I didn't ease up on the pedal and got to the mortuary with no time to spare. I parked across the street. The Cutlass was still in the parking lot. A few moments later a big-hipped black lady exited the mortuary and made a beeline for the Cutlass. She was wearing a shiny taffeta dress and sneakers. She moved deceptively fast for such a big woman. She roared out of the lot with me close behind. She headed straight for the café on Broadway. I watched her turn into the café's parking lot and make her way inside before pulling in next to her Cutlass.

She was seated at a corner table as far from the windows and door as one could get. I slid into the opposite side of her table and put on a smile of smiles to try to disarm her icy stare.

"Hi, I'm R.C. Bean. I want to thank you in advance for taking the time to meet me and sign the paper. This way we don't have to get a court summons compelling you to come to court to sign the paper about Mr. Jimmy's will change in front of the judge." I paused to let my words sink in. Most folks are extremely nervous about having to testify in court and afraid of judges. She looked like a scared walrus stuffed into her chair. I didn't inform her that if the second witness to the codicil signed a verification form, hers wouldn't be necessary. Fear and confusion were written all over her furrowed brow.

"Now, Mrs. Brown where did you actually sign the paper saying you saw Mr. Jimmy sign a change to his will?" I passed her a copy of the attestation clause to the codicil which she had signed. She looked at the paper with her signature and frowned.

"I don't really remember whether it was Mr. Jimmy or Mr. Tony who asked me to sign it."

I tried to mask my surprise. "It's not important who asked you to sign it. What counts is that you actually signed the paper. Is that your signature?" I pointed to her signature.

"Uh-huh, yeah that's my signature."

"Now try to think carefully about the circumstances. Did you go to a lawyer's office to sign?"

"Un-uh. I never went to no lawyer's office or to Mr. Jimmy's house. I signed that paper at work."

"But you don't remember which brother asked you to sign? How can that be?" I said in a disbelieving voice.

"They just asked me to sign the paper and I signed it."

"Did Mr. Jimmy tell you he was changing his will and that's what you were witnessing?"

"Naw. Nobody told me nothin' about no will. They just said sign this here paper. They just said they needed a signature from the mortuary, that's all."

"Do they often ask you to sign forms like that?" I was fishing.

"I do fill out a lot of forms as a part of my job. There's a lot of paperwork to do with the burials, so it wasn't no big deal to sign this here paper for Mr. Jimmy," she said pointing to her signature.

I caught sight of the waitress out of the corner of my eye and waved her off.

"Was anyone else in the office when you signed the paper?"

"I don't think so. I would've remembered that."

"Was Mrs. Simmons or her housemaid there when you signed?"

"No, it was just Mr. Tony or Mr. Jimmy what asked me to sign the paper. Does that mean I have to go to court?" She asked looking worried.

"Well, if no one asked you to read the new will and no other witnesses were around to watch you sign, then it's pretty sure you won't have to go to court if you sign this here paper," I said pointing to the Declaration I had prepared. "But, if you sign this paper and change your story, the judge will probably throw you in the slammer and throw away the key. So you better be sure to tell it like it was just like you told me."

"Yeah, well I sure don't wanna go to no court and get in serious trouble. That's why I didn't wanna meet with you today.

You really need to talk to Mr. Tony about this. He's gonna know more about what's best to do."

"No, I can't talk to him. See, I work for a lawyer's office. I can only talk to the persons who signed the papers. Nobody else will do. You signed the paper and your ass is on the line if you change your story as far as the judge is concerned. It'll be just you, me and the judge." I decided to pour it on and I could smell her fear as she started to sweat profusely.

"So, let's see if I have your story straight. Just answer yes or no to my questions so I can tell the judge." I took a legal pad and pencil out of my briefcase to make it look more official as I scribbled squiggles on the pad after each of her answers.

"This is your true signature on the paper?"

"Uh-huh, I mean yes, that's my name."

"Did you sign the paper in your office at work?"

"Uh, I was at work but I don't think it was in my office."

"Whose office was it? Take your time. We don't want to have to go through this again in front of the judge, do we?"

"Well, I think it's coming back to me. I, uh, signed it in Mr. Jimmy's office."

"That's better. Now was Mrs. Simmons or her maid, Maria, present when you signed?"

"No, Mrs. Simmons wasn't there. She hardly ever comes to the office. I don't know no Maria, so she sure wasn't there."

"Good. Now we're getting it straight. The judge will be pleased. Now, think carefully. Who asked you to sign the paper?"

"Well, I could be mistaken, but I think it was Mr. Tony who asked me to sign the paper for his brother."

"So, Mr. Tony asked you to sign as a favor for Mr. Jimmy. That's what you recollect, right?"

"Yeah, that's what happened. They was real busy. We had a lot of work at that moment. The two brothers work close together. They ain't got no secrets, so I didn't think nothing of it at the time. Only after Mr. Jimmy passed did I get to thinkin' about it."

"What made you think about it then?"

"Well, my son asked me and my husband to make a will a couple of years ago. We went to a lawyer's office and he said we all got to sign at the same time for it to be any good. So, I was surprised nobody else was signing when I signed. But I figured they knew what they was doing."

"Did you mention it to Mr. Tony or Mr. Jimmy? The judge might think it's important."

"No, I don't want to get nobody in trouble. I'm afraid to do the wrong thing."

"Don't be afraid. Answer truthfully and I'll make sure with the judge that nobody, including Mr. Tony, will know what you told me."

"I never said nothin' to Mr. Tony about my worries. Wasn't my place. They just asked me to sign a paper and that's what I did. I figured they knew best."

"Yes, you're absolutely right. Just don't say anything to anybody at work about what you did and everything with the court will be fine. That's what the judge wants." She looked relieved and had stopped sweating. I probably had come on too strong about what the judge might do. It bugs me that people believe this kind of nonsense. Alice Brown was living proof that fear of the judge was about as strong as fear of the Lord for lots of folks.

It was time to finish my little scam. I pulled out the declaration of proof of signature from my briefcase with a flourish and indicated where she should sign. She was between a rock and a hard place. Her signature on the declaration I'd drafted stating that she'd not witnessed Jimmy Simmons or Maria Benevides sign the codicil in her presence would be a bone of contention between Mrs. Simmons and Tony Simmons. Her hand was shaking too much for her to read it. We both knew she didn't want to sign it. She was worried she would lose her job.

She hesitated with the paper clutched in her paw. "You have to sign it. The judge requires it. Best just sign it and not tell anyone you signed it. We probably won't have to use it. The judge will just keep it in the file and no one will know what you signed." A glimmer of hope flicked across her visage but didn't stick.

She finally heaved a big sigh and scrawled her John Henry on the declaration. I snatched it out of her hand and stuffed it into my briefcase. I pulled a twenty from my wad and dropped it on the table. I thanked her for meeting with me and invited her to order herself some food with the money. She hadn't gotten those heavy thighs by pushing away from the table.

Chapter 25

I WAS PLEASED WITH THE INFORMATION I HAD EXTRACTED from Alice Brown and the affidavit she had executed stating she had not signed the codicil in the presence of the testator and the second witness. It was still unclear which brother had made her sign as a witness at the mortuary. It didn't make much sense for Tony Simmons to insist she sign because he stood to lose a major interest in the mortuary business. But why would Jimmy Simmons nullify the premarital agreement in favor of his wife? It gave her a prime reason to want him dead, especially if he was getting hooked on Jennifer Wong and wanted to dump his wife for any reason.

I was almost in front of the Berkeley Police Department when I realized I had failed to clarify when the attestation clause was signed by Alice Brown. The date on the codicil might be wrong. Had the document been prepared recently and backdated? It was even possible it was prepared after Jimmy Simmons was snuffed. It wasn't in Nate's file before I left for Las Vegas.

I wasn't pleased with such an obvious investigative failure on my part as I climbed the steps to the Hall of Justice and was directed by the duty officer to Detective Walker's office. Walker looked up briefly from the file he had his nose in and nodded for me to take a seat. His desk was piled high with various dossiers and his large ashtray was full of cigar stubs and ashes. A plume of smelly cigar smoke hovered above his head and more was on the way as he puffed on the panatela wedged in the side of his mouth. Walker prided himself in buying American; he was addicted to cheap American cigars that were more like stink bombs than genteel tobacco.

Walker had an office all to himself. I suspected even die-hard smokers on the force had no stomach to work in his smoke house. He'd nailed the window shut to make his point.

Walker lowered his file and wasted no time in formalities. "What do you have for me, R.C.?"

"Look at these." I handed him copies of Jimmy Simmons' will, premarital agreement and codicil. He examined the signatures for a good while before resuming eye contact and signaling he expected more.

"I think the codicil's a fraud. I don't believe he would've signed anything giving his wife a half interest in the mortuary businesses in Oakland and Las Vegas where his current girlfriend was discovered murdered. The prenuptial and will give his wife only thirty-five hundred a month on his death or divorce." Walker was all ears now.

"Who gets the other half with the codicil?"

"Jimmy Simmons' brother, Tony."

"Who would've got the wife's share without the codicil?"

"As there's no children, Tony gets all his brother's share."

"I suppose you want our handwriting expert to compare the signatures for fraud."

I laughed. "Yeah, it would give her a pretty good motive to kill her husband, wouldn't it?"

He laughed, too. "It might give her a motive if I had the original documents. It's gonna look strange ordering a handwriting analysis on copies, isn't it?"

"You know my confidentiality problem. Once Nate files the originals with the court, you can order or subpoena a certified copy as part of your investigation with the Oakland police. Meanwhile, knowing Jimmy Simmons' signature on the codicil is forged may lead us directly to the killers." Walker regarded me intently as he sucked on his stogie and pondered my bait.

"Who else do you think was involved?" Walker demanded.

"The wife's boyfriend could have written the codicil and orchestrated the hit on her husband and his girlfriend."

"You know if you want my help, I gotta have a name. Who do you think rubbed out the mortician and his Chinese girl-friend?" Walker's face was set in an "I mean business" mode.

"My theory is complicated. What I know is that the Simmons brothers are transporting dope from the Oakland docks to a distribution point in Las Vegas in hearses from their two mortuaries. They also can move their dead enemies and rivals the same way. They are working with Asian partners who placed their bookkeeper in the Oakland mortuary to keep tabs on drug profits and the loyalty of their black associates. She was the girlfriend I found in the Las Vegas freezer along with the animals being cut up for sale in Asia by the taxidermy across the street; they also processed the drugs for the market. There should be some local rumblings about the Chinese trying to muscle in on the local drug dealers' turf. It should leave a trail to the shooters in the drive-by at the mortuary," I said optimistically..

"It sounds good in theory, 'cept our informants say they don't know anything about the hit at the mortuary involving the Chinese or black gangs. Maybe the wife and her boyfriend wanted to make it look like the boys from the 'hood were responsible?"

Walker's news was upsetting. I had a hard time picturing a Bonnie & Clyde team with Gloria Simmons driving and Royce Bronson filling her husband full of holes. I wasn't about to tell Walker that I was present at the time of the shooting doing a bag job and had failed to make out the shooters or their car. There was also the problem of the drugs and cash I'd recovered at the scene. Walker wouldn't be amused at my taking mate-rial evidence related to a homicide, either. I didn't have much choice other than to give him Royce Bronson's name as Mrs. Simmons' boyfriend if I wanted his assistance.

"It's possible that Mrs. Simmons and her boyfriend, attor-ney Royce Bronson, committed the crime themselves, but I don't think a direct action drive-by would be their style."

"You ask either one what they were doing that night?"

"No, I haven't." I hoped Walker wasn't going to probe where I was that night. My alibi that I was at my parents' house wouldn't hold up to scrutiny. I decided to broach another subject and hope he'd not come back to press me on my activities and involvement.

"I took blood samples from the bookkeeper and left them with a drug testing lab in Vegas before leaving. I should have a report in the morning. I'm pretty sure they shot her up with the drugs the gangs have been moving. The only marks on her body were needle holes. Did you get a preliminary report from Vegas?" I asked Walker.

"Yeah, your account fits what the detective on her case knows. The autopsy is scheduled for late today. What else do you know about her that could be useful to our investigation?" Walker said while firing up another stink bomb.

"The autopsy should show she OD'd on ice, the designer drug the gangs were moving. Both she and Jimmy Simmons were hooked on it and it's a clever way to kill a junkie."

"Why did you test the sample when you knew there'd be an autopsy? You should have mentioned it when you called from Vegas. They're gonna know someone tampered with the crime scene." Walker was not amused. My future as a private investigator and license with the State Bar were squarely in his hands.

"I took the blood sample before I was attacked. I wasn't sure there was foul play and I was afraid they'd dispose of the body and there'd be no autopsy or investigation. I took two samples – one to test in Vegas and one to give to you to if the mortuary made the body disappear. I was feeling the pressure. They were looking for me and I felt I had to make the shooters before they got to me. I've been real nervous since they messed up my little studio on Fulton Street."

Walker dropped his frown and eased up his face. "I heard about that. What were they looking for?"

"I'm pretty sure they were after my investigation notes on

the Simmons case. I'd been snooping at the mortuary. I even did a little theatre piece pretending to arrange a burial for a relative. I don't think the acting job went too well and they were on to me."

Walker smiled ever so slightly at my account. "I suppose you had a set of picks in your pocket at the time?"

I didn't answer his question. If I said no, I would be lying, and if I said yes, I would be admitting to a felony of attempted burglary.

"That's probably one of the things the brothers at the mortuary were looking for when they tossed my apartment. How long will it take to get signatures analyzed?" I asked.

"How sure am I the original documents are gonna be filed in court like you say?"

"Right now, I'd say it's ninety-nine percent sure they'll be filed this week. If not and you believe you need them to get a conviction, I promise someone will mail them to you anonymously." It was a promise I'd have a hard time keeping if Nate squirreled them away somewhere outside the office.

"Okay, I'll go with that. You know it's your ass on the line. I'll get you a report sometime tomorrow. Call me after noon. If the codicil's phony, we're gonna want to re-interview Mrs. Simmons."

"Where'd she tell you she was the night of the shooting?"

"She said she was home all evening. The live-in maid supports her story and her brother-in-law stopped by to speak with his brother that evening, but left after waiting for a while."

"I wouldn't trust the maid. She's one of the witnesses to the codicil. The other witness works at the mortuary and says neither the maid nor Mrs. Simmons were present when she was asked to sign the amendment to the will." Walker was real focused now and looked at me with renewed interest. Maybe he wouldn't oppose my application for admission to the California Bar when I got around to passing the exam.

It was getting late. I needed to pick up some food and change clothes before meeting my brother and heading over to the Simmons' residence. I wanted to see how far Walker would go to help me if I got in over my head. I was still leery about taking a cab to the Simmons residence as instructed. "What more will you need in order to put a collar on the wife and the boyfriend?"

"Right now, we ain't got diddly-shit that puts her at the scene of the crime and she's got two people backing her alibi. If your codicil comes up smelling, then we got a motive, but nothing concrete to go with it. She's gonna claim what she said to you and your boss is privileged communication. It's real neat. Maybe now you see why us cops hate lawyers worse than you private dicks. Slick bastards!" He blew two smoke rings in my direction.

"If the autopsy proves a homicide, then we're gonna start putting a lotta heat on the mortuary staff until somebody cracks. When the shit hits the fan over the mortuary peddling drugs, we're gonna catch us some drug middlemen willing to finger the perps for some probation time."

Walker seemed convinced he could force a speedy resolution to the case. I feared he was blowing smoke to keep me playing on his team. It was time to claim a favor for risking my butt.

"I need you to call me with the autopsy results just as soon as you get them."

"Yeah, will do. You earned the right to know what they pumped into her. That was quite a piece of guerilla theatre you produced in Vegas. The guys at the station and our Oakland partners have been laughing their heads off every time they view their bulletin board with the photo of the guy you left in cold storage."

"Well, let's keep 'em laughing. I gotta go."

"Be sure I'm the first to hear anything that might connect the wife and the boyfriend to the murders. I'm the liaison with the Oakland police on this case."

"I sure will." We shook hands and I couldn't wait to get some fresh air in my lungs. It felt like I'd just smoked several packs of cigarettes.

I had debated whether to tell him I was meeting Mrs.

Simmons tonight. I didn't because I was afraid he'd insist on my asking her certain questions that might clue her to my game plan. I was already scared shitless about meeting her, even without Walker's parrot sitting on my shoulder.

Chapter 26

I WAS RUNNING LATE AS I SKIPPED AWAY FROM WALKER'S office and made a beeline for my cottage. I phoned an order for a large pepperoni and mushroom pizza. The pizza arrived after I'd showered and dressed up for my meeting with Mrs. Simmons. As she was being billed for my new Armani threads, I figured the least I could do was to model what her money had bought.

I was surprised and even impressed with my new duds. It had been years since I was dressed to the nines. No way I was going to wear a tie, but my silk, French foulard gave me a jaunty air. I couldn't resist preening in front of a large mirror and winking outrageously at my natty ensemble. I was laughing so hard that my antics startled my little brother when he popped through the front door and skidded to a halt. I was bent over holding my sides with one hand and trying to wipe away tears with the other. L.C.'s deep frown confirmed his suspicion that I'd just gone off my rocker.

I don't think L.C. had ever seen me dressed up. He spends most of his money he makes working for me on stylish clothes and entertainment. His taste runs to casual elegance and the latest sports fashion, but he has a good eye for style and quality. Once he realized I hadn't gone bonkers and was just cutting up, he gave me a thorough once over.

"You do be lookin' good big bro.' 'Spect you musta' got hot with the dice in Vegas. You got a new, hot mama you plannin' to squire around town?"

"You know I don't play sucker games. I got a new client who sprung for the threads so I could look my best while representing her interests." Next to nice clothes, my brother is very partial to sharp looking ladies.

"Uh-huh. Figures you be steppin' out with some hot mama. You bess be careful. When they start buyin' yo' duds, they're usually thinkin' how nice you'd be lookin' wid a ring on yo' finger."

I laughed. "The lady who paid for these threads is a foxy lady, but she sure isn't looking for a husband at the moment. She's a cool mama, but strictly business." I was reluctant to tell him more than he already knew about Mrs. Simmons. What I told him would make the rounds of his associates and I didn't think that was a good idea for now.

While we demolished the pizza, L.C. brought me up to date with his surveillance activities. He confirmed Walker's claim that there'd been no rumbles from the drug gangs on the streets or in Oakland's Chinatown after the drive-by hit on Jimmy Simmons. I needed to rethink who the actual shooters might be and who they worked for. It was a very worrisome flaw in my theory, but I was too pressed for time to deal with it now.

I asked L.C. to put a tail on Royce Bronson. I was afraid he might slip up on my back when I met with Mrs. Simmons. I was more and more anxious about meeting with her as the time approached.

I planned to have the cab drop me off as close to her door as possible. I instructed my brother to engage one of his crew with a late model car and station it unobtrusively so he could monitor who came and went from her residence after I arrived. He was to verify I left on my own power and he was to follow me back home to ensure I arrived safely.

I had no idea why she insisted I come after dark and by cab. There was no way I planned to stay at her place even if she made an offer she thought I couldn't refuse. Marcie's words of warning jangled around in my head. L.C. would be in contact with his team shadowing Royce Bronson. I still had doubts that Royce Bronson had arranged the hit on Jimmy Simmons, but then again, anyone who got seriously hooked on Gloria Simmons was probably capable of doing that and worse. I couldn't afford to take any chances. My sweet ass was on the line.

By the time I had L.C. squared away on his role, it was time to head over to Oakland and face the music. My brother dropped me off near the downtown entrance of the Berkeley BART station where there's a cabstand. I browsed the latest detective novels in a nearby bookstore in order to give my brother a head start to the Simmons' residence. I didn't want him and his buddy following or racing my cab. Most cabbies can spot a tail and I didn't want to advertise my plan. Someone might wave some big bills in front of the cabby's nose and learn all about my brother's car after he let me off.

The cabby at the head of the line turned out to be an Afro-Cuban immigrant who proceeded to burn my ears off about how the U.S. trade embargo was hurting his family in Cuba. It must have been the Armani suit. He'd pegged me for an imperialist flunkey in spite of my dusky skin. I grunted my agreement to his views from time to time as he gave me no opportunity to get a word in edgewise. I didn't want to get him more worked up by contesting what he said.

He shifted his political rhetoric into high gear once we got into the pricey area of the Oakland hills. His political views were now punctuated with expressions like, "Power to the people," "Viva La Raza," and "Fight the power."

I was relieved to spot my brother's stakeout car in the shadows of the tree-lined street as we pulled into the driveway entrance to the Simmons' estate. I asked to be let off directly in front of the elegant house. I'd watched the meter and prepared the fare and a healthy tip to compensate for having to drive me into the lair of Yankee *imperialistas*. I don't know much Spanish, but I do know the derogatory term *gringo* which my cabbie spit out about every fifth word.

I shoveled the fare and tip at him the moment we skidded to a stop. I hoped he'd focus on the gringo's dollars and not spot the hitching posts with Negroes dressed in servants' livery. He'd no doubt be convinced I was visiting the descendants of real slave traders. Fortunately, he was still jawing me out about my responsibility to Cuba as he gunned his motor and took off with his back to the offending antique horse ties.

I adjusted my foulard which had slipped during the taxi ride and was just about to lift the ornate bronze door knocker in the form of a cupid when the door eased open and away from my raised hand. I was surprised to find myself eye to eye with Mrs. Simmons and not her maid. She was dressed casually, but elegantly in black, silk, bell-bottom trousers and a sexy top that blew me away. It was filmy and gauzy and did little to mask Mrs. Simmons' full breasts. The only solid band of material was in the collar around her neck. The front of the top was comprised of small lozenges stitched together at angles that let one see her creamy, mahogany-textured skin from many angles and allowed her pert, erect nipples to poke through the stitching.

I don't how long I stood there mesmerized and staring like a chump. She was in no hurry to end the spell she'd cast. She watched my reaction with a bemused smile. The ceiling lights in the entryway were diffused but strong enough to let me see how her breasts stirred with each movement as the filmy little lozenges allowed her nipples to peek through. Once again she'd caught me by surprise to her advantage.

I had laughed at Marcie's tale of the commotion Mrs. Simmons had made at the Oakland Museum with her see-through top. Now the same woman was tantalizing me with a private, peekaboo showing. I was frustrated to be so discombobulated. Why couldn't I just be like those cool dudes in the magazines who sat around in restaurants or on boats on the French Riviera or in Monte Carlo drinking and chatting while topless babes in thongs sunned themselves at their feet?

Mrs. Simmons broke into my train of thought and

interrupted my gawking. "What do you think of my latest fashion design?" She did a pirouette in front of me to demonstrate how her slinky top shimmered and swayed as her bosom rippled under the gossamer lozenges which sought to flow with her movement, then cupped her breasts like slippery cobwebs trapping prey. I could feel sweat pearling on my brow, but I didn't dare wipe it off. I knew I must look like a fool in a fancy suit with a silly-assed grin like a kid sneaking a peek at his big sister stepping out of the shower naked for the first time.

"Probably going to cause a riot in Slims," I replied. It was the only thing my addled brain could come up with. Slims was a local rhythm and blues club that catered to the black community; it was a place to take your lady when you wanted to put on the dog.

I was thinking of Bobby Bland's song, "Get Real Clean." Bobby's lyrics instruct his girlfriend to get dressed up in her tight, designer jeans and not forget to wear "her see-through top, 'cause tonight we gonna pop." He also reminds her to bring "her Gucci bag to carry the Mag." Anybody planning to squire Mrs. Simmons to Slims or any other club in her present attire should consider hiring private guards armed with Uzis and transport her in an armored car. I kept my thoughts to myself. She motioned for me to follow her down the hallway. I would have wagged my tail if I had one.

She led me down a set of stairs off the hallway and we arrived in a sunken living room. The central brick fireplace was flanked by plate glass windows with sweeping views down a woodsy glade lit by outdoor spotlights. The interior décor reminded me of a pick-up fern bar I've been to in San Francisco. The room was divided into cozy nooks and corners with plush chairs and recessed loveseats separated by large ferns and miniature trees in redwood tubs and large, colorful pots.

The wall décor was a splash of modern fabrics in rich colors and abstract designs. African masks, shields and spears were cleverly interspersed among the framed fabrics. The overhead lighting was soft and subdued throughout the room. Each African artifact was illuminated by its own spotlight embedded in the ceiling. The fireplace added its own diffused light and the scent of oak logs burning.

Mrs. Simmons motioned me to be seated on a loveseat directly in front of the fireplace. I would have preferred to take a seat on one of the easy chairs on either side of the loveseat where I could view the door which was now to my back, but I was still following my mistress's orders like a good doggy. She pulled up an ottoman and seated herself at an angle to me. She was so close that I could smell the musky fragrances with which she'd anointed her hair and body. The play of light from the fire on her large, gold hoop earrings was dazzling. I was trying without much success to ignore the tips of her nipples which peeked out at me through the fabric of her flimsy top.

"Would you like a drink? There's Courvoisier in the decanter, or I can get you anything you like from the bar." She pointed to a large crystal decanter and two brandy snifters on a massive silver tray on a side table. She'd thought of everything to keep me in her thrall.

"A brandy'd be just fine. Thanks," my voice croaked as I sought to clear it.

She flashed me a seductive smile and poured us each a hefty snort of brandy.

I took a healthy slug of the firewater to settle my nerves and prepare for the interrogation I knew was coming. The liquor's throat-burn and heady fumes helped me to relax and eased the tension I was feeling. However, I knew I would need all my wits about me; it was no time to get lulled into complacency.

"I like your suit, R.C. The foulard's a nice touch. I hoped to have a new collection of eveningwear designed and ready for marketing, but my husband's unfortunate death interrupted my work. Still, I'm glad to see you followed my advice and bought a stylish outfit." She looked directly at me and I tried to keep my eyes from following the enticing movements rippling across her bosom as she spoke. I nodded my agreement and diverted my gaze to the crackling fire. She continued after a pause and a sip of brandy.

"Nate and I were both concerned when you left town

without notice after my husband was killed. Nate mentioned that you were following important leads to some of my husband's hidden assets. What did you find?" Her tone was more curious than accusatory.

I took another hit of brandy before replying. I felt in better control now and able to answer her inquiries.

"I traced your husband's movements in Las Vegas. You told me he went there regularly to gamble. I learned that ownership of the Oakland mortuary was transferred into the name of a Nevada corporation shortly after the death of your husband's father, Booker T. Simmons. I was surprised to learn that the same corporation owns another mortuary in Las Vegas, the Lone Pine Mortuary. Did your husband ever mention it?" I was letting out my fishing line to see if she would bite. She did.

"No, Jimmy never mentioned another mortuary. He did say he had business in Las Vegas other than gambling, but I always assumed that it was related to the Oakland mortuary." She didn't seem upset or surprised at the news.

"Well, in a way it was related to Oakland. Your husband and his brother owned both businesses jointly." I didn't believe her denial; I wanted her to entangle herself in a web of lies that might lead away from queries about what I was really doing in Las Vegas.

"What did you learn about the second mortuary that could help my case?" Her tone was pointed.

I hesitated while deciding to reveal only what I'd learned from public records. So far, there had been no mention in the press of my role inside either the Lone Pine or the taxidermy. I wanted to keep it that way. I took another hit of brandy to boost my resolve.

"The corporation owns both mortuaries outright and there are no mortgages. So, your husband's interest in the Las Vegas mortuary will be part of the estate to be probated. It should double the value of your husband's assets."

"Did you visit the Las Vegas mortuary?" She locked her eyes on mine.

I finished the brandy in my glass, then helped myself to

another healthy tot from the decanter before replying . Maybe
it was the alcohol, or possibly my strategy to be cool was working; either way, I was feeling bolder and less intimidated. If
guys in Hollywood could sit in restaurants, at parties or in public with starlets and act natural while they paraded their breasts
and other charms under the noses of admirers, then so could I.
I purposely let my eyes rove slowly over her coyly dancing nipples to meet her gaze. I was playing with fire, but I wanted to
send a clear message that I was no longer titty-whipped. Mrs.
Simmons responded by raising her eyebrows and throwing me
a quizzical look.

"I checked out the mortuary a couple of times. It's about
the same size as the one here. As there are only two others in
Las Vegas, they were doing a pretty good business from what I
observed and read in the obituaries. Lots of heart attacks and
strokes with all those out-of-town gamblers getting worked up
at the tables and overexerting with all the available goodtime
girls. What surprised me most was that a local attorney named
Royce Bronson was the attorney for the corporation that owns
both mortuaries. I discovered the legal address of the Vegas
mortuary was a mail drop." I let my voice trail off to gauge her
reaction.

"Are you sure it was Royce Bronson?" She stammered.

Time for the clincher. I whipped out the letter I'd lifted
from the mail drop and handed it to her. I'd removed the form
letter announcing some corporate rules changes and inserted a
copy of an amendment to the articles of incorporation of the
Las Vegas holding company that I'd found in the company's
filings with the Nevada Secretary of State's office. The amendment had been drafted by Bronson and filed three months earlier. It dealt with a change in voting rules that could favor one
of the two brothers and of course, Royce Bronson as well.

Mrs. Simmons's visage became more and more perturbed as
she read the document. By the amendment, Attorney Bronson
now held two percent of the shares issued by the corporation. It
would give him the swing vote between the two brothers who
now held forty-nine percent each.

"I don't believe the son-of-a-bitch! How did he get an interest in the business and not tell me!" She sounded furious. She was either a good actress or legitimately outraged.

"Attorneys often take a small piece of the action in corporations they manage," I said tongue-in-cheek. "Usually, it's in exchange for reduced fees during the startup phase of a new business." Mrs. Simmons did not appear amused.

"Now maybe you understand why I came to Nate instead of having Royce Bronson probate the estate. He just can't be trusted. I knew the Bronson law firm had done work for the mortuary and the father did an early will, but I'm sure Jimmy never knew the son had an interest in the business. Royce is furious with me for giving the probate to Nate and frankly, I'm afraid of him."

I was perplexed. What she just said didn't add up from what Marcie had told me of her relationship with Royce Bronson. Was she lying or sincere? Her next move surprised me even more. She'd somehow triggered a tape player and a velvety voice crooned a soft melody that beckoned a slow dance. She leaned forward on her ottoman and said, "Close your eyes and get comfortable, R.C."

With one hand she pushed me gently back into the deep, soft recesses of the loveseat; her other hand slowly snaked up the inside of my trouser leg until it reached the mound of my crotch. I thought I had been doing fine until now. Her soft kneading through the fabric produced an immediate erection which she skillfully caressed until I was gasping for breath. I knew I had to stop her before she rendered me helpless. She whispered softly, "Time to dance, R.C."

I was trying to rise up into her arms when it hit me. I knew as the lights flickered out slowly that I'd been sapped from behind like a sucker. That'll teach me to go dancing with the Ice Lady.

Chapter 27

MY EYES FELT LIKE LEAD SINKERS AND MY EYE-balls seemed to be trying to lift ten pound weights in an attempt to focus on my surround-ings. As my eyes finally emerged from a blurry test pattern, I wished I hadn't bothered. Brother Thomas' ugly mug grinned directly in front of my face. I tried to lift myself up, but couldn't.

I was strapped to some kind of table; my arms and legs were pinned like a candidate for experimental surgery. The pungent smell of formaldehyde announced that I was back in the Simmons' Brothers mortuary. I faced the far wall with my back to the door.

My head ached and throbbed. I gladly would have traded all my physical discomfort for a friendly face. It didn't take much brainpower to figure out I'd made a monumental miscal-culation in my analysis of the case. Now that I'd been played for a sucker, most of the missing pieces flooded into place with a rush.

Brother Thomas' presence confirmed what I should have known all along; it was Tony Simmons, not Royce Bronson, who arranged the pop on Jimmy Simmons. I had asked my brother to watch the wrong suspect and it was probably going to cost me my life. My troubled introspection was rudely interrupted by my guardian.

"So you see, li'l brother, we do meet again," Brother Thomas said with a leering grin.

He added insult to injury by shoving a long-barreled automatic pistol in my face and letting it rest on the tip of my nose. I needed to get my addled brain to focus on a way out of my predicament, but instead of calculating possible escape routes, it only flashed on the smell of gun oil and the horrendous hole a dumdum bullet would make in my head at close range.

I cringed at the knowledge of what such a bullet would do when it entered my nasal cavity and crashed its way through bone, cartilage and brain tissue before blowing a hole out the back of my skull twice as big as its entry. I'd read enough autopsy reports to know the grim details by heart. As Brother Thomas grinned and pressed his cold death machine into to my face, I knew I had to conquer my fear of immediate death which had paralyzed my speech.

"I'd shake yo' hand if only I could get it up," I uttered in a hollow voice. I knew I sounded lame, but it was a step towards mastering my fear of dying at his hands. I had to play for time if I hoped to live. As I was strapped securely to a gurney in a mortician's morgue, my mouth was the only weapon I could use to distract my enemies. My brother must have witnessed my abduction and I hoped he'd put two and two together and summoned help.

"Glad t' see the cat ain't got yo' tongue, little brother. Don't want ya dyin' wid'out appreciatin' what we doin' fo' yo' black ass. Ya ain't gonna need no hep from yo' Auntie. No siree. Yo' funeral's on the house. Be my personal pleasure t'mix yo' ashes wid d'trash," he said with a venomous leer. He pulled his cannon back a couple of feet from my nose to make his point. I had to keep him talking and jiving if I was to live for much longer.

"I can accept dyin' when it's my time, but I shore do think you got the wrong guy. What'd I do to get y'all so riled up and mad at me?" I tried to sound serious.

"You shore got sum cheek li'l brother! Come in here shuckin' an' jivin' 'bout how yo' po' Auntie be needin' a nice fun'ral when she pass. Didn't fool nobody 'round here. Had y'all figur'd fo' a plant. An' you know how curiosity done killed da cat. Gave yo'self away snoopin' an' sneakin' up dem stairs."

So far, Brother Thomas' words gave me a little hope. He hadn't referred to my illicit entry the night of the shooting or my more recent capers in Las Vegas. My glimmer of hope didn't last long. He was just about to speak more when the door behind us creaked open.

I got an upside down view of the man I'd seen briefly in the parking lot on my first visit to the mortuary. It had to be Tony Simmons.

"Take a break, Thomas. I'll watch him until you get back. When you come, bring the syringe and the speed. We want Mr. Bean to enjoy his last trip. We're going to enjoy watching him die from pleasure."

I was sure he'd ordered Jennifer Wong killed the same way. So neat and clean. One little hole and another recreational drug user overdosed to an early death. As Thomas departed, he turned his attention to me.

"You were presumptuous to think we wouldn't figure it was you who broke into the Lone Pine. You were spotted in the casino and we should have taken you out then and there. Unfortunately, my workers were tired from the long road trip and passed on the opportunity to waste you and your girlfriend."

I was shocked that he had a bead on Miss Rita. If I didn't get out of here alive, she'd be in even more danger because of me. I had to get my tongue working quickly and try to postpone the fate that had claimed Jennifer Wong. It didn't take much imagination to see them packing my ashes along with a phony death certificate from a crooked doctor for a trip to the rubbish dump, or even worse, to fertilize Mrs. Simmons' roses.

"Since I'm destined to die, do you mind filling me in on some of the details that escaped my investigation?"

"Shoot away. You've got until Thomas comes back from his break with your joy package," he said with a self-satisfied smirk.

I was tempted to retort that I couldn't shoot with my arms

pinned and strapped, but I feared he had no sense of humor. A condemned man shouldn't push his luck too far. He'd offered more than a final cigarette and I couldn't afford to lose sight of my objective to play for time in the hope my little brother was getting Jim Dandy to the rescue.

"I was just trying to do what Mrs. Simmons hired me to do and discover whether your brother had hidden assets she didn't know about in case they separated or divorced. She didn't think very highly of you and said not to trust you or your handling of the account books." I didn't know why she had teamed up with Tony Simmons to rub out her husband. I thought maybe I could drive a wedge between the two by suggesting she was playing him for a fool. Tony Simmons just looked at me and guffawed.

"You and your horny boss aren't going to win any prizes in the smarts department. I couldn't believe you'd be dumb enough to work on first her divorce and then her probate case when Gloria suggested the idea. Your boss followed her like a three-legged dog chasing a bitch in heat and you weren't far behind the pack," he said mockingly.

"Frankly, it didn't make much sense to me either until I learned she was shacking up with Royce Bronson and they planned to double-cross you with their fifty-one percent of the voting shares. The idea was for him to avoid a conflict of interest on the probate and when Mrs. Simmons got her shares, finger you for the drug business. It was a neat plan to get you behind bars while they consolidated all aspects of the businesses. She was playing you for a chump all along." His expression had changed. I could see concern on his face and perhaps a trace of jealousy for his younger and better looking rival. I pressed on.

"At first, I thought your Asian drug partners must have arranged for the drive-by hit at the mortuary. Your brother's relationship with the attractive bookkeeper wouldn't sit well with very conservative Tong leaders anymore than the lovers getting hooked on the product. But word on the street didn't point that way. That meant it had to be either you or Royce Bronson who'd teamed up with Gloria Simmons." Even though

I was blowing smoke, I now had his undivided interest. He had to wonder how I knew Miss Wong was addicted to the drug.

"I took samples of her blood and turned them over to the Las Vegas coroner and the police here. You slipped up. You should have had her smoke the ice until she passed out instead of shooting her full of speed and leaving the needle hole. If she was addicted to speed, her arms would have been full of tell-tale needle tracks. It was too neat and obviously staged. It proved she'd been murdered with the same dope recovered from your drug lab across the street. When I spoke with the Oakland police this afternoon, they'd already secured arrest and search warrants for you, the mortuary staff and your partners; they were just waiting to assemble a large SWAT team and the arrival of FBI agents with more firepower. They've undoubtedly seen you arrive with me and have the building surrounded at this moment. They're probably just waiting for you to come out so they can pick you off one-by-one and avoid storming the premises." I really had his full interest now and doubt furrowed his brow. While my story was mostly wishful thinking, I could almost hear his alarm signals blaring like a series of auto alarms.

"You're bluffing," he uttered in a shaky voice. It was enough to give a condemned man a ray of hope.

"Why should I bluff? I knew when I was instructed to come to her house alone and by cab that you guys were running scared after the fiasco at the Lone Pine and planned to snatch me. I agreed to come because I knew the Oakland Tactical Squad would have raided the mortuary by the time I got there and be shaking down your hit men to learn your whereabouts and movements. Even though the timing was off, I know for a fact the police have the mortuary surrounded at this very moment. Kill me and you get a one way ticket to the gas chamber unless you prefer a lethal injection."

My neck was cramping from the strain of speaking upside down on a gurney. Tony Simmons was between me and the door. I caught him taking a peek behind him at the closed door. He was nervous and looked ready to bolt for somewhere safe. He was in survival mode.

I was just about to continue my self-serving fantasy tale when we heard the unmistakable sounds of a car racing around the back of the mortuary. Next came the sound of screeching brakes followed by a series of loud pops that sounded like cannon fire accompanied by breaking glass and splintering wood. From my upside down view of the world, I could see Tony Simmons frozen with fear. Then, he abruptly dashed for the door and was gone.

My heart was pounding so fast I was afraid I was going to have a heart attack right there on the gurney. I struggled with my bonds anew, but I was securely pinned. I heard more loud popping sounds and muffled yells and cries of a battle going on outside. I had no idea who the parties were or who was winning or losing. I could only hope it was Jim Dandy come to my rescue and not the two drug gangs in a showdown.

Tony Simmons had left the door wide open. I could now hear voices and feet running down the hallway inside the mortuary. I wanted to cry out for help but was too afraid. I didn't want any of Tony Simmons' goons thinking about me. I hoped they were all hauling ass out of Dodge. So with my back to the door, a racing heart and bulging eyes, I awaited my fate.

Suddenly, two figures dressed in black and wearing ski masks skidded around my gurney brandishing ugly-looking automatic weapons. They looked like members of a rival drug gang ready to take care of business until one of the faceless dudes pulled up and let go with a raucous laugh.

"Looky what we got here, Ted. I'll be damned. This must be the dumb shit that kid was hollering about." From my topsy-turvy vantage point, I had to agree with my saviors. I must've looked like a turkey, trussed up and ready to have his head chopped off for Thanksgiving.

The taller of the two masked bandits whipped out a badge and flashed it at me. "You're under arrest. You have the right to remain silent, to have legal counsel appointed to represent you if you can't afford your own. Anything you say can and will be used against you in a court of law."

I didn't know whether to laugh or cry at the irony of the situation. When I finally stopped shaking, I broke into a big-assed smile and croaked out a simple request.

"Could you officers be so kind as to untie me from this gurney so I can accompany you to jail?"

My willingness to cooperate in my own arrest must have been a first for these hard-boiled police operatives. They released me, then cuffed me and prodded me down the hall and outside where they stuffed me into the back seat of a waiting police cruiser. I managed to catch a glimpse of Tony Simmons and brothers Thomas and James spread-eagled on the ground while flak-jacketed commandos from the Tactical Squad roughly cuffed and patted them down.

As the cruiser I was in pulled out with a squeal of rubber, we passed another vehicle with three young black men squeezed in the back seat. One of the heads belonged to my brother, L.C. I couldn't wave, so I just flashed him a big-assed grin as we zipped past. Hopefully, it would all get sorted out in time.

Chapter 28

THE POLICE STATION WAS A MADHOUSE AFTER OUR arrival. The Oakland police were furious and determined to throw the book at my brother and his associates. They'd unwittingly busted up a police stakeout of the mortuary by attacking the premises in an effort to free me. I tried in vain to explain that my brother was so desperate to stop my kidnappers from harming me that they attempted to take on the mortuary's goons by themselves; they believed the police might arrive too late to save my life. The police were convinced that we were all members of a rival drug gang trying to settle a score or muscle in on the action. Who could blame them?

As none of the detectives were getting anywhere with us and planning to ship us all to the Santa Rita jail facility, one finally agreed to call detective Johnny Walker of the Berkeley Police Department. Even though it was late evening, Walker agreed to come to the station and counseled our captors not to jail us yet.

Walker explained my role in busting the drug enterprise and the murder investigation involving Jimmy Simmons. While they agreed not to charge me, they were reluctant to drop charges against my brother and his friends who'd messed up their operation. They had detonated large, illegal Chinese firecrackers and fire bombs outside the mortuary and hurled large ball bearings and muscle-pumping weights through windows and into doors to simulate an armed attack by a drug gang or law enforcement agency. As they didn't know about the stakeout, their objective was to scare my kidnappers and attract police intervention.

After much hemming and hawing back and forth, Walker persuaded the police to release us all without charges. The clincher was that L.C. and his friends were witnesses to my kidnapping and would be needed as witnesses to help nail Mrs. Simmons in the murder/kidnapping conspiracy plot. L.C. made it quite clear on my advice that he was not signing any witness statement or agreeing to testify for the "Po-Po" unless all charges were dropped and we were free to leave.

Detective Walker took me aside after I was released. He informed me that the autopsy report on Jennifer Wong had caught up with him after I'd left his office. It confirmed she died from an overdose of speed. It also established that she was three months pregnant when she was murdered.

Bingo! Suddenly all the pieces fit. No wonder Mrs. Simmons had jumped off Royce Bronson's speedboat for Tony Simmons' scow. Jimmy Simmons' will and codicil provided that all his property would go first to any surviving child of his. Jennifer Wong's little bastard stood to disinherit both Tony Simmons and Gloria Simmons. The prospect of their Asian partners owning and controlling one-half of the two mortuaries and the drug business must have cemented their alliance. They'd arranged the hit on Jennifer Wong to kill the kid in her womb.

It didn't take much imagination to see why I was next on the hit list. Alice Brown must have reported my heavy-handed threats to invalidate the codicil shortly after our meeting. She also may have told her boss about Ms. Wong's pregnancy. Tony decided to take me out before I rocked the boat. He used his black widow to entice me into her web and snare me with her charms. They must have had a good laugh at my expense at how easily I fell for the bait. Mrs. Simmons had another notch to carve on her ebony cane. My weakness for the flesh nearly cost me my life. It also ruined my new Armani suit which somehow got torn when I was unceremoniously loaded onto the gurney.

I treated my brother and his associates to a late night snack at one of their favorite hangouts on Telegraph Avenue and listened to them crow about they had single-handedly beat both the drug dealers and the "Po-lice." I gave them each a crisp one-hundred-dollar bill out of Mrs. Simmons' expense money for their night's work. L.C. dropped me off at my cottage where I tumbled into bed like a lump of coal. Needless to say, my sleep was not restful. All sorts of bad guys chased me in my fitful dreams. Just when they caught up with me, Miss Rita turned up to save my skin. I woke up with a start as the sun was rising..

I knew that I had to wrap up my case and then take care of some important business. I couldn't face the thought of meeting with Nate to tell him how I'd cut a deal with the police to finger our client. The morning papers wouldn't have an account of last night's events, but the radio and TV news stations would be blaring and embellishing the story of our escapade for days to come. Marcie and Saundra would be on top of it by the time they arrived at the office and would expect to hear my account. Nate would be furious with me, but that's the way the cookie crumbles. News reporters would scour the police blotter for the names and addresses of all the participants in the mock shooting and kidnap and come knocking on my door for a scoop.

So, instead of facing the music, I penned a report to Nate and left a message for my little brother to deliver it in the afternoon. Next, I hustled over to my studio apartment and retrieved the thirty thousand dollars I'd hidden from Jimmy Simmons' pouch.

By early afternoon I was well on the way to Las Vegas. I stopped for lunch in Barstow and visited a branch of my bank. I bought two cashier's checks—one for twenty thousand dollars payable to the Oakland Rescue Mission as an anonymous gift to feed and house homeless and displaced persons in downtown Oakland. I figured it was a better use for the drug money than paying Mrs. Simmons' legal expenses.

The second cashier's check in the amount of seven thousand five hundred dollars was in the name of Rita James, I enclosed the bank draft in an envelope addressed to her and note saying the check was a scholarship gift to be used for tuition, books and living expenses at the college of her choice. The scholarship was in recognition of her help in liberating the animals at the Lone Pine Mortuary and shutting down the animal parts traffic at the adjacent taxidermy. The note was signed, "Gratefully Yours, Members of Eco-Terrorist Unit #13."

The remainder of the money was earmarked for my expenses. I planned to catch up on some sleep, treat Miss Rita to a weekend in a high-class resort of her choice anywhere other than Las Vegas if she was in a forgiving mood for my lack of communication over the last forty-eight hours.

I didn't call Rita as I didn't want to have to explain things over the phone. I was racing my Chevy a little faster than I should, but I needed to get to the Dry Tortuga Casino before she finished her shift. I planned to mosey into the bar and order a double shot of Johnny Walker black straight up and take my chances. Walker had told me my testimony at Tony and Gloria Simmons' preliminary hearing wouldn't be needed for several days. I planned to hang around with Rita, take Annie to a steak dinner and just cool my heels until things calmed down in Berkeley and Oakland. My job and the pile of unanswered messages would just have to wait their turn.

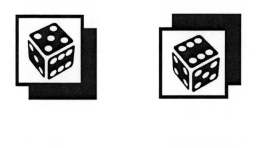

Coming soon, the next
R. C. Bean Murder Mystery.
Enjoy the following preview of
Murder In The Campanile
to be published in late 2017.

MURDER IN THE CAMPANILE

CHAPTER ONE

I still worked for Nate Green, but no longer as his employee. I'd set up my own shop and hung out my shingle in Berkeley as a private investigator. I did contract work for several local attorneys who practiced both civil and criminal law. I also handled investigations for private parties. Nate sat across the desk from me droning on about finding a deadbeat and newly disappeared husband in a messy divorce case when I noticed the red eye of the office intercom blinking furiously. It was Jaunita's signal I had an urgent call on hold. I assured Nate that I'd check out the allegations of child molestation in his case and locate the husband who'd skipped town. I waved him out the door to take the call in private.

"Hello, Mr. Bean? Are you there?" The woman's high-pitched, desperate voice sounded ready to crack. She was obviously nervous and stressed about something.

"I'm R.C. Bean. How can I help you?"

"Thank God you're there. I have to see you. I'm desperate and it's very urgent. I have to see you right away."

"Let me look at my calendar and see when I can fit you in. Hang on a sec." It was Friday afternoon and I wanted to get out of the office. It had been a long week and the unfinished cases littering my desk all needed immediate attention as some were scheduled to go to trial or deposition next week. I had planned to spend the rest of the afternoon out of the office sipping a cool one and getting a handle on the most urgent cases.

"How about sometime Tuesday morning?" I'd need all of Monday to get the info Barney Schultz needed for a trial next week. I'd also have to make some noises in response to Nate Green's case so he could get a contempt citation and arrest warrant for the husband who'd skipped his court appearance. As I mentally ticked off all I had to do, the snuffles at the other end of the line grew louder and louder.

"Are you okay?" I asked.

"No. I'm desperate. I need your help right now; next week will be too late. Please help me! Sharon Miller said I could trust you and you'd be able to help me before things get out of hand. She said you'd understand," the voice pleaded.

The mention of Sharon Miller caught me by surprise. She'd been one of Nate's divorce clients for whom I'd helped secure a tricky alimony agreement that allowed her to complete her degree. I had also helped her celebrate her victory with a roll in the hay in the back seat of my old but comfortable Chevy Impala. I'd not kept in touch with her after our night of spontaneous and frenzied lovemaking. It seemed strange that she would refer me a client after my seemingly caddish behavior in not asking her out again after promising to do so.

I glanced at my watch. It was after 3 P.M. "Look, what say we get together for coffee in thirty minutes at a café not far from my office. It's been a zoo around here today; it'll be more private at the café. Is that okay?"

"Yes, thank you! That'll be fine," she said in a trembling, but grateful voice. I gave her the address for Reggie's Place on Martin Luther King Way.

Reggie's Place is a friendly oasis for Berkeley's eclectic residents who like to banter with the proprietor and who enjoy his down-home Creole cooking. I often use his café to meet with certain clients or to ponder what to do on a case.

"Hey, Juanita. I'm gonna meet a new client right away. I won't be back in the office before ten on Monday if anyone asks."

Juanita Torrres is a petite twenty-four-year-old bundle of energy with fiery brown eyes and cinnamon-colored skin the texture of soft deerskin. She was born in Mexico and raised in East Los Angeles. Her English is heavily accented and her Spanish is peppered with the slang of her barrio. She's what her people call *buena gente*, good people, but she can be a real tough cookie when she needs to be. She raised her black eye-lashes and rolled her beautiful nutmeg-colored eyes to say, "I know what you're up to, Meester Bean." I shook my head "no way" to the implication I was hustling a new lady friend and beat a retreat out the door before she could chastise me on my dereliction of duty this early in the day. It wasn't the first time I'd left her to deal with the wrath of clients who'd not received return phone calls from me as promised.

Juanita manages my appointment book and time sheets for billing, so she knows what I'm up to both in and out of the office. Nate Green's receptionist and assistant, Saundra Joiner and Marcie Louis, had wasted no time apprising Juanita of my many failings when I'd left his employ and struck out on my own. I figured my time was my own as I was no longer under the thumb of an employer and his minions. The fact that Nate still relied on me to work for him on a contract basis at a much higher rate than he had paid me irked Saundra and Marcie no end. However, the fact that they couldn't get Juanita to tattle on me vexed them even more.

I realized as I drove to Reggie's Place that I hadn't asked my caller her name. I'd also forgotten in my haste to slip away that I'd not taken Nate's file from him as promised. I'd have to stop by his office Monday morning to pick it up and face Saundra's wrath. It was real easy to get to the top of her shit list. I felt she'd unfairly pegged me as a spoiled, no account northern black boy with a rovin' eye and a penchant for procrastination as she'd said many times in her Deep South accent, "You just caint be relied upon, R.C. You're jess back to yo' same ol' ways. Say you gonna do sumthin', then don't even show yo' face 'til it suits you."

Then again, I might get lucky on Monday. She'd only chew

me out in our down-home lingo if we were alone. She was part of the reason I'd left working for Nate Green where I did skip-tracing and investigating for his divorce practice. I was grateful to be my own boss and work for several lawyers. I sub-rented my office space from Attorney Barney Schultz and we shared Juanita as our receptionist and office assistant.

I parked my car in a two-hour metered space across the street from Reggie's Place. I cranked eight quarters into the bandit to take me up to six P.M. when Berkeley's meter maids are supposed to stop nailing citizens to fill the city's bloated coffers. I pulled my radio out of the car and jaywalked across the street. I could see through the window that there were only three customers at this slow time of the day.

One elderly patron with grey-streaked, nappy hair was seated at the counter shooting the bull while Reggie cut and diced vegetables for one of his Creole specialties. Another sil-ver-haired pensioner dawdled over his cup of coffee in a front booth as he pored over the discount coupons in the well-thumbed local papers Reggie puts out every morning. The third occupant was a very attractive young white woman who I immediately pegged for my client.

She was seated at a table near the door, playing nervously with her coffee spoon and was hunched over her coffee mug with elbows resting on the table's oilcloth. Despite her furrowed brow, her face was pleasing – a straight, finely tapered nose, rosy cheeks and full, fleshy lips that she alternately moistened with the tip of her tongue and then bit gently. She'd tied off her hon-ey-golden hair with two red bows, one at the top of her loose-weaved braid and the other near the small of her back.

I couldn't see her eyes from her hunched position, but I would've bet a twenty they were the kind of deep blue that would melt your heart if they were shining on you. She looked like the kind of old-fashioned All-American Girl gracing the cover of *Seventeen* a few years back. I couldn't but wonder what worry could make this lovely young woman seek my services so urgently.

I waved at Reggie as I entered and headed directly to the

woman's table. "Hi, I'm R.C. Bean," I said with a smile. I motioned her to stay seated as I took a chair opposite her and she gazed at me with royal-blue eyes flecked with gold. She had all the ingredients to be a heart-breaker despite slightly puffy lids from crying recently.

I noticed a thin gold wedding band but no engagement ring as she expended her hand for me to shake; it was wet and clammy. She looked to be in her mid-twenties. She wore no jewelry or makeup, but she didn't really need any to enhance her beauty.

"I'm Melanie Richards," she said in a voice so soft I had to crane my head to hear.

"What's troubling you, Mrs. Richards?" I asked.

"I don't know where to begin. It's all so complicated," she said with her eyes down and probing the dark coffee in her mug as if it would reveal a course to follow.

"Why don't you start at the beginning. Tell me about what precipitated your present problems."

"It's not that easy for me to talk about it. I'm ashamed about what's happened and it's made me very frightened."

"What are you afraid of?"

"I'm afraid if my husband finds out I'm talking to you and not him, it will destroy our marriage," she said glumly.

I took her hand gently in mine and looked her in the eye. "Don't worry about talking to me. I work for attorneys and anything you say will be kept in the strictest confidence. If your husband ever learns you met with me, just say you consulted me and the attorney I work for, Barney Schultz, to draft a will."

What I said with such conviction was, of course, not really true. Even though I have a J.D. degree from a Bay Area law school, I haven't yet taken the bar exam and can't practice law. However, if Barney covers for me and claims I met with Melanie at his behest, our conversation would be covered by attorney-client privilege.

My little white lie worked. Melanie heaved a sigh of relief and seemed determined to get her troubles off her chest. I suggested that we move to a secluded booth as far away from prying ears and the café windows as possible for privacy. Soon early-bird diners would be arriving to take advantage of Reggie's daily special. Today he featured a shrimp gumbo *à la creole*, whose aroma was exciting my stomach juices.

I signaled Reggie for two beers and some finger food as we made our way to a back booth. I was thirsty and thought a beer might help loosen my client's tongue. Reggie brought two bottles of San Miguel and a platter of shelled shrimp with a small tub of New Orleans hot sauce. Reggie knows how much I like his spicy cooking. The plate of shrimps was his way of saying "Welcome" and complying at the same time with his liquor license that required alcohol be served with food.

I took a long pull on my bottle of San Miguel and focused on Melanie. "Now, tell me what has upset you so much that we need to do something about it."

"Well, I'm a graduate student in the Human Resources Program at Cal where I hope to get my Ph.D. and then teach college courses. Something terrible has happened and now I know I won't get my degree." I could see her eyes tearing up and threatening to flow.

"It's okay; you need to talk about it. Tell me what's happened to threaten your degree," I said gently.

"My dissertation director is pressuring me to have sex with him. And, if I don't agree to it, I'm sure he'll hold it against me and never sign off on my dissertation; so, I'll never get a doctorate degree." Her words were full of both anger and resignation.

I tried to feign surprise. It's a story I've heard from others. "I'm not too familiar with the ins and outs of the graduate schools at Cal. You need to explain it to me so I can figure out how best to help you."

Actually, I know a lot about how the system of patronage and student dependence works. My mother still rails about the sorry lot of graduate teaching assistants which has not changed much since she was a T.A. during the Free Speech Movement in the mid-sixties.

"What makes your dissertation director think he can proposition you for sex and not lose his job if you denounce him to the proper authorities?" I wanted to know what leverage he had in the situation. She gave me a funny look before continuing. She hadn't touched Reggie's shrimps and had only taken a small sip of her beer. She appeared to be debating what to tell me.

"I can't bring a complaint. He's a full professor with a national reputation in his field. I'm just an aspiring graduate student. He would deny everything and I'd be left hanging out to dry. Jesus, I'd be the laughing stock of the department. All the professors in the department would figure me for a dangerous and vindictive bitch. They'd all be only too happy to help him get rid of me."

"How could they do that?"

"It's very easy. All they have to do is give me B minuses and C pluses on my papers and exams, or, fail me on my oral exams. It's unfair as hell, but they have all the power they need to shaft me."

"I don't understand why the other people in your department would conspire to protect your professor in light of the seriousness of the charge."

"It's not just me. This shit happens all the time. Suppose by some miracle I managed to expose Dr. Jones; it would send a signal to every other female grad student who's had a professor hit on her that's it's okay to rebel and denounce him. They don't dare let it happen. They'll stick together like glue out of self-interest to discredit me, and then dump me," she said bitterly.

"Do you know other students who've been propositioned by their profs for sex?"

Melanie gave me a disbelieving look at my naïve question. "Yes, I know several."

"Why do they buckle under to this kind of thing?"

"Many do it out of fear they'll get washed out of the doctoral program and given a terminal Master's degree and be relegated to teaching high school or at a junior college the rest of their lives."

"Surely, there must be some sympathetic professors who

could help you. What about women professors in your department or in the administration?"

Melanie managed a small ironic laugh. "You must be kidding," she said in a tone full of sarcasm. "There's only one tenured woman in the department and she's tough as nails. She
had to buck the same system to get her Ph.D. She had to take
them to court to get her tenure. No way she's gonna stick her
neck out for me. She's got too much to lose."

"Surely, she isn't the only woman in your department ..."
She cut me off.

"The untenured women in the department are even more
vulnerable. They're lucky to have a job at all in these hard times.
Nobody is going to say boo if I upset the apple cart. Most are
untenured lecturers who must be reappointed every year."

I was starting to think we were checkmated. I decided to
try one last tack. "I thought one could file a sexual harassment
complaint with the university that's confidential."

"Yeah, that's good in theory. You can complain to the
ombudsman, but each department is a closed little world. It's
like a small town; everyone watches everyone else. It's a very
competitive environment. Some students will do anything to
get ahead and are all too happy to assist in the demise of a
competitor." She paused to take a sip of beer and gauged my
mounting frustration written all over my mug.

"Anything? Does that include sleeping with their professor
to get ahead?"

"Yes, some do that to curry favor, but it's not limited to
that. Some will badmouth a competing student to a prof or
other students. Some will spy and tattle on students and other
profs if they think that will help them get ahead."

"I see," I said deflated by her grim words. She was lectur-
ing me on the subject of sexual politics at the university. She
appeared to know all too well what she was talking about. It
was time to learn of her present dilemma.

"Tell me about how you were propositioned by your dissertation director."

"I met him when I first enrolled in the Human Resources

Program. Allister Jones is one of the best known experts on designing retraining strategies for displaced workers and professionals. That's the area I chose for my dissertation."

"Then he must be familiar with EEOC guidelines on sexual harassment in the workplace."

Melanie threw me a disbelieving look. "Yes, but he knows damn well that a lowly woman grad student would be crazy to accuse him of sexual harassment. Look what happened to Anita Hill and she was a tenured law professor." Melanie was struggling to suppress her tears. She pulled a paper napkin from the metal holder on the table just as they started to cascade down her face.

"I have to use the restroom." She grabbed her purse and dashed for the restroom door.

To Be Continued

ABOUT THE AUTHOR

Ken Salter is a Bay Area native who earned his degrees at U.C. Berkeley. After graduating from Boalt Hall, U.C.'s law school, he directed an undergraduate writing program at Cal for several years. He is professor emeritus in Communication Studies at San Jose State University where he taught persuasive writing and critical thinking courses. He also prcticed law in Berkeley, California. He is the author of several books about famous legal trials including *The Trial of Dan White, The Pentagon Papers Trial* and *The Trial of Inez Garcia.* He has also authored the *Gold Fever* trilogy about the problems faced by immigrants during California's Gold Rush years from 1851-1860. He lives and writes in Berkeley, Californbia. See his web site at www. salterken.com.

CPSIA information can be obtained
at www.ICGtesting.com
Printed in the USA
LVOW10s1619250817
546379LV00001B/114/P